Under the Mink

Under the Mink

A Novel

Lisa E. Davis

alyson books
los angeles | new york

© 2001 BY LISA E. DAVIS. ALL RIGHTS RESERVED.

MANUFACTURED IN THE UNITED STATES OF AMERICA.

THIS TRADE PAPERBACK ORIGINAL IS PUBLISHED BY ALYSON PUBLICATIONS,
P.O. BOX 4371, LOS ANGELES, CA 90078-4371.
DISTRIBUTION IN THE UNITED KINGDOM BY
TURNAROUND PUBLISHER SERVICES LTD.,
UNIT 3, OLYMPIA TRADING ESTATE, COBURG ROAD, WOOD GREEN,
LONDON N22 6TZ ENGLAND.

FIRST EDITION: APRIL 2001

01 02 03 04 05 🄰 10 9 8 7 6 5 4 3 2 1

ISBN: 1-55583-556-2

LIBRARY OF CONGRESS CATALOGING-IN-PUBLICATION DATA
    DAVIS, LISA E.
        UNDER THE MINK: A NOVEL/LISA E. DAVIS—1ST ED.
        ISBN 1-55583-556-2
        1. GREENWICH VILLAGE (NEW YORK, N.Y.)—FICTION.
    2.TRANSVESTITES—FICTION. I.TITLE.
    PS3554.A93535 U53 2001
    813'.54—DC21   00-053595

CREDITS
COVER PHOTOGRAPH FROM *LAST CALL AT MAUD'S* COURTESY OF FRAMELINE.
COVER DESIGN BY PHILIP PIROLO.

In Memoriam,
Eileen

Acknowledgments

Thanks to Gail and Buddy for talking about the good old days.

And to Elise for her unconditional love and support.

And to Joan Nestle for Elise and everything else.

And to Sonia Pilcer for teaching me.

"I lived a few weeks while you loved me."

—*In a Lonely Place* (Columbia, 1950), Gloria Grahame

"America was still the 'Land of Plenty More
Where That Came From.'"

—Polly Adler, *A House Is Not a Home*

July 1949

Week One

PROLOGUE

Uptown on Park Avenue, Skip sat on the edge of his bed—antique Venetian, supported head and foot by gilded leaping dolphins. He was clad only in a polka-dot silk dressing gown with velvet lapels. A loose strand of hair, bleached almost white by the summer sun on low-lying beaches, swept across his forehead. He was beautiful, with a sweet beatific aura, and his skin was very fair. The cheeks were soft and radiant. It was the kind of face that tricks went crazy over.

Skip dangled his bare feet off the bed and opened his robe. A pale naked image with dreamy hyacinth-blue eyes looked out at him from the tall mirror, like the center panel of some Renaissance triptych. His chest and legs had a buttermilk sheen and shimmered in the hothouse light. He ran his hands down his thighs. He was restless and tired of being alone. If his sister had come home, they could've gone out on the town, but it was too late to expect her now.

He went to his closet and fingered the light blue silk tulle, then a strapless pink satin with seed pearls. They were all his sister's dresses, let out for him at the waist and the hem with a few tucks here and there. She was no prude. If her baby brother liked to dress up in her clothes and said he was gay, that was all right with her. She loved him and found his friends charming. They had lots of laughs. Of course, if his father found out, the old man would have a screaming hissy fit. And Mummie would really take to her bed for good with a whole thermos of hot toddies.

Skip's hand lingered over the metallic threads of a floor-length gold lamé he'd worn the night he won first prize at the Paradise Casino on 125th Street. It was a big drag to-do, almost as big as Phil Black's Funmakers Ball. A long stairway with a shiny brass railing led up to the door where Skip had slipped the maître d' a generous tip for a good table and champagne.

After the competition, his friend Titanic, a drag queen who entertained at the Candy Box Club, had come by to congratulate him. "You look just like Dietrich, dahling," Titanic said, swishing a fan of real ostrich plumes in one gloved hand. "A natural beauty wonder!"

Titanic could be a sore loser, but he hadn't allowed Skip to feel guilty about winning. Skip already felt self-conscious about being filthy rich, and Titanic had told him a thousand times how silly that was. "For Chrissake, I don't know why you're ashamed of all that moolah," he'd say. "If the fur coat fits, wear it. Poor is tacky!"

Clutching the gold lamé, Skip thought maybe he'd drive down to the Candy Box and say hello to Titanic and the other kids. He'd go backstage and have a few laughs. It seemed like ages since he'd been there. Titanic had told him to have nothing to do with the trade that hung around the bar—a lot of creeps, all closet cases. "I oughta know," he'd grin. But Skip wanted to suck a dick. Maybe he would try to pick up somebody anyway.

He carried only the money he needed, no identification, in case his trick turned out to be an undercover cop. Because his family was well-to-do, he couldn't afford to be recognized.

The picture of bandbox elegance, Skip stared again into the mirror, his eyes a haunting blue. He'd dressed simply for his visit to the Candy Box, in a Savile Row suit and silk shirt from Sulka, with a foulard tie and pocket square. He shuffled down the balustraded stairway into the apartment's circular polished-marble foyer and pressed a button. A white-gloved attendant popped up in the small velvet and gilt cage of an elevator, like a diver emerging from the deep. He opened the door and rode Skip down to the building's wide vaulted vestibule.

Red damask covered its walls halfway down, with dark wood panels to the floor. Paintings in the beef-gravy colors of the Royal Academy represented English cathedrals and Italianate ruins. Beneath them sat pleasant groupings of low sofas, wing chairs covered in striped satin, and mahogany tables.

Ruggles, the doorman, touched his cap. He was gap-toothed and elderly, liveried in gray to match the fortresslike, pre-World War I building. Thirteen floors of stone with sharp cornices, false architraves, and fluted pilasters.

"Will they be bringing the car around, sir?" Ruggles asked. He noted that the boy was wearing a proper suit and no makeup. Maybe someone had warned the father or the sister that people in the building were beginning to talk.

"I'll need a taxi," Skip replied. They stood beneath a green awning that stretched to the sidewalk. Unquestioning, Ruggles stepped off the curb. His shrill whistle sounded up and down Park Avenue.

Skip's Checker cab bounced downtown. Red taillights bobbed on either side, taxis and limousines picking up fashionable people at their doorsteps. On a mild summer night like this, no one would sleep until dawn. Skip watched the city flash by and wished he'd gotten into the chorus line at the Candy Box.

"It must be wonderful to be in show business," a stagestruck Skip had hinted to Titanic in the dressing room. "What could I call myself?"

"Oh, something aristocratic," Titanic replied, "like Alexis, Georgette, Lalique."

"Howzabout Dolly Dimples?" Blackie Cole had suggested, and flashed him one of her sensational smiles. In her white tie and tails, she looked like a swashbuckling Errol Flynn starring in the new show at the club.

Back at home, when Skip had talked to his sister about the Candy Box, she hadn't shared his enthusiasm for a stage career.

"You can't use your own name," she warned. "You know how stuffy Father and Mummie are...and terrified of scandal."

Titanic confirmed the warning. "Don't be so sure you won't meet up with somebody you know!"

"Everybody gets down here sooner or later," Blackie Cole added.

Skip hated being in the cab with no one to talk to. He looked out the window and wondered if he'd ever do anything with his life. His sister would know what to say to raise his spirits, but she was out on the island with Mummie. Another one of the crises that Mummie had managed to prolong through the weekend.

A roll of thunder threatened summer showers. Skip got out in front of an unmarked door on Eighth Street just off Sixth Avenue. To find the Candy Box, you had to know where you were going.

Three steps down from street level led him to the dimly lit bar. Skip stood silhouetted in the entrance until the shapes inside took on firm contours. Slender young men leaned against the bar or sat on stools. Older guys, some with women on their arms, sat at tufted wraparound banquettes along one wall. Beyond the bar was an oblong performance space, white-draped tables in a semicircle around the stage that glowed like a distant star, with red and blue gelatinous shadows. In dresses of frothy pink chiffon, a chorus line of long-haired boys, including Titanic, swayed in time to an old standard. They sang,

Life is such a drag....

Short-haired girls in tuxedos knelt beside them.

Skip liked the Candy Box because it wasn't seedy like some bars he went to down by the river or uptown in the shadow of the Third Avenue El. The floor show inside gave it glamour, and Titanic said they had the best protection money could buy. A straight audience of highbrows, racketeers, celebrities, out-of-towners, lawyers, and Wall Street brokers gave the club an air of respectability. They came for the novelty and to spend money. But management allowed gay boys to gather in the bar, which was cruisy and more than a smidgen adventurous.

Skip ordered a drink and leaned on the bar. He felt the caress of eyes on his flesh. A guy in a bomber jacket at the end of the bar caught his eye. He could have been a gypsy, swarthy with longish black hair. All he was missing was the golden earring. His eyes were like burnt-out cinders, where Skip read experience and mystery. If Titanic had decided the guys in the bar weren't worth the trouble, it was because he hadn't seen this one.

The man looked up, returned Skip's blue-eyed stare, and flexed his shoulders. The boys and girls in the show wailed to the music, "When I'm not with you."

Now Skip and the man stood side by side. Skip took in the man's hands. Heavy veins, and knuckles like walnuts.

Blue-white sparks seemed to play around them with the promise of power and a tantalizing hint of danger. The hands cradled an empty glass.

"Can I buy you a drink?" Skip asked.

"Sure." His warm, sweet breath broke over Skip's cheek. "I'll have what you're having."

Skip carelessly threw a 10-spot on the bar. When he pocketed the change, he touched his money clip, 18 karat and sculpted with his initials. Titanic had always warned him to keep his money out of sight.

"Bottoms up." The man raised his glass in a toast. He was a connoisseur of backstreet brawls and barrooms, his voice coarse and self-assured.

Skip leaned closer, offering up all his youth and good looks for inspection. "You like the show?"

"What can I say? If those fairies want to dress up like that..." He glanced over his shoulder. "Great legs, though— and lotsa laughs!"

The answer made Skip uncomfortable, but he longed to touch the face, burnished olive skin like antique bronze, and flaring nostrils above fleshy lips.

The man drained his glass. "I gotta go inside," he said.

He skirted the crowd watching the show and hesitated for a moment on the far side of the room in front of a red velvet curtain. Then he lifted the curtain and headed for the Gents.

Skip's body hummed with desire. He made his move, legs racing out from under him. He tried to slow down. Titanic would be green with envy when Skip told him about this number.

The men's room was lighted by a single incandescent bulb under milk glass. The glare flattened the porcelain urinals against the wall and threw dark shadows into the corners.

Skip came in as the man, stroking his cock, turned away from the urinal. When they faced each other, Skip wanted to say something easy and joking. He moved closer and tried to kiss the man, who averted his mouth and pointed toward the two metal stalls.

The last one had no door. Ancient phone numbers and hearts pierced by Cupid's arrow were etched into the walls. Skip slipped inside and tried another kiss.

"No." The man pressed Skip onto the enamel toilet seat.

Skip liked some show of tenderness but buried his disappointment in a throbbing erection. Coaxing with his tongue and lips, he murmured, "You're beautiful."

Skip wrapped his arms around the man's narrow hips as he took the cock deep into his throat. He nursed greedily until an explosive spasm shook them both.

The man stepped back, zipping his fly. "That's 20 bucks you owe me, kid."

Skip took out a silk handkerchief and wiped his mouth. You had to expect these things, Titanic had said.

"Don't be like that," Skip said, leaving himself room to maneuver. "There's plenty of time. Let's go somewhere."

"I've got to meet some people, kid."

"Don't be afraid," Skip said. "We could have a few more drinks."

"Why should I be afraid of you?" He ruffled Skip's shining hair and put out his hand palm up.

"Well, maybe some other time."

"I don't make dates with faggots." The man spread his feet into a hustler's stance.

Skip laughed into the narrow space. "Who are you calling a faggot? You could've fooled me."

"C'mon, I saw you got money on you." He grabbed for Skip's pocket.

Skip shielded it with both hands. "You oughta pay me. You got what you wanted."

"Hey, don't get highfalutin on me." The man nudged

Skip's chin with his fist. "Rich boys, fancy dressers like you can afford it. I know who your old man is, and whatcha can't afford is for somebody to put a bug in his ear: 'Hey, did ya know your little Lord Fauntleroy is queer?' "

"You don't know anything about me," Skip muttered. "I'm going back to the bar." He stood up and tried to push his way out.

The man pushed back, and the flimsy stall rocked as their bodies ricocheted against the walls. Skip lowered his shoulders and landed a surprising uppercut, a lucky sucker punch, as he twisted away. He wanted to smash something.

Taller and heavier, his opponent recovered and collared Skip. "Whazzamatta with you?" He stunned Skip with an open-handed slap.

Another punch sent Skip crashing back into the stall, and he fell for what seemed a long time. The scarred metal walls rose up on either side. A black hole gaped in the plaster ceiling. Finally the back of his head cracked sharply on the cold enamel of the toilet seat. Everything went silent and dark.

The man straddled Skip, lifting him by the lapels of his suit. "Well, ain't you the pretty one?" he whispered tenderly, and dug deep for the money clip with its wad of bills. He pocketed Skip's money and gave him a shake.

"Get up, for Chrissake!" The kid was lying too still. Behind his head a pool of thick blood was forming.

Along Skip's neck and over his heart, there was no pulse. The man seized Skip's shoulders and shook the body harder. Blood spattered the stall. Skip's left hand, flashing a ring with several carats of square-cut diamond set in platinum, waved convulsively as his life drained away.

The man backed away fast. Blinded by sweat, he stumbled over Skip's legs. "A dead kid wasn't part of the deal," he muttered, sirens wailing inside his skull.

Skip's ring flickered ghostlike in the shadows, a crystal will-o'-the-wisp. The man stopped and cautiously reached across the body. If this was real, a couple of easy grand. He was forcing it over the knuckle when he heard the dull thud of footsteps outside the door.

One

Blackie Cole was beautiful, and everybody at the Candy Box Club wanted her. Women in the audience shouted pledges of devotion. The men, bored stage-door Johnnies who liked a new twist, all stood up and applauded. Murmurs of "fabulous" spread over the crowd. Blackie Cole was no freak. She was what they'd come to the Village to see.

"Isn't she stunning?" the customers rhapsodized at their tables about the slender figure in white tie and tails. They watched her doff an iridescent top hat. Under a tangle of short black hair slicked down with Vitalis, her face was an androgynous mix of movie-star gorgeous and handsome. Cheekbones soared above a chiseled jawline.

Blackie flashed her audience an extravagant come-hither smile and took a bow. One arm cradled an ivory-tipped cane. "You're such a great crowd," she drawled in a breathless baritone, "that I wanna sing a couple songs just for you."

She nodded to the orchestra leader who, elbows high, pulsed his baton. The spotlight dimmed to pale pink as a single muted trumpet blew the opening heartbroken bars. The strings glissandoed up the scale. Piano and bass came in behind Blackie's shimmering alto. She sang of loneliness and the chains that bound her to a lost love.

Saxophones wailed under the lush bluesy voice. The drummer got in a few hot licks, tux riding up and sticks spinning. Blackie crooned,

Passion's the rule
And I'm passion's fool.

She could've written those lyrics herself. She should've gotten over Renee by now, her last girlfriend with the creamy bisque complexion and strawberry-blond curls. But love had a way of holding on until it was through with you for good.

The trumpet took over the melody, bright then sultry. Sauntering away from the stand-up mike, Blackie grazed a woman's bare shoulder with a trailing hand. It was part of the show. The swooning patron reached up to clasp it. Her lips brushed then devoured the fingers with kisses. The woodwinds droned mysteriously.

Wide-eyed, the audience shivered deliciously at the shadow world of lesbian lust before them. They clapped wildly and at ringside stuffed double sawbucks into the pockets of Blackie's pants with the perfect creases and a satin stripe down each leg.

It was more money than she'd ever seen in her life. Just out of high school, she'd netted $15 a week roller-skating messages for AT&T, from where they came off the electric belt to the teletypist. At the club she could make $200 on weekends alone, all in tips. No tax, no questions asked. She could've saved money, but she bought clothes and a red Ford coupe instead.

All that was heady wine for a kid from Brownsville, a poor Jewish neighborhood in Brooklyn where Blackie Cole had been Blanche Cohen. Her parents still lived on the third floor of a wooden tenement that smelled of cabbage and onions. The Candy Box was about as far away from there as a subway ride could take you.

Happy to be a hit in a business where the boys usually got top billing, Blackie bowed and gave the crowd another generous dose of that sensational smile. Her hazel eyes, flecked with green and gold, beckoned from under sooty brows.

Her mother had been the first woman to fall for those eyes. "Her grandmother's eyes," Mrs. Cohen told the other ladies showing off their babies on Pitkin Avenue.

"Such a beautiful child," they said.

"It's all in the bone structure—the image of my sister Gussie when she was a girl."

Blackie's Aunt Gussie had been a little wild, of course, but good looks were also a blessing. "You'll be able to pick and choose," Mrs. Cohen had encouraged her daughter, "and not get stuck with some schlemiel."

If Blackie could tell her folks the truth about what she was and what she was doing, her mom might be proud. At least she'd love the applause and all the people dressed up in tails and long dresses like in some black-and-white movie. But not her father Sam, fierce and incorruptible. He had always preferred failure to success in a rotten world.

Blackie was looking for more out of life and didn't expect his approval. When no one was hiring Jews, she changed her name. And instead of working all her life for peanuts, she took a job tending bar in the Village at a place called Ernie's, on Third Street between Thompson and Sullivan, in the shadow of the Sixth Avenue El.

For a while Blackie's father had been proud of her for wanting to help out during the war. In the WAC, she'd been assigned to the motor pool at a base north of San Francisco. When the war ended, she came back to her old job at Ernie's and sang for tips.

Then she got lucky. Stevie the Frenchman, manager of the Candy Box, discovered her. "Whaddaya wanna work in this homo dive for?" he asked in his nutmeg-grater voice. "With that face, you can make it big. Not only dynamite looks you got, but talent too." His wire-rimmed spectacles flashed like silver dollars under the lights. "You'll give the joint class." A little butch for his taste, he thought, but there were lots of customers who went for her type.

"Hey, Blackie," Stevie would say in a lighthearted moment, "you got the looks. Why, if you was a girl, I could go for you myself!"

"Same here, Stevie," she'd reply, and he'd roar with laughter.

Maybe the Candy Box wasn't Broadway, but it wasn't your Aunt Tillie's living room either. And if you wanted to be in showbiz, you had to start somewhere. Even the Andrews Sisters hadn't been an overnight sensation.

That night Blackie also played the role of emcee, warming up the crowd. "Ladies and gentlemen," she wooed them, "I'd like to welcome you to the Candy Box, the gayest night spot in New York."

"We're the High Hat Revue," Blackie said as she replaced the top hat on her head at a rakish angle and gave it a tap. Maurice Chevalier had nothing on her. "We promise you lotsa laughs tonight, and some very special entertainment."

"Now that summer's here," she leaned on her ivory-tipped cane, her feet planted wide apart like Fred Astaire's, "we invite you to sit back, drink up, and cool off."

The sassy music that had droned softly in the background reached crescendo. A single line of queens in wide picture hats emerged gracefully one by one onto the stage. They sang, *Life is such a drag....*

"And remember," Blackie said, winding down, half sorry to give up the spotlight as it shifted from her to the boys, "we're here at the Candy Box every night for your pleasure, so relax and enjoy the show."

As she initiated her fade-out into the wings, she knew she

had them eating out of her hand. Backstage, she turned to watch the dark-eyed boy in pink chiffon who led a procession of female impersonators center stage between two potted palms. He had skin as smooth as an Ivory Soap baby's and a pretty turned-up nose. A dusky wig with fake diamond clips curled over his powdered shoulders, firm and rounded like a young ballerina's.

At the Candy Box everyone called him "Titanic." Because he goes down, somebody joked. Others claimed it was because he was very large in the downstairs department, struggling to pull it back and strangle it between his butt cheeks so he could wriggle into his costume. As a drag name, Titanic stuck.

A long, undulating sweep from narrow waist to tapering legs propelled him across the dance floor. His partner, one of the short-haired tuxedoed girls who served drinks between shows, grasped his hand in hers. The customers were on their feet applauding.

"You for real?" one of them shouted, while his wife tugged at his coattails.

Titanic gave an impromptu high kick. "Wouldn't *you* like to know, dahling," he replied in a stage whisper, overlaid with a fake British accent he'd recently adopted. He sounded like Vivien Leigh with a vodka hangover.

Blackie laughed. Titanic had been her best friend since she'd started at the Candy Box, green as grass but determined to succeed. He hadn't gotten along so well with her girlfriend Renee, who one night preached some cockamamie drunken sermon about how drag queens gave queers a bad name.

"I don't know what you see in those nellie guys," she'd said to Blackie.

Titanic called Renee a bitch and a slut, and warned, "You'd better watch your step, sister." After that he ignored her but took Blackie on as his protégée.

"No, no!" he'd cautioned, as she skimmed the tip of a black wax pencil through her eyebrows. "You're not behind a bar anymore. You want to look glamorous. Watch me!"

He took the eyebrow pencil, made her arch her brows, and fattened them into a dark line. "Like that." He dusted her cheeks with a marabou powder puff, then carefully sketched a white line in greasepaint inside both her lower eyelids. "This'll make those big Kewpie-doll eyes sparkle."

He kept after her. "This isn't a pitcher's mound you're walkin' out to. Fans can be so veddy veddy demanding. Give 'em lots of leg, hips, and lips." He demonstrated, sailing up to the microphone with a lush Anna May Wong grace.

Blackie felt like she had two left feet.

"As close as you can come, sweetie," he said. "Like a debutante on her way to dinner at the Stork Club."

Then Titanic had helped her develop her spiel and delivery.

"Breathe from the diaphragm," he'd holler from the back of the club, "like they do at Dramatic Arts." And her voice would drop into a low register while she fished around for the right intonation.

Just before her debut at the Candy Box, Titanic looked her over. "Now pucker up for the mirror," he said, a dab of rouge on his finger.

"Hey, that's enough."

"Onstage you'll be perfect," he clucked. "It's the illusion that counts, dahling, the illusion!"

He traced a ruby arch under her cheekbone, blending and lifting toward the temple, and smoothed a last touch over her lips. "Oh, you're so elegant, I could die!"

Wild applause greeted Blackie's act, the audience calling for encores. She took one bow, her knees wobbly. He bullied her back onstage.

"Get back out there and take another bow!"

"I don't feel so good."

He pulled out a bottle of brandy. "Take a belt of this. You'll feel better."

The audience wouldn't let her go. She sang two more songs.

Stevie, the boss, congratulated himself when the money really started to roll in. Did he know talent when he saw it, or what?

Out onstage the kids sang,

When I'm not with you.

Titanic and his partner sashayed left, big Judy Canova smiles plastered across their kissers.

From the wings Blackie applauded. She'd stay on at the Candy Box for as long as Stevie would have her. He was making her a star, and Titanic was her friend. When she and Renee had called it quits, Titanic was the only one she could talk to. She could do a helluva lot better than Renee any day of the week, he told her, then held her when she cried.

Two

Backstage at the Candy Box, glamour evaporated like a soap bubble. The space was a narrow corridor, dark and cramped. Yards of duct tape bandaged pipes that looped along a low ceiling. It reverberated with the boys' music.

Blackie hummed along as she walked down to the makeshift dressing room. In the center of the door, a nail secured a ragged gold star cut from shiny paper. She heard no sound behind her. Only when a hard white hand clamped down on her arm did she realize she was not alone.

"Hey, buddy, this the men's room?" came a slurred question from the spongy darkness.

The drunk was a heavy-smelling damp mass crowding her, drawing her toward him. He seemed to Blackie all open mouth and spiky mustaches sprouting above it, like an angry gray walrus. She pulled away from his grasping hand.

"Hey, whazzamatta?" he said, his neck as broad as a woman's waist. "Do they want me to piss on the floor?" He clutched affectionately at his crotch.

"Other side of the club," Blackie muttered. She knew this joker was drunker than 16 million dollars and would never make it all the way across the dance floor, then down another hallway to the Gents. It wasn't her job to play nursemaid, but nobody needed this big lug passed out cold in front of the dressing-room door. She could handle this.

"Come with me, pal," she said in a husky voice, feeling cocky. "I'll show you."

Blackie laid an arm across his meaty shoulders. A red velvet curtain separated the narrow hallway from the performance space. She lifted the curtain and measured the distance she had to cross. Most of the customers had their eyes fixed on the stage. The kids pursed their lips and sang.

Breaking trail, Blackie edged the drunk along the back wall, away from tables he might upset. A few patrons giggled and toasted the two. Blackie and her companion zig-zagged toward the opposite side of the club. Another curtain in red velvet loomed up through a haze of cigarette smoke. It concealed a broader passageway that led to the Gents and the powder room.

As the drunk hunched under the ruby curtain, he got a closer look at Blackie. "Hey, you're not a man!"

His head jutted forward, and he rocked on the balls of his feet like a Golden Gloves contender past his prime. His face was one big boozy grin. "You one of those lezzies that sits at the back tables?"

Blackie fumed. Being taken for a man was safe and respectful. Being taken for a dyke whore who jerked men off during the floor show was risky. She'd told Stevie those girls gave customers the wrong idea. "They think we're all whores."

"Don't be so touchy. The girls are part of the operation," Stevie had answered. "They pay their dues. In business you gotta live and let live."

So she'd learned to turn down offers with a smile but not always in control.

"Nuts to you, buster!" Blackie said, and shoved the drunk ahead of her up to the door. "Here's the men's room."

"Aw, what's your rush?" he slurred, and fumbled with his fly. "Everybody says you girls are great cocksuckers. I ain't askin' you to do it for nuthin'!"

Blackie gave the drunk a stiff arm to the chest. "Sorry, bub, but I got a number to do. Why don't you go on inside, like a good guy?" The next drunk she tangled with, she'd call Charlie and Waxy, two button men Stevie kept around to handle troublemakers.

Just then another man lurched out of the Gents. The face was handsome but craggy, with hard lines. Blue-black hair and soft olive skin brushed by Blackie's shoulder close enough for a kiss. The eyes smoldered with rage and panic. They held Blackie's for a moment before the apparition fled, broad shoulders blurring down the hallway.

Blackie knew she should've looked the other way, like she'd been warned to do at the Candy Box. "The less you know," Stevie had told her with a significant nod of his head, "the better."

The drunk took advantage of the moment to sober up dangerously. He slapped Blackie's arm away as though it were a pesky mosquito. A spark of indignation lit his glassy eyes.

"My dick not good enough for you, cuntlapper?" he mumbled, and leaned toward her again, his stenchy breath against her cheek. "You like to make a buck, don't you?"

"I don't care what your dick's good for." She turned to go.

An arm like a meat hook caught her from behind and spun her around. The red sulky face blurred in front of hers, as he pinned her against the wall with his weight.

She pushed back like a game streetfighter, but he seemed rock solid. She'd seen a lot of rough stuff, and she'd heard, "Hey, lezzie, wanna suck my dick?" so many times that she'd forgotten to be afraid. But violence had never come so close. With the energy of awakening panic, she pushed harder at her assailant.

"Cut it out." Her voice rose in pitch.

"Don't try to be a hero, girlie." His eyes shone like silver thumbtacks. He'd stopped slurring. "Down on your knees, if you wanna keep your pants on."

Blackie's breathing slowed to shallow. Somebody would come around the corner any minute. They had a full house, and the boys' number was winding down.

The drunk pushed at the men's room door, dragging Blackie along. "Now you're gonna give it to me for free."

Numbness crept over her. She screamed once as loudly as she could. Outside, the crowd applauded the end of the boys' number.

Suddenly, her tormentor's jaw went slack, eyes fixed on a spot beyond Blackie. "No colored in here!" he hollered, pointing a stubby finger in the air. "No colored!"

Out of the semidarkness, a length of something hard came down across his forearm. A howl broke from his mouth.

The fight was brief, around and above her. A powerful Joe Palooka–style left hook flashed and connected with the drunk's face. KO'd, he reeled as his knees buckled.

Blackie watched him sink against the wall. "Tyrone, was I lucky you came along!"

"You all right, Blackie?" replied a rangy young man, thick wrists and big hands jutting from the sleeves of a starched white jacket. He held a broom in one hand and a dustpan in the other.

She kept her eyes down so Tyrone wouldn't see her tears and how scared she was. She'd heard girls talk about being roughed up by neighborhood thugs or the cops. She'd told herself she was savvier.

"Oh, he's just some drunk son of a bitch," Blackie murmured.

The muscles in Tyrone's soft nut-brown face tightened. "You gotta be more careful around here." Nobody knew better than he did about the drunks at the Candy Box. When he found one passed out in the men's room, he was supposed to haul him to his feet and splash water in his face. But the drunks called him worse than colored, wounds deep as an ice pick to the heart. He couldn't quit because his Aunt Sundown, his mother's sister, had gotten him the job. "You pay attention to your aunt," his mother had told him when she sent him up north. "This is your chance to get somethin' better outta life."

"I'll be OK," Blackie told Tyrone. "You know what Stevie says, 'This town is full of lunatics.'"

Tyrone poked the drunk to make sure he was out cold. "You want anything, Blackie?"

"Some water maybe." Her voice was steadier.

"You keep an eye on him."

Blackie watched the drunk where he lay unconscious, his rumpled trousers unbuttoned. Her toe itched to give him a swift kick in the slats.

Tyrone pushed his way into the men's room. He took a paper cup from an upside-down dispenser near the sink. The place was empty for a change, except for a pair of legs sticking out from the last stall. He didn't need any more screwballs right now, but he'd have a look-see. Mr. Stevie had said passed-out drunks were part of the job.

Tyrone strained the seams of his starched jacket as he bent over Skip's body, then quickly sucked in air. There'd been a fight, bright patches of blood on the walls, more seeping from his head onto the tile floor. Younger than the Baby Jesus, Tyrone thought. This boy lay too still for somebody sleeping it off. He wasn't breathing.

Tyrone's first impulse was to make a run for it. He'd been dumb enough to slug that ofay who was picking on Blackie out in the hall. But dead white people, he knew, were even more trouble than live white people.

Just do what they tell you and keep your mouth shut, he heard his aunt's voice in his head. *Never ask questions and don't talk back.*

Her advice didn't cover dead bodies of boys as pretty as girls. God only knows what this one had been up to and how he'd ended up like this. Tyrone thought he would've been better off if he'd stuck to sweeping floors and emptying wastepaper baskets. He had to get back to Blackie.

Then Skip's big diamond twinkled up at him like the star on a Christmas tree. Tyrone picked up the one hand in both of his own. The ring sat practically atop the knuckle, like somebody had tried to get it off.

Whoever it was had the right idea, Tyrone thought. If the rock was real, he could get some money for it.

"Nobody's gonna miss this ring, least of all him," he muttered as he knelt beside Skip. No point in leaving it for the next guy or the cops.

A couple of tugs and the ring slid into Tyrone's hand. He looked at Skip. Leave it alone, something told him. Even as pretty as he was, it hadn't done this white boy no good. And if he was rich, somebody would be out looking for him. It was risky.

But there was nobody to see, nobody to tell.

He heard his mother: *We don't take things that don't belong to us.* But he'd found out that was what smart people did to get ahead in the world. They sure didn't haul garbage for Mr. Stevie or mess with stinking, evil drunks every night of their lives.

Tyrone stood up and popped the ring into his pants pocket. Here at last was a little bonus, he thought, and maybe the something better his mother had wished.

Or maybe he'd cooked his own goose the moment he found the body. The police would be looking for somebody to pin it on, and nobody had to tell him how happy they'd be to lock him up and throw away the key. Unless Blackie would stand up for him.

He opened the door a crack. "Blackie," he said. "C'mere a minute. We got a little trouble."

"What kinda trouble?"

Fear was fast closing around Tyrone's throat. "Please," he answered hoarsely. "Somebody's hurt."

Blackie hesitated and looked over at the drunk in the corner, who was snoring. She wished she'd taken the night off. "I can't leave this creep."

Tyrone poked out his lower lip. "He ain't goin' nowhere, and there's nobody in here but me."

She read panic in his big dark eyes. "You want me to get Charlie and Waxy?"

"No, no," he pleaded. "You c'mon." His hand trembled on the doorframe.

Tyrone had stuck his neck out for her. "I'm right behind you," Blackie said.

He opened the door wide and pointed her toward the metal stall where Skip lay. She stared at the slender young body. "Is he?" Her mouth gaped in a kind of prayer. Except for the blood spreading like a crown around his head, the only mark on the boy was a rose-colored welt along one cheek. Otherwise the face was luminous like that of a child or an angel. She'd seen that face before at the club. She never forgot a face.

Tyrone nodded. "Musta been a fight. He musta fallen some way and hit his head."

Nobody would've ever expected trouble at the Candy Box, Blackie thought. Everyone came for laughs and a good time. Even mobsters who didn't flinch at bumping off whoever got in their way behaved themselves at the club.

Blackie stood very still, recalling another moment, a face that had passed her in the hallway. Enormous desperate eyes, olive skin. She'd bet a bundle that guy had been up to no good. She should've caught up, found out what he was running away from.

"Did you see a dark-haired guy runnin' down the hall before that bastard out there jumped me?" she asked Tyrone.

"He passed me goin' about 90 miles an hour. Feet not even touchin' the ground." Tyrone paused. "You think he did this?"

"Who else?" Blackie felt like sitting down beside the dead boy for a good cry. She'd let a killer get away. With her description, maybe the police could nail the fugitive. But they only showed up at the Candy Box to collect their payoffs.

"Wait here, Tyrone. I'm gonna get the boss." Stevie was the only law and order at the club. He'd know what to do.

Tyrone's eyes were wide, like a diver's searching for the loose hose. "Please don't tell Mr. Stevie nuthin' about me hittin' that man, findin' that body."

"You got nuthin' to worry about, Tyrone," Blackie said. "You just sit tight."

He had to trust her. She knew Aunt Sundown, who'd told him she was a decent white woman. He followed her out the door of the men's room. No sap, he stuck an OUT OF ORDER notice on the doorknob, took out his keys, and locked it up tight. The drunk stirred in his corner, keeping Tyrone company as he hunkered down to wait.

THREE

Stevie the Frenchman, kingpin of the mob's downtown night-club operation and manager of the Candy Box Club, took off his wire-rimmed glasses. He rubbed his eyes by the light of a brass table lamp that flattened out his elongated shadow against a blank plaster wall.

In the club's back room, which Stevie called his office, he'd just gone over last week's receipts. Business was good, but you had to be on your toes. When some crackpot shot up the Moroccan Village, a club just down the street, they were closed for a month. Thirty-eight-caliber slugs all over. The Candy Box couldn't afford that.

Stevie read the papers too. In June, crusading Manhattan District attorney Mike Duggan had thrown his hat into the ring when incumbent mayor James O'Malley chose not to seek a second term. Or so the story went.

The mob wasn't pleased. DA Duggan had a reputation as a troublemaker, sticking his nose in where it wasn't required. He'd caused a ripple or two going after their horse parlors and crap games last year before things settled down to normal. So the big boss, Uncle Fred Capotello, had let those punks down at the Hall know—Duggan for mayor wouldn't wash. "Give us O'Malley," Capotello said, and the kingmakers squirmed.

DA Duggan was supposed to be tough on crime. With front-page headlines screaming every day about murder and mayhem taking over the city, he could count on a lot of support. Stevie glanced across an expanse of weather-beaten desk at a two-column photo of a garbage can up on 94th Street in Yorkville.

"Look at this," he said to Smash Nose Babe, his colossal bodyguard. "Some Irish girl got herself murdered, a parochial-school girl. Slashed her and left her in a garbage can."

"Sure thing, boss." Babe's massive teeth floated above Stevie in the dim light, a wide Boris Karloff smile splitting his face from ear to ear.

"Whaddaya grinnin' about?" Stevie mumbled in a voice like a wood rasp. "This has got a lotta people hot under the collar."

He crossed himself piously. " 'The work of a degenerate,' it sez here. The church's demandin' a full investigation." His finger meandered down the column. " 'Flaws in sex crime laws...' it sez here, 'and softness in enforcement have left degenerates free to prey on women and children.' "

Stevie patted his crisp gray hair over a couple of balding spots. "Just the kinda grist Duggan needs for his mill."

Babe looked glum.

"Doesn't take a Svengali to figure it out!" Stevie ranted. "Nobody's safe in this town anymore, what with all the cops so busy collectin' their payoffs."

A flurry of blows, like an amateur boxing match, pelted the door to Stevie's office, interrupting.

"Yeah, who is it?" Stevie called out, motioning Smash Nose Babe toward the door.

Babe took a peek through the peephole. "Blackie, boss."

Stevie nodded that she was welcome. And why not? The swell-elegant show he'd built around her was packing them in, customers lining the street waiting for the next show. More than a few high rollers had asked Stevie why she wasn't available for a little hanky-panky after hours.

"You know how it is, boys," he'd replied. "Some girls are shy at first." That made them want her more.

Blackie burst in. A curly lock of hair, loosened by her dash across the club, dangled over those fabulous eyes. Her trousers barely disguised long, shapely legs.

Stevie sat up in his armchair. When he'd first seen Blackie at Ernie's, he'd asked her to come out from behind the bar. "Since you ain't wearin' a skirt, sister," he said to her, "you'll have to drop your drawers."

"To see your legs," he explained when she blushed crimson. "With good legs and that face, you can make it big."

Blackie had breathed in a sharp sour smell like the stench of a tenement alley. "You want me for the chorus line?"

"You could do worse." He shrugged and straightened the brim of his fedora.

She watched him turn to walk away and felt a riptide of despair. He was right. She didn't want to spend the rest of her life behind a bar. "OK, sure." This wasn't kid stuff. It was business, show business.

Blackie unzipped her slacks. He ogled the trim thighs. From below the edge of her shirttail peeped men's boxer shorts with printed red hearts.

"Dizzy dykes," Stevie chided. But oh, those legs! "You get some women's underpants before you come to work at the Candy Box!" He paused. "Otherwise, the cops'll have you up for impersonatin'."

He wondered what kind of underpants she was wearing now. Plenty of johns would pay big money to see them.

"Hey, boss!" Blackie puffed.

"Whazzamatta, kid?" Stevie asked, then spread his arms paternally. "Siddown over here."

"There's no time. We got trouble."

Part of Blackie's charm, Stevie mused, was she was hot-blooded, got all excited over nothing just like any other broad. That could be a real plus. He adjusted his myopic gaze away from her crotch.

"Hey, what happened to you?" he asked. "You're a mess."

"Aw, some stinker got the wrong idea, like me and him was gonna be pals."

"He got fresh? Who was it? We don't allow none of that."

"Yeah, well, tell *him* about it. He's passed out over in front of the Gents." Blackie paused for a breath. "But that's not the biggest problem. What's inside is worse."

Stevie gave her a questioning look. "Whaddaya mean?"

"In the men's room...a customer's turned up dead!"

"A stiff? In the Gents? You sure?"

"I saw him. Tyrone's keepin' everybody out of there."

"Tyrone?" Stevie's eyes misted over like smoked crystal. "Who the hell's Tyrone?"

"Sundown's nephew, boss," Blackie reminded him. "You gotta come quick."

"That colored kid?" Stevie's face sagged like a Saint Bernard's. "Killed somebody?"

Stevie made the sign of the cross again, exonerating himself for hiring Tyrone as a favor to Madam Lucille. In 20 years he'd never been able to say no to Lucille, and Tyrone's Aunt Sundown had been Lucille's maid for longer than that.

"You got it wrong," Blackie said. "Tyrone didn't do nuthin'. He's watchin' the body."

Stevie rubbed his glasses with the end of his tie and replaced them on his nose. "Body, huh? We'll see about that."

Short but dapper in a chalk-striped gray suit with wide lapels, he rose and lifted a splayed palm. "Babe, get me Charlie and Waxy over to the men's room, and make it snappy." His lips scampered rapid fire over the names of obscure Christian saints, invocations to the mother of God, and insults to the mother of the stiff in the men's room. "Whadda we waitin' for?"

He followed Blackie out. If the cops got wind he had a dead man at the Candy Box, they'd close him down for sure. That would suit DA Duggan just fine.

Stevie couldn't let things get out of hand. He'd promised Tony the Hawk—"Mr. Hammer Lock," they called him—before Tony left for an extended vacation to Italy.

"Stevie, my boy, you're in charge," the Hawk had admonished. "I'm depending on you to mind your P's and Q's—pimps and queers." All the boys roared with laughter. "Nobody gets outta line."

Stevie imagined the hot water he'd be in if the cops closed down the club. When he reached the door of the Gents, his frigid stare fell on the drunk in the corner. "This shitheel the one who got fresh witchya?"

Blackie nodded, and he raised his hand again. "Charlie, Waxy, get him outta here."

Crazy Charlie, whose head was patched by a steel plate, stored a lead pipe under his jacket. His sidekick Waxy wrestled the drunk up into a viselike half nelson while Charlie frisked him. An inch or two of pale striated tongue lolled between the man's lips like an aging tomcat's. They were playing for keeps.

"We don't want no cheapskates around here botherin' our girls," Stevie threatened. "You pay, or you don't play."

The drunk's eyes opened wide as Waxy towed him through the red velvet curtain. Charlie followed, the light framing his dented head in a shifting halo. They left a trail of cheap aftershave.

"OK, that's taken care of." Stevie mopped his brow. "Now where's the stiff?"

The word grated on Blackie's ear like a cold wind blowing sand. She didn't like this side of Stevie. "In here," she mumbled, and Stevie hurried past.

Skip lay on the floor where he'd been left. A pool of blood had congealed behind his head. Smash Nose Babe prodded the body with his foot.

"He's a goner, boss."

"Miss Suckoffski!" Stevie rasped. "Dead in the toilet, like some animal." He recrossed himself. "That's why I don't want no gay boys comin' around." He raised a fist against the affront. "One don't like somethin', he starts a fight, like they was husband and wife. Sick sons of bitches." Easier to keep the girls in line.

A flush rose to Blackie's cheeks. This wasn't the Stevie who passed around free champagne at holidays, laughing and patting the boys on the butt.

"Aw, Stevie," she dared, "he's just a kid—and pretty as a picture."

Stevie's face went blank like an ice cube. "Not anymore he ain't!" He signaled brusquely to Smash Nose Babe. "Any ID on him?"

Tyrone nervously rolled the dead boy's ring around in his pocket, between thumb and forefinger.

Babe bent down. "Clean as a whistle," he grunted back.

Well, one thing for sure, this was no lowbrow, Stevie reflected. Not with those looks, those clothes. Everything about him spelled class. Maybe he'd even had a coming-out party. "Anybody ever seen him around here before?"

Blackie racked her memory.

Stevie didn't wait for an answer. "Forgedaboudit then! Capisce?" He carved up the syllables. "Nobody talks about this to nobody."

He paused and turned to Blackie. "You go on and get ready for your number."

Singing was the last thing on Blackie's mind. What was Stevie gonna do with the body? And who was the guy who'd passed her in the hallway? A killer, on the loose and free to kill again.

She knew better than to complain, but the look on Blackie's face told Stevie not to trust her silence. He took off his spectacles and shined the splotched lenses again.

"Easy does it, sweetheart," he clucked like a den mother. A house full of people had paid to see her. "You know what they say: The show must go on!" He gestured to Smash Nose Babe, who took Blackie by the arm.

She flinched at his touch. "Hey, what's the big idea?"

"Babe'll make sure you get backstage," Stevie promised. "You just got time to get cleaned up."

With desolate eyes, Blackie gazed back at Skip's body. There was nothing she could do for him. Renee, her ex who'd been in show business a long time, had given her some advice. "I wouldn't shit an old timer, honey," she'd confided to Blackie in a low smoky voice. "The first lesson you gotta learn working for the mafia is don't cross the boss."

Blackie decided to call it loyalty. She owed Stevie. A bartender she was, and he'd made her into a headliner. He made hamburger out of the drunk who'd roughed her up. "Sure thing, Stevie," replied Blackie, who only wanted to go home and crawl into bed. "I'll do my best."

Silence hung in the air as Blackie was led away. Stevie's jaw hardened. Whirling around, he got down to business, pointing a finger like a derringer at Tyrone, who froze to attention.

"You," he mumbled something into Tyrone's ear, "On the double."

Tyrone exited in a hurry as Charlie and Waxy returned from their first assignment.

Steadying his hands, Stevie indicated the metal stall. "OK,

boys," he commanded, "let's get this mess cleaned up and hustle him out of here."

Waxy took some towels off the cotton roll that hung on the wall, and bound up Skip's head. Charlie brought more, dampened in the sink, to wipe up the floor and walls. They held their breath, and both squeezed in beside Skip. When they were ready, they lifted him between them, straightening and adjusting.

Stevie announced that the coast was clear. They were steering the body into the hallway when Waxy staggered and slipped to one knee. "Oops. Sorry, boss!" he groaned.

"For Chrissake," Stevie barked, "keep it down!" All they needed was a curious customer in search of the Gents. The procession crept along the hall in silence.

At the other end was the Candy Box's kitchen, where Tyrone waited. Beyond swinging doors, stacks of square and round packages wrapped in butcher paper overflowed the tables. Tyrone had followed orders to a T.

"Plenty of room now, boss," he told Stevie, with a phony smile like the Great White Way. He lifted the heavy lid of a Philco store-size freezer and shivered. It was the latest model, about the size of a coffin.

Stevie nodded his hard-boiled approval. "In here, boys. We're putting him on ice."

Charlie and Waxy dangled their burden in mid air. "Great idea, boss," Charlie said. "I saw this once in a movie."

"The one with Joan Blondell?" Waxy asked, breathing heavily. "Where she's a nurse?"

"Will you cut it out! We ain't got all night!" Stevie pressed a handkerchief to his temple. "And this ain't no movie."

These two had loyalty but no brains. Sometimes he wondered how a guy with his reputation had gotten stuck with them when there was so much talent around.

"Sure thing, boss," Charlie and Waxy chorused. Puffing like weightlifters, they hefted Skip over the edge and into the freezer.

Stevie shook his head and made the sign of the cross again, this time over the Philco. He couldn't afford any mistakes, not where Tony the Hawk was concerned. "Close that thing up—now!"

The lid descended with a whoosh and shut with a clunk that brought everything in the kitchen to a standstill.

"Tyrone!" Stevie beckoned him out of the lineup of bug-eyed cooks and dishwashers. "You go on home, and take some of that meat too. It's just gonna rot."

"Yessir. Thank you, boss," Tyrone mouthed, eyes on the ground. He began bagging a pile of steaks and chops.

Stevie drew closer. "And take tomorrow off, boy—on me."

To the kitchen crew, he said, "The rest of you, back to work, and keep your mouths shut."

Tyrone didn't waste time quibbling about the price of his silence. His arms encircled the groceries. He felt lucky to get out of there. The kitchen's back door opened into an alley-way, which he followed around a corner and back onto Eighth Street.

Charlie pulled out a chair for the boss, who slumped into it. Stevie was in a pickle. His head throbbed, and he needed a drink. He closed his eyes to dodge the memory of the lifeless form on the cold tile floor. Nobody would believe, God forgive him, a stiff at the Candy Box. At least there'd been no shooting, no shiv. He shuddered to think about guns going off and gushing fountains of blood. They'd never have been able to cover all that up.

Four

Blackie managed to put her number over, but her throat was scratchy. Her performance felt hollow, her movements stiff and rehearsed. She tried to sound like she was pining for everyone in the audience as she sang,

It's no use caring
For someone who can't be true.

It worked. She was a trouper, like Stevie said. "Bravo!" the crowd shouted as Blackie stumbled back to the dressing room.

She'd tried to shake the blues, but the song reminded her of Renee, her hair like a hammered sheet of red-gold spread over the pillow. Blackie had never wanted to leave her, hadn't wanted any more betrayals in her life. But Renee had been a bombshell, a smoking stick of dynamite when she drank. Their love affair had turned into a bad dream.

Titanic passed Blackie in the hallway. He wore a quicksilver-blond wig and skimpy tutu outfit, bare shoulders aglitter. "Whazzamatta?" he asked. "You look like hell!"

She wanted to pour out the story of the drunk and the dead boy in the men's room. But he had only seconds to spare before his cue, and Stevie had warned them all to keep their mouths shut.

"I just got a touch of the jitters," she replied.

Titanic could be motherly. "Lie down for a while," he said, then pranced onstage. She heard him belt out the opening bars of his slapdash Betty Grable routine.

Hold me, squeeze me....

Not much of a voice, Blackie thought, but he certainly had the legs for it. She closed the dressing room door. Sinking onto a shabby divan that sat in one corner, she longed to rest her head on someone's shoulder.

The dressing-room mirror was lined with photos, black-and-white glossy 8-by-10s. Most were of the kids posed with customers for the club photographer, who did a land-office business every night. Visiting firemen, butter-and-egg men from Toledo or Oshkosh, took the photos back home to show folks what nightlife was like in the big city.

There was one of her and Titanic with a straight couple from Havana. They'd invited them both down to stay at their 25-room seaside cottage. There were publicity shots of Titanic alone. First came the cheesecake poses. Then the Gene Tierney look and finally Dorothy Lamour. His "road pictures," he called them.

Blackie snatched up a powder puff from the dressing table. In the mirror she studied the shambles of her face, the color of the rice powder she dabbed on her chin. A little more here would soften the jawline.

Somewhere deep inside the ceiling a pipe whined, and Blackie gasped like a slug had taken her by surprise. She knew in a flash where she'd seen the dead boy before.

They'd all been in the dressing room in front of the mirror. He was trying on gaudy costume earrings in the shape of miniature Japanese lanterns. They bounced against his cheeks as he twisted his pretty head from side to side.

"It must be wonderful to be in show business," he was saying. "I just wish I was good enough to make the grade."

Titanic was making up, pressing false eyelashes, thick bands like little feather dusters, onto his eyelids. He offered advice.

"It's all in the way you move," he said as he thrust one shoulder forward, then the other. "We'll walk through a routine. You'll be sensational!"

The boy had fluttered pale lashes. The Japanese lanterns danced saucily.

Blackie would have to tell Titanic, who knew who the dead boy was, maybe knew his friends. There would be family to notify. Who would tell them and what? And if anything ever happened to Blackie at the Candy Box, how would her own family find out? Mom, eyes the clear blue of glass marbles, and Dad, his dark unruly hair like hers, only straight and stiff, going gray.

She'd told them she worked at an all-night coffeehouse in the Village, run by Italians. Her father would say she was a fool to be mixed up with the mafia and would never forgive her for helping to cover up what looked like a murder.

A few feet away from the dressing room, Stevie was on the phone in his office. It seemed to him it had rung a zillion times. Finally, Madam Lucille's maid, Sundown, answered at the uptown house, an 11-room apartment on 55th Street just off Madison Avenue.

"Hi, Sundown," Stevie growled. "Whaddaya know? Whaddaya say?"

"Oh, not much, Mr. Stevie," Sundown answered sweetly. "Pretty quiet tonight." Her skin was café au lait. Her hair had a red tinge to it. On the phone she didn't have to smile at those dumb lines he always greeted her with, like he was some comedian.

"Tell Miss Lucille it's me," Stevie said. Another eternity passed before a voice came on the line.

"Stevie, honey," it drawled in a leathery Barbara Stanwyck, which for years had made men forget they were paying for it. "How's everything by you?"

Lucille Martin wasn't as young as she used to be. She often rested while her girls turned tricks in the bedrooms, or milled around on the Aubusson carpet downstairs, sizing up the trade. Her room was at the top of the staircase that led up from the high-domed entrance hall with its rock-crystal chandelier.

She took Stevie's call sprawled on a chaise lounge of carved walnut. Pink satin pumps, dyed to match her low-cut gown, pointed at the ceiling where fat cupids floated, tangled up in rosettes and ribbons. Layers of silver-blue silk curtains covered the 12-foot French windows.

"Things ain't so good down here," Stevie confessed. He wouldn't have said that to just anybody. He trusted Lucille. His good-luck charm, he called her. They went back a long way, since Prohibition.

Stevie told the story of the dead body in the Gents, no ID, and the Philco freezer. "I didn't want no cops snoopin' around."

"You did the right thing," Lucille said. But she always said that, even if things got botched up. Part of her job was to make him feel good. He was the boss, and his protection kept her operation afloat.

"Now I gotta get him outta here," Stevie added anxiously. "We need to get some food in to serve, and he could start stinkin'!"

Lucille flipped her hair out of her eyes. She wore it peek-a-boo style like Veronica Lake, long and bleached blond, a very good, very expensive dye job.

"Well, you oughta get a move on." She signaled Sundown to pour her a drink. Her waistline had spread a few inches in the last few years. It strained at the seams of her dress.

"What's the rush?" he asked.

"Don't you read the papers?"

"Sure, the Yankees are two games out."

"Very funny, Stevie." Lucille was a Yankee fan too, another bond between them. "But I'm talking about front-page news. With Duggan runnin' for mayor, some Irish girl got herself murdered up in Yorkville."

"Yeah, yeah, I read all about it. So?"

Lucille remembered him from when he was a strong-arm man, quick on the trigger. But dumping bodies in the river didn't teach you the finer points of the sex trade.

"OK," she explained, "*The Daily Journal* sez it ain't normal the way they rubbed out that girl. Only deviants and degenerates go in for that kinda thing." She paused. "Then farther down it sez, 'These degenerates are in little neighborhood nests, and a few bars and nightclubs that are famous for sex deviants.'"

A slight tremor shook the bottle Stevie took out from the desk drawer. Fog condensed on his eyeglasses as he poured himself a whiskey.

"So the cops think I got prime suspects in the chorus line?" he squawked. "The Candy Box is a family show, lotsa laughs!"

"Some people think different."

"Who cares what they think? We got protection!"

"Tell it to the judge." Lucille's voice thickened. "I've already heard rumors from our boys on the police force that the purge is comin'."

"What purge?" Stevie was beginning to sweat. "They got their money."

"Sometimes that ain't enough, with an election comin' up

and DA Duggan chompin' at the bit," Lucille confided. "You get rid of that stiff!"

"Before you can say Jack Robinson."

"That's the spirit. Ain't I your good-luck charm?" Lucille's voice mellowed. "And how's Blackie Cole doin'?"

So innocent it sounded, the question caught Stevie off guard. He hemmed and hawed.

"OK, I guess. We had a little trouble down here with one of the boys. Got fresh with her."

"Well, you said she was a big draw," Lucille giggled.

"Yeah, yeah."

"When she gets tired of workin' for you, tell her to give me a buzz."

"You got a lotta nerve," Stevie snarled. "Blackie's my bread and butter."

"I gotta have a lotta nerve," Lucille replied coolly.

Well, that much was true, Stevie reasoned, a smart businesswoman like her. Maybe it was natural she wanted a piece of Blackie. But she couldn't make a move without the OK she wouldn't get from him.

"Gotta go," he said, and mumbled good-bye.

Lucille planted a big kiss on the receiver and hung up.

Stevie leaned back uneasily in his chair and watched some dufus moth batter its wings inside the shade of the brass lamp on his desk. He didn't feel so lucky as he replaced the phone in its cradle. Cops and women, they were always up to something. But this was no time to go off half-cocked. There was work to be done.

"The paper," he said to Smash Nose Babe, who'd been keeping silent vigil near the office door. "Bring me the paper."

"Which paper, boss?"

"Any paper!" Stevie snapped his fingers. "Now!"

Babe returned in an instant with the *Times*. "This do?" he asked.

Stevie was already leafing through to the marine and aviation schedules. The heat was on, and he didn't want this stiff washing up somewhere next week.

"Our friend in the Philco," he jerked his head toward the kitchen, "needs a little sea air, a nice long voyage." He ran a finger down the listings, soliloquizing. "We're a little late for tomorrow's departures. But there's plenty more where that came from. Would he like Europe or South America better? And here's the best one yet. Around the world. Too bad, don't leave till Friday, and he won't keep forever. Look here, Babe."

Stevie spread the departure listings across the table. "Day after tomorrow, we've got one at the mornin' tide, North River piers.... Noon, West 44th. 11 a.m., West 14th, Cunard. In the evening, West 24th, Canal; West 50th, Moore-McCormack." Stevie took a pen and marked one entry with a big X. The stiff would go as cargo. "This is it. Pier 53, right here. We'll load him up early. I'll just make a few calls."

He snapped his fingers again. "I need a phone number for Local 428."

Babe supplied it from a small black book.

"And get me Charlie and Waxy," Stevie said. "We'll need a trunk, a big one, to get him over to the waterfront. Longshoremen'll be waitin' to pick him up. We scratch their backs, they scratch ours, and vicey-versey."

Stevie grabbed the phone again and started dialing with a flourish.

"Hey, boss," Smash Nose Babe cautioned, "you're gonna wake those union guys up."

"You think I give a damn?" Stevie shook a fist in Babe's face. "Who ever said Stevie the Frenchman was gettin' to be a cream puff?"

FIVE

Uptown, all the talk about dead bodies and police raids had left Lucille nervous. Even if she preferred taking it easy, out of the line of fire, she decided she really needed to have a look-see downstairs. It was a busy night, and things were going full blast. She rose off her couch.

Resting one hand on the curved banister, Lucille tilted her neck back, sagging muscles stretched taut. She remembered the many times she'd descended this staircase before. One night years ago when her high jinks were the talk of the town, she'd started out a little tipsy wearing a full-length mink buttoned up around her neck.

"Aren't you a little warm in that coat?" a customer had asked. Music was playing in the background.

Lucille had replied that yes, she was, and dropped the coat to the floor. Stepping over it butt naked, she chose a partner. They snuggled close and danced off to a chorus of oohs and ahs.

She chuckled and thought that none of her girls seemed as fancy free as she had been at their age. Too interested in money, they were, and dreaming of getting to Broadway or

Hollywood. Especially that new girl Renee. But Lucille couldn't complain. Renee was great for business.

Done up in a dark strapless satin gown with matching elbow-length gloves, and with her strawberry-blond hair hanging loose, she looked enough like Rita Hayworth to play Gilda. Lots of big tippers were in a tailspin and asked for Renee by name.

Once downstairs, Lucille peeked into the living room. Two Louis XVI-style loveseats, upholstered in pale silk with embroidered country fantasies, flanked the marble fireplace. Towering mirrors on opposite walls repeated the opulent curves. In one corner a foursome of highbrow johns with fat wallets played no-nonsense poker at a mahogany-and-leather card table, while a couple of Lucille's girls kibitzed. The game was winding down.

"Some bluff, Jack," said a busty redhead in a champagne-colored marquisette gown to the man with the winning hand. He had a mane of light hair streaked with silver. The blue eyes were deep set and haunting, the forehead high and smooth.

"I'm afraid you've cleaned me out," the man across the table added without any fuss. Paunchy and balding, he wanted Jack to enjoy himself and didn't mind losing. He had a nose that could've slit envelopes.

"You're always such a good sport, Judge," said Flo, the brunette who sat beside him. She could've stood in for Hedy Lamarr, with her hair almost black against alabaster skin and her great soulful eyes.

A blond named Marie, with perfumed curls, powder-blue eyes, and a kittenish Lana Turner air, leaned over the judge's shoulder and whispered, "The party's all set if you wanna go in."

Judge Randolph Valerio, a staunch friend of Mayor O'Malley, did want to go in and stood up.

"C'mon, Jack," the auburn-haired girl said to her companion. He was John Jay Fletcher-Payne, owner of *The New*

York Daily Journal, but he insisted the girls call him Jack.

Her saltwater-taffy pastel dress clung to her like flypaper, revealing the voluptuous body of a stripper. "You're gonna love the party, Jack."

He didn't budge. Strictly upper crust, with a family tree a mile long, John Jay was also an inveterate gambler. "How about another game, Judge?" he offered. "I wouldn't deny you a chance to get even."

While pretending to be generous, John Jay felt his heart beat frantically. His luck had changed at last, and if he could keep the game going, he might recoup yesterday's losses at the track. A hot tip on a horse at Aqueduct, a 15-to-1 shot, that never got out of the gate. Pete the bookie would be calling about his tab, and John Jay was fresh out of excuses.

The judge had had enough. He could only afford to invest so much in keeping the old boy amused. The redhead would have to take up the slack.

Lucille moved over to the table. "Everything all right, boys?"

Tall and imperially slim, John Jay rose gallantly to his feet. Good breeding kept him from insisting on the poker game. He put a youthful spring in his step so Valerio wouldn't guess his disappointment.

"A great evening, Lucille," the judge said as he draped an arm around his poker buddy. "Jack says he hasn't had such a good time in years." He paused. "You can't buy influence like that."

"That so, Jack?" Lucille smiled. The horses, the cards, dice, cockroaches, you name it, word was Fletcher-Payne would bet on it. "You know you're welcome any time. We've always got a game goin'."

John Jay Fletcher-Payne nodded with a patrician elegance, but his turquoise eyes were playful. He'd spun roulette wheels from Jersey to the Florida Gold Coast. He'd once met Lansky himself. There was nothing like a smart Jew.

For now, he consoled himself with the redhead the judge had set him up with. "Shall we go in, Renee dear?" John Jay said, offering her his arm.

She smiled demurely, like butter wouldn't melt in her mouth, as she led John Jay past the dining room, set with 50 chairs in oyster-white leather and hung with coral-and-gold draperies. In the adjacent taproom, decorated in black and zebra-striped leatherette, the party Lucille had arranged was in full swing.

Judge Valerio drew Lucille aside. "Thanks again," he said, and pressed a wad of bills into her hand. "Renee's just what the doctor ordered. She oughta do the trick." The party bosses badly wanted *The Daily Journal*'s endorsement for their candidate.

"I'm glad you're pleased with Renee, Judge," Lucille said, reflecting on her good luck. She watched the partygoers disappear into the taproom, then slipped around back to the kitchen. A window in the swinging door gave her a view of the judge, Old John Jay, and other society types at small tables with young hostesses. On a postage-stamp stage up front, the show was underway.

The first performers were three queer boys completely in drag—wigs, false eyelashes, high-heeled pumps, and evening gowns. The crowd was under their spell, in stitches and begging for more.

"You can't make me believe those aren't women," one patron sputtered with alcoholic abandon.

Suit yourself, Lucille thought.

Next up was a hefty black woman dressed in an extra-large white tie and tails. She wore her hair nappy, trimmed close to her head, and clinched an unlit cigar between pearly white teeth. She sauntered to the piano and made a deep bow.

"Good evenin', ladies and gentlemen," she said in a rich

alto. "My name is Mabel, and my first number I calls the 'Copulatin' Boogie.'"

The kitchen door sighed as Lucille pushed her way into the taproom and hovered at the back to catch Mabel's act.

Mabel didn't disappoint her, leaning into the keyboard with the full force of her considerable girth. Her big hands glided into a deep rolling bass with lightning-fast fingering in the upper register. The boogie throbbed soulfully, filling the room. At intervals Mabel accompanied herself by growling out the muted tones of a trumpet. Anyone would've sworn it was the real McCoy.

"Hear that?" one member of the group shouted over the applause. "Hear" ended in a broad aristocratic A. "Only a nigger could do that."

Mabel's cynical glance took in, then dismissed him. The boogie rhythm faded to a steady blues cadence as she swung around on the piano bench to wail out a sad story of love's frustrations. She glided up the keyboard and sang,

My man named Lou
Didn't know just what to do
Where to put that thing
That ding-a-ling.

The crowd applauded and guffawed. Lucille knew the routine, and when Mabel sang again about "that thing," she led them in "that ding-a-ling."

Mabel picked up the refrain.

I say, what's wrong with that thing?

And the crowd bellowed back, "that ding-a-ling." Down front, Judge Valerio, with Flo and Marie on either side of him, exploded in laughter.

Mabel's song tapered off in silvery arpeggios. Lucille came forward and took her around to shake hands with all the big-time spenders. The judge laid a large bill in Mabel's outstretched palm. John Jay slipped something into the breast pocket of her jacket. She nodded graciously. Yes, they could see her at an after-hours joint in Harlem called Monroe's.

When the show was over, Sundown came out in her black dress with a white apron and cap. The seamed wedge of her elbow was ashen, ankles swelling over her shoes. All discretion, she took Mabel's arm and guided her swiftly out the back door.

John Jay Fletcher-Payne, Lucille observed, had discarded his tie, his face red and distended. One arm around Renee's creamy shoulder, he pulled her closer, thin lips smiling, and mumbled something into her ear. She laughed at his joke, and a bolder hand slid down the front of her dress.

Lucille chuckled as she turned away. Whether his name was Fletcher-Payne or Joe Blow, in the dark all johns were the same.

Down at the Candy Box the show was still going on, the chorus line hoofing it across the stage. Blackie stood in the wings waiting for the finale. Stevie sidled up and motioned her back into the shadows. His eyes blinked narrow and glassy like a panther's caught in a camera flash. He needed to know what was on her mind.

"How ya feelin', kid? Great number you did out there for the folks."

"Thanks, boss," she said, with a hint of her winning smile.

Beneath the smile he sensed she wouldn't level with him. It didn't matter. "I'm glad you're OK. I wouldn't wanna see ya mixed up in any trouble."

"Yeah, me neither. But you know, the boy in the Gents..." She paused, and Stevie rotated his head her way like a lizard. "I remembered where I saw him from. He used to come down a lot, wanted to be in the show. He was harmless."

Stevie wagged a finger at Blackie. "Nobody's harmless, and do I look like the missin' persons bureau?"

"If somebody wanted to identify the body..." she began, then clammed up quick.

"They can identify all they want as long as it ain't here," Stevie sulked. "They find that body, it's curtains for the club. They'd close us down tight as Dick's hatband."

That got Blackie's attention. She scrunched up her forehead and felt queasy.

Stevie saw her waver. "You know," he went on, "the cops ain't gonna pound the pavement lookin' for the killer of some faggot. And even if they found him, they'd wanna pin a medal on him."

It had been a long night. Blackie coughed into her fist. None of that was news.

"Yeah, the cops'd be much more interested in you dressed up like that." He pointed to her trousers. "If they ever got their mitts on you, they'd run you in. Call it disorderly conduct, disturbin' the peace. Whatever pops into their head. Capisce?"

Beads of perspiration glistened on Blackie's forehead.

"And once they get you inside," Stevie harangued her, "they throw you dykes in with the men. It's been done."

He paused to let his words soak in. "We took care of the stiff already, and you oughta stop worryin' about what you *thought* you saw."

Smart girl, she played dumb. Stevie couldn't be sure she'd leave well enough alone. He'd had trouble with dames who blabbed before. In fact, the only one he'd ever known who could keep her mouth shut was Lucille.

The first few bars of the finale blared across the club. Blackie had plenty of good reasons to play it safe. She could forget about the lifeless boy on the tile floor, even the dark-haired man in the hall. "Sure thing, Stevie. You can trust me."

"Attagirl!" She knew which side her bread was buttered on. His old self again, Stevie gave Blackie a playful shove toward the stage. "You just go out there and knock 'em dead."

He watched her join the promenade. She'd turned out to be a great little entertainer, great legs. But between the stiff in the freezer and crusading DA Duggan running for mayor, Stevie reflected, his luck seemed to be wearing thin. The feds had run Tony the Hawk out of the country, and the queers and hookers were getting a little too hot for Stevie the Frenchman to handle.

"Fangool," Stevie muttered to the universe, pressing his right forefinger and middle finger into his thumb. Blackie Cole had better keep her trap shut.

Six

A white gown with chiffon skirt and narrow sequined straps was draped over a chair in the little furnished room Blackie rented on Christopher Street. Gauzy open-work patches sprouted like flowers on the bodice. Rita Hayworth had worn a dress like it in *Cover Girl*.

Blackie dreamed she reached out to caress the fabric, then turned to the cloud of strawberry-blond hair on the pillow next to hers. She was wearing her tux, a satin stripe down the seam of her pants. Damp thighs gripped her leg.

A voice like breaking glass mumbled, "Down on your knees, girlie," and something about a toilet.

In her dream the narrow window above the bed opened. A shoddy cloth pull-down shade billowed. It filled then flattened, snuffing out the air in the boxy room. Hands like silken threads entwined themselves in her hair, and she shifted around to make room for the closeness. A breeze from the courtyard stirred the shade.

"Don't leave me," another voice said. "Don't ever leave me."

"I'll never leave, sweetheart," Blackie replied, just as a

siren sounded from the street. When she woke up and opened her eyes, she saw only the blank wall. But her crotch throbbed, a pungent dampness spreading between her legs. The pleasure she and Renee had wrung from each other still bound them together. Renee's black lacy nightie hiked up around her hips as she spread her legs urgently, Blackie's tongue probing Renee's silken lips.

Blackie moaned and squeezed her eyes shut again. All that love come to nothing, the promises broken.

The sun had already dropped behind the shabby building next door when she woke up alone a second time. Long shadows filled the room. She let go of her fetal grip on the pillow and unwound her legs from the sheet. When she flipped onto her stomach, she saw the clock.

Blackie never slept this late. But the last couple of nights had been almost sleepless, filled with nightmares about the body in the men's room and the drunk. She hadn't been going to breakfast with the rest of the kids after the club closed. Said she didn't feel like it. She was tired, the dead boy dragging at her heart. No one had shown up looking for him, and she hadn't told Titanic anything. It wasn't safe.

The mattress dipped as Blackie sat up. Built into the opposite wall, the galleylike Pullman kitchen glistened—tiny sink, cabinets, and refrigerator. In the ancient bathroom, a pipe rattled. She slumped under the weight of her loneliness, then put coffee on.

Since Renee had moved up to Lucille's, no empty beer bottles crowded Blackie's counter. They used to spin around with an angry clatter when she backhanded them into the sink. At the noise, Renee would shout, "Whaddaya doing? You break a bottle, we've got glass all over."

And Blackie shouted back, "Do you hafta get up every day drinkin'?"

The coffee perked, and she poured herself a cup. She

started for the big chair where Renee used to spend Sundays sprawled in a sheer nightgown reading the paper, long silky legs thrown over the plump arm. Those were the good times.

Renee hadn't been such a lush at the beginning. But after the police closed down the Club 181, she didn't want to go back to stripping in those joints in Jersey.

"Strippin', hookin', it's all the same thing," Renee had argued between swigs of beer. "And there's more money to be made in hookin'."

Blackie spat back at her, "Call me old-fashioned, but you're talkin' about workin' for a lousy whore!"

Still a sucker for a pretty face, Blackie picked up a pinup magazine and leafed through the cheesecake photos. That's how she'd ended up with Renee, who'd strolled into Ernie's one night in her low-cut beaded dress. Glamorous chorus girls and hookers fussed around the bar every night flirting with Blackie, but none of them could hold a candle to Renee. She'd invited Blackie to catch her act at the 181 on Second Avenue just below 14th Street—a swell joint with a chandelier and plush red carpeting. Blackie and Renee closed the place down and then went back to Renee's.

Blackie put down her magazine. The furnished room on Christopher faded into a soundless haze. Renee had been like a sunny meadow full of flowers. After her, Blackie had kept to herself. She especially wanted nothing to do with the sometime showgirls who came down to the club—and she wanted even less to do with hookers. She'd told Titanic she felt like a washed-out rag, that he didn't understand about love.

"Whadda *you* know, Miss High and Mighty?" he'd replied. "Why, I've been faithful all night long."

Titanic probably had the right idea. She didn't want to be a prude, but she couldn't stand the idea of sharing Renee like a rented tux. She didn't want to hear any stories from

Lucille's—no jokes, no more assurances that none of it meant anything.

"What you don't understand," Renee had told her over and over, "is that you can hate men and still take their money." Her slippers had a narrow band of fake fur across the top and made a soft clip-clop noise as she walked away.

She was right about one thing. Blackie *didn't* understand.

Of course, Renee had promised, "I'll be out of Lucille's soon, like my mother used to say, 'as soon as I've got some money saved.' " Her voice rose in an Irish lilt. "Then you and me, we'll get our innings in."

Blackie had pushed her away, eyes brimming with fury. "Do me a favor, and don't wait till it's too late. Remember your mother and your brother never got out of the old neighborhood."

Despair had washed all other emotions off Renee's face. Her mother was dead, and before that her kid brother had been mortally wounded in a Hell's Kitchen crossfire. Renee told the story when she'd had a few drinks.

"A half shot of whiskey after every meal, the old man gave my brother. Said it would make a man of him. It made him a bum instead."

Sometimes Blackie felt like a heel for leaving Renee when she knew how much sadness lay just underneath Renee's bluster. Now there was another dead boy. An emptiness settled into the pit of her stomach, and she remembered her last meal was yesterday before she'd gone over to the club.

There was a leftover Danish in the fridge. The sugar was cool on Blackie's tongue. A sip of coffee dissolved it. She sat down at the old enamel table where she used to divvy up meals—a plate for her, one for Renee. Chop suey from the Lotus Garden, sandwiches from the deli downstairs. The image of Renee sitting at that same table, in a golden silk robe with big flowers on it, skittered through her head.

At Lucille Martin's, Renee was saying, there'd be Broadway directors, even Hollywood producers. She was bound to get that big break. And where did Blackie come off preaching sermons? Wasn't she working for the mafia? She could save her goody-goody spiel.

In the bathroom Blackie tried to unwind in a tub that rested on white claw feet. Steam frosted the window and curled around her shoulders. As she eased into the tub, rivulets of water sloshed over her belly and breasts, eddying around her thighs. She was too tall to get really comfortable. Her knees jutted above the surface as she slipped lower. She opened her legs so the warm water could run between. Her hips flared slightly, firm not fleshy. She liked the way her smooth muscles rippled under the skin.

Renee's voice whispered in her ear: *Let me show you how beautiful you are.*

Blackie's mind drifted to nothingness. All that mattered was the sensation between her legs. Under the water she started a steady circular motion with her index and middle finger. The kids at the club said only nuns and old maids masturbated. She didn't care.

Her fingers moved faster, in circles wider, then narrower and more intense. Every cell in her body strained toward that point. At last she quivered and felt a warmth like hot liquid suffuse her body. She rested her head on the back of the tub and closed her eyes.

Blackie woke an instant later. The water had cooled. She jerked out the tub's round stubby plug to let some drain out, then added more hot water. Somewhere a clarinet practiced scales, and she settled back to soak again.

After her bath, she dressed quickly for work. Her tux was tailor-made, her shiny black shoes purchased from the boy's department at Macy's. Since she was fairly flat-chested, she didn't have to bind her breasts tightly. On the street, people didn't look too hard at her crotch.

Outside on the corner she stopped by a pushcart and bought an apple. "Keep the change," she said, leaving the kid a tip worth twice what she'd paid.

"Thanks, mister," he replied.

She didn't really like being taken for a man, but she liked the feeling of ease and power she got from wearing men's clothes. It was safer.

By the time Blackie came around the corner of Greenwich Avenue munching her apple, tiny drops of sweat borne in the roots of her hair trickled onto her stiff shirt collar. The city was having a sample of tropical weather, a record-breaking summer heat wave. The humidity matched the temperature.

Behind her a bright red sun plunged over Village rooftops and into the Hudson River. It spawned high flamingo-colored clouds and a spectacular sunset. As evening fell, lights blinked up and down Eighth Street.

Everything promised another hot night at the Candy Box. Blackie would sing her heart out to charm the audience, and the memory of the body in the men's room would vanish from her conscience like puffs of smoke from a stale cigarette.

SEVEN

Debonair in tux and tails, Blackie leaned on the bar at the Candy Box and sipped a beer. Stevie wasn't around, which was fine with her. The stirring of the early crowd boosted her spirits.

Voices hummed against a background of romantic music and laughter. Glasses clinked in a toast to good times. The club was in her blood now. She couldn't resist the table hopping, shaking hands with friends, old and new. She put down the beer, slicked back her hair, and went out to hobnob.

Blackie worked the room like a pro. She stopped first at a table of entertainers, headed up by Harry Ting and the seductive Miss Nanky Poo. They were headliners from the floor show at the China Doll, uptown on Broadway. On their night off, they came to the Village.

"You down here stealin' my stuff?" Blackie joked.

"Sing one for us," Harry Ting replied, and kissed her cheek. Show people loved one another, and the kids from the China Doll always made a great audience. Maybe because they knew what it was like to be a novelty act, a bunch of "singing and dancing Chinks." That was a rung or two up on the showbiz ladder from a chorus line of dykes and drag queens.

At the next table Blackie said hello to Henny, a two-bit numbers runner who greeted her like a buddy. "Long time, Blackie," he said. "How you been?" A floozy he must've picked up along the way, with tousled flame-red hair, sat beside him.

Henny used to hang around Renee when she worked the Club 181, buying her and Blackie drinks.

"Does Henny know the score?" Blackie had asked Renee one night.

"Sure, he knows what I like." Renee set her jaw in a hard line. "But it's his nickel. Let him pay."

Blackie didn't give Henny a chance to ask about Renee. Maybe he didn't know she'd gone to work for Lucille Martin. He was low on the mob's totem pole and didn't exactly move in the circles that frequented Lucille's.

"Great to see you at the Candy Box," Blackie said with a smile. "Hope you like the show."

She turned away and spotted the maître d', Miss Freddi, towering above the crowd. She was seating a shapely unescorted female at a ringside table, a young woman dressed to the nines in a swirl of some sheer fabric that fluttered around her like a silver kite. The frothy gown outlined the elegant arch and swell of her bosom. Her hair was golden topaz pulled back from her face. Blackie knew class when she saw it.

Her mom always said that Blanche got that from her side of the family. "We weren't peasants," she would scream at her husband when they fought. "My father was a learned man."

"We're not poor," Blackie's father would shout back. "We're socialists."

That argument hadn't kept Blackie from longing for a little

grace and refinement. This dame had all that. She was a soft-focus mystery like Ingrid Bergman in *Casablanca*, but strictly Park Avenue. She must've slipped Miss Freddi a big tip.

Blackie was seduced. Women like this one didn't drink whiskey like Renee, didn't curse or make scenes. They drank champagne and slept on silk sheets. Blackie drew up tall, then felt a little foolish, glad no one but her could hear the dull whirring of blood pulsing in her head. It never hurt to look, she told herself, even if this nifty blond dish was a little out of her league.

A burst of canary-yellow flame lit the young woman's cigarette, and Blackie got a good look at the face. It was a soft oval, bisected exactly by a delicate nose. The skin was so fair it was almost translucent. Pure and sincere, like a spunky Ann Sheridan, this doll was certainly a change from the same old crowd of painted faces.

Blackie batted her eyes and gave her bow tie a quick tug. Slicing past waiters and drunks, she drew closer to the table. By that time something like a summer storm was breaking over her. She saw lightning flashes and felt the oppressive heat.

It couldn't be, Blackie thought, but it was. A face enough like the face that had lain lifeless and silent on the floor of the Gents to be its twin. A few strands of golden hair hung loosely across the young woman's forehead. Just a hint of puffiness under the eyes, a haunting sapphire blue. Her cheekbones arched away from her temples like a fashion model's.

If she hadn't seen the boy dead, Blackie would swear this was him in drag. Instinctively, she started to backpedal. But she wasn't fast enough. Titanic brushed past and caught her arm.

"C'mon!" he said, drawing Blackie over to the young woman's table. "There's someone here just dyin' to meet you!"

Tonight he was masquerading as a Jean Harlow lookalike in a bobbed blond wig. From narrow straps over his shoulders, a white silk crepe gown fell away to the floor.

Blackie's face was as pale as that dress—or the ghost she thought she'd seen. "I can't," she muttered. "Previous engagement."

"Break it!" he commanded, tightening his grip on her arm. He bent over the mystery woman and bubbled, "Didi, dahling! What a surprise! It's been ages!"

The blond raised gilded eyelids, her face flushed with sparkling wine. "Far too long," she said in a breathy New York–debutante drawl. She talked out of the side of her mouth and had perfect teeth.

Goose bumps stole up the back of Blackie's neck, and her heart pounded.

"Well, aren't you the lucky one," Titanic went on, "'cause we've got a whole new show and a brand new star. Let me introduce you to Blackie Cole. She sings like an angel."

A flexible necklace of ribbed gold, studded with diamonds, lapped over the blond's collarbone. She twirled it like a rosary between her fingers. China-blue eyes darkened into pools of lapis lazuli, and she looked at Blackie so hard that her eyes could've gone right through and buttoned in the back.

Blackie stood rigid as a bayonet.

With the self-assurance of one used to things going her way, the young woman thrust out her hand. Her introduction was schoolgirl precise and symmetrical, like small whacks to an anvil.

"I'm Diana Fletcher-Payne," she said, and studied the androgynous cast of Blackie's face. "My friends call me Didi."

Blackie looked shaken. Everybody knew who the Fletcher-Paynes were. "Charmed, I'm sure," she replied weakly and sat down when Titanic pulled out a chair for her.

As usual, he needed no encouragement and babbled on like a waterfall. "Remember that party," he said to Didi, "the drive out to the island and all those people soused to the gunwales." Titanic loved nautical terminology the way he loved sailors. "A squadron of houseboys serving drinks on that lawn the size of Central Park."

Blackie was trying to keep her wits about her. "Definitely your kind of layout," she joked to Titanic. His fondness for money—and for the people who had it—was common gossip at the Candy Box.

"Nothing makes people feel as guilty as being filthy rich," he'd often explained to Blackie. "And I make them feel better by helping them spend all those simoleons."

Didi sipped champagne. "That was the same night Skip wore those adorable see-through harem bloomers."

Titanic giggled. "And it was his idea we all take a sunrise dip in the pool to sober up before breakfast."

"You know decorum's not our family's strong suit," Didi laughed.

Blackie sized Didi up and felt something like her heart rising into her throat. Was this just another Park Avenue bubble-bath dame—too much money out for a good time? Was she straight as an arrow, or did she swing both ways? One thing was for sure: She was trouble.

"Do I know Skip?" Blackie asked, gliding over the words nervously.

Didi inspected Blackie with big indigo eyes. She didn't know much about dykes. At the gay haunts she'd been to with Skip, the girls seemed to swim around the edges of the action like alligators and didn't smile. They didn't seem safe like gay boys, but this one was devastatingly attractive with a contagious grin. Didi was curious and excited.

"Skip's my younger brother," she confided. "His real name is Owen, and Father *will* call him that." Her lips were a fleshy pomegranate red. "Some people say Skip and I look a lot alike."

"Don't be modest," Titanic replied. "You and Skip are both natural beauty wonders." He paused and turned to

Blackie. "You know Skip. He comes around a lot. Wanted to be in the show."

"He loves the Candy Box," Didi added. "He's so theatrical, you know. Even as a child, he danced, made up plays and poems." She'd always known Skip was different.

"He can be a real ham, you mean," Titanic said.

By now, Blackie's eyes were big as half-dollars. What kind of nightmare had she stumbled into? And how could she have been such a coward? If she'd talked to Titanic about the body right away, maybe Stevie would've let them contact the family. But that was stupid. Stevie liked to make his own arrangements.

"Where's Skip tonight?" Titanic asked.

Didi's smile puckered into a frown. A life of ease hadn't prepared her for doubts and frustration. "That's why I came down, actually."

"Oh?" He sat forward. "What's up with Skip? Trouble in paradise?"

"No, no, nothing like that," Didi assured him. "You know, if the family ever found out about Skip, they'd go into spasms."

Skip had begged her not to say anything to their father. "Don't be silly," she replied. Knowing how much Old John Jay disliked bad news, she didn't intend to give him any. "You know that whatever you do is fine with me."

Didi paused and measured her words. "It's just that I was out on the island this weekend, and when I got home, Skip's bed hadn't been slept in. The servants knew nothing, and he hasn't called since."

Titanic chuckled. "He's met someone! It was bound to happen." There was an uncomfortable note of envy in his voice. Everybody was falling in love.

"You haven't seen Skip then?" Didi seemed to wilt like a rare magnolia blossom in a chill wind. "Last night I dropped by the Howdy Club and the Ship Ahoy, but no one had seen him." Going out with Skip, she'd gotten to know the Village bars as well as any hustler. Skip's charming friends made a fuss over her and were lots more fun than the namby-pamby society types she got stuck with most of the time.

Over the rim of her champagne glass, Blackie observed Didi and heard her speak as though from a great distance. Waves of panic slapped inside her chest. There was no explaining what had happened without putting her life on the line. The cops could send her up the river, or Stevie could send her to the bottom of it.

Titanic was optimistic. "There's nuthin' for you to worry your pretty little head about," he consoled Didi. "Boys will be boys. Skip'll show up."

"But he could've called at least!" Didi's response caught in her throat. "Something must be wrong."

Blackie felt her world shift on its axis. If you got choices, she wouldn't have chosen to find Skip Fletcher-Payne dead in the men's room at the Candy Box. When the truth came out, Stevie would be in for a big surprise and big trouble. Cops would be swarming the place. She had to warn him.

But the rush of sympathy for Didi that swept over Blackie far outweighed her concern for Stevie. Didi seemed as cool as marble, but those sad turquoise eyes gave her away. Under all Didi's fluff and palaver, there was a heart that Blackie wanted to shield, the way she'd always wanted to protect Renee. The force of that desire stunned Blackie. She bit her lip and wondered what Stevie had done with the body. Didi would want to identify it and take her brother home.

Inches separated Blackie from Didi, whose hypnotic doe eyes Blackie imagined brimming over with an endless flow of tears. Titanic dissolved into a sequined blur.

"I worry about Skip because he's generous and naïve," Didi was saying. "Someone people could easily take advantage of." Her voice rose to a childish soprano. She'd never sat this close to a woman like Blackie Cole and felt suddenly shy. "What will you sing tonight?"

"Whatever you'd like!" Blackie answered. Her eyes met Didi's like black magic. This was a face like something conjured up out of a fairy tale, fragile and pink-cheeked.

Titanic recognized that look, and swelled with pleasure. At last Blackie was showing a little interest in somebody, and it didn't hurt that she had more money than God. He estimated the potential of the drama in progress. Certainly he wouldn't want Blackie to marry just for money. But rich or poor, it was nice to have.

"Oh!" Didi's pursed lips molded her sigh into a circle. "I can't stay for the show." Her befuddled gaze drifted back toward Titanic. "I want to drop by the Lantern," she said, "and ask if they've seen Skip. Then I'd like to be home in case he calls."

"That's a good idea, dahling." For Titanic's money, Didi Fletcher-Payne was smitten with Blackie. He thought how that harlot Renee, looking like the wrath of God, would smart when she heard the news.

Didi took another cigarette out of a gold case by Fabergé.

"Let me get you a light," Blackie said, rummaging through all her pockets. She struck a match as Didi puffed.

"Thanks," Didi replied. A shaky hand betrayed her emotions.

"Sure thing." Blackie was trying to keep both her feet on the ground. The stakes were high. "Do you live with your folks?" she asked to keep the conversation going.

Didi hesitated. Under any other circumstances she wouldn't have shared the details of her private life with a stranger. But she was beginning to feel pleasantly sloshed, and like she'd known Blackie for ages.

"Oh, Mummie's mostly out on the island. She isn't well."

Didi paused. "But Father likes to keep a hand in. He still goes to the office."

Blackie imagined the Fletcher-Payne apartment: A living room like an art deco movie set and a bedroom all swirls and white lace. About a million miles from the walk-up she called home.

"Mummie's in the city sometimes for shopping and the opera," Didi added.

"I'm sure your place is fabulous," said Titanic, who'd wanted an invitation for a long time.

Suddenly Blackie sat up stiffly in her chair. Over Didi's shoulder she saw Stevie entering from the bar. His head swiveled slowly from side to side, smugly surveying the club. Smash Nose Babe tagged along, his crocodile grin hovering above Stevie's head.

Like a checkered warning flag, Miss Freddi's pompadoured head leaned over their table. "C'mon, guys and dolls," she chirped. "Fifteen minutes to show time."

"I'd better be going," Didi said, "and let you two get ready."

In the nick of time, Blackie thought. If Stevie got a load of Didi, he'd notice her resemblance to the dead boy. She imagined him staring pop-eyed, his jaw dropping a few inches. "Who's the broad?" he'd ask her, and what was she gonna tell him? Harry Truman's mother? She didn't dare lie. If Stevie gave the order, she could leave the Candy Box feet first.

Blackie got up and checked the creases in her trousers. "I'll get you a cab," she said to Didi.

Titanic wallowed in Blackie's gallantry. She seemed thoroughly smitten too. For her part, Didi realized she didn't want to go. But she wasn't prepared to feel that way and held her tongue. She'd had considerable experience with restraint, absorbed from Mummie, who'd inherited it from generations of aristocratic ladies deceived by worthless husbands.

"Oh, don't bother," Didi said to Blackie. "I have my car."

"No bother. I'd like to get a little air before the show."

Didi smoothed her ballooning skirt around her as she stood up.

"And if Freddi shows up again," Blackie told Titanic, "tell her I hadda go somewhere in a hurry. I'll be right back."

Didi let herself be maneuvered through the bar. A beaded purse dangled from her wrist. Blackie moved briskly. She led Didi up the steps into the damp evening, where a breeze swirled her gown around her knees. Didi's hair shone silver-white on the darkened street.

Thunder rolled in the near distance. More showers were predicted. Music drifted over the sidewalk from a bar across the street. Blackie looked down at Didi across what seemed to her a gulf of tragedy and deception. The best Blackie could hope for was that if Didi ever found out, she wouldn't hate her.

A dove-gray town car pulled up to the curb. The chauffeur came around and doffed his cap.

Blackie gazed vacantly at the man's trim uniform, the car's chrome bumpers and leather upholstery—the kind of luxury most people only dreamed about. This was Didi's world.

"It was wonderful meeting you," Didi said, one foot up on the running board. "Be careful. It's going to rain."

Didi was right. Thunder boomed down Eighth Street, just ahead of a downpour. Blackie thought about all the people around town hurrying to pull their mattresses inside, off the fire escapes, where they slept on muggy nights: the tenement penthouse.

Inside the car, Didi looked like a princess in a fairy coach. She gestured for Blackie to come closer. "I'm really worried about Skip," she said, anguish written across her face. "Would you let me have your matchbook for a moment?"

Blackie fished it out and handed it over. Didi scribbled a

phone number. "If you hear anything at all, please call me," she said. "This is our private line."

"Sure thing." Blackie put out her hand for the matchbook. It dropped soundlessly into her jacket pocket where she felt it smoldering, the number etched in flames. Here was the solution: an anonymous phone call to let Didi know Skip wouldn't be coming home.

The first heavy raindrops pelted the car. "I'll be waiting for your call," Didi whispered.

"If I hear anything..." Blackie's voice was an empty echo. The car door slammed, and gritty exhaust engulfed her.

Eight

In the kitchen of the Candy Box, a small contingent gathered respectfully around the Philco. Stevie the Frenchman slouched. Smash Nose Babe flexed his ankles, while Crazy Charlie and Waxy stood at attention.

"After closing time," Stevie said, "we'll load him up." A steamer trunk with leather handles and tarnished hinges waited in the corner.

"Think he'll fit in there?" Charlie asked, measuring with his eyes. "Stiff and all?"

"Whaddidya expect?" Stevie drew a bead on Charlie with basilisk eyes. "A stiff shouldn't be stiff?"

Charlie and Waxy laughed, giddy and nasal.

"It's your job to make him fit," Stevie added and gave them all another drop-dead stare.

Out onstage, in front of the mike, Blackie punched the lyrics with a steady beat, her voice mellow as a slide trombone. She rounded off every note the way she'd been coached, and the song rambled to its end.

The last chord faded. Blackie bowed low to her audience and threw kisses. Flashing a glitzy grin, she scanned the house and saw another party had taken over Didi's table: two good-time Charlies with their dates.

Blackie told herself it was better Didi hadn't hung around. A dame like that, the scent of wild flowers reaching for the sun, didn't belong at the Candy Box, didn't belong in Blackie's world. Just like her kid brother hadn't belonged.

It wasn't something Blackie liked to think about. She trembled and was glad to get offstage without a bobble. As she stepped down, the orchestra switched to a tropical beat. In the hallway, she passed Titanic, who'd changed into a long flowered skirt. He wore a fruit-laden turban.

"I see you got along fine with Didi." His hands darted like hummingbirds.

"It's not that kinda thing." Blackie acted cagey. "She's straight."

"I saw the looks she was givin' you." Titanic waved double-dyed fingernails and outsized pinky rings. "And you know what they say: 'This year's trade is next year's femme.'"

"Cut it out," Blackie said, but she knew Titanic was right about the looks. She didn't dare hope for more.

"You oughta know better than anybody that love is as blind as a friggin' bat," Titanic added, and congaed out onstage. A flurry of drums, rattles, cowbells, and serrated gourds accompanied him. Blood-red lips and sunburst eyebrows: This was his big number.

Like a fireworks display, Carmen Miranda burst upon her fans. The bare midriff pulsated. Platform sandals flapped. She moved centerstage, chirping, "I hope you weel not mind that my hat is tutti-frutti. Ees just a few knacks-knicks I had around the refrigerator."

The crowd roared with laughter.

"You so beaudifool audience," Carmen continued, "you swoop me off my feet. I teenk you like me, and visa-visa, I'm gonna like you too." She plucked at her turban. "Everybody like bananas. They are my business."

Titanic dropped the accent and added, "I've had these damn things on my head for years."

More laughter.

"I'm liking doing ozzer zings, believe me!" Carmen resumed in fake Brazilian. She took a banana in one hand and peeled it suggestively. Taking a nibble, she said, "But I'm singing for you now a song tasty like bananas."

The trumpets picked up the familiar melody, blasting over the percussion. A shaky falsetto belted out,

Ay-ay, ay-ay, I love to dress so gay
When I dance the South American way.

As the rhythm accelerated, Carmen rhumbaed, sambaed, and sang at a torrential clip. She paused, at last, to draw in a deep breath for the last chorus of *Ay-ay, ay-ay.*

Music, laughter, and applause drowned out a distant rumbling from the back of the club. Titanic stripped off his turban and took bow after bow in his own wavy brown hair, plastered down with sweat. Curtsying awkwardly in the skintight skirt, he failed to see the menace approaching across the dance floor.

By the time he realized what was happening, a getaway was unlikely. A swarm of bluecoats led by a plainclothesman had almost reached the stage. A cry rang out, "Police! This is a raid!"

Customers shrieked, "Gangway!" and surged away from the ruckus like a startled school of fish. *Batten down the hatches,* thought Titanic. The other kids, including the orchestra, scurried for cover. All the lights came on.

A police whistle, like a steam locomotive barreling through the club, alerted Stevie in the kitchen. About that same time he heard Smash Nose Babe's low, desperate cry: "Boss, you'd better come quick!"

Stevie broke into a trot the length of the hallway, and swept aside the red curtain. Cops at the Candy Box had seemed to him about as remote as the San Francisco earthquake. And tonight of all nights, with the stiff in the freezer. He gasped.

Lucille had warned him to ditch the body, but he hadn't been quick enough. Somebody must've ratted. That bastard Tyrone—and after Stevie had given him a day off too. Or Blackie. But she was loyal and no fool.

The blue line snaked across the dance floor like a Texas sidewinder. Stevie cursed his luck. A few hours and that punk's body would've been gone for good.

To keep the bulls away from the kitchen, Stevie moved up to intercept them. "Good evening, officers," he bluffed. "This is my place. Is anything wrong?"

The detective in charge was straight from central casting, red-faced and stocky in a tan trench coat. "Excuse me, sir, we've had some reports about State Liquor Authority violations."

"SLA violations?" Stevie thought he'd heard wrong.

Centerstage, the flatfeet with tin shields were already rounding up Titanic, Blackie, the other boys, and short-haired girls. Two rookies, twin giants with cherubic smiles, shoved them into formation with their nightsticks.

"Howzabout it, sir?" the detective repeated to Stevie. Turned up, the collar of his coat almost reached the brim of his porkpie hat. "Could we talk in back somewhere?"

Stevie squared off against his adversary. "Yeah, in back," he muttered, "we can talk in back." Stupid coppers! They didn't know about the stiff. Stevie's luck was holding.

The plainclothes officer removed his hat. He had thinning hair the color of tobacco and a little mustache to match.

So nobody should get the wrong idea, he thundered back to his patrolmen in a voice like Bogie's, "*Youse*, keep an eye on the freaks."

Two more he dispersed to cover the exits. The zealous rookies squeezed the circle of entertainers tighter, jabbing at bare arms and shapely rear ends.

Titanic's head bobbed like a bird on a sprung wire. "I don't think I can stand goin' to jail," he confided to Miss Jackie Mae. "Not in this outfit."

Miss Jackie Mae danced ballroom style with a dyke named Larry. Their performance was an orgy of spins that would have put Fred and Ginger to shame—a big crowd-pleaser at the Candy Box.

"Stevie's people don't go to jail, honey," Jackie Mae assured Titanic. "The boss never welshed on a payoff in his life. This is a low-down double cross."

Pressed up against Titanic's backside, Blackie hoped Jackie Mae was right on all counts. She'd never live it down if her parents found out she'd spent a night in jail. Not to mention Didi Fletcher-Payne, if they should ever meet again. But the chances of that were slim. Blackie remembered to breathe. Now it was up to Stevie to square things with the cops.

Fortunately the stroll to Stevie's backroom office took the detective to the opposite side of the club, far away from the kitchen and its secret. Stevie prayed nobody should start asking questions, sweating the kids or the kitchen help for what they could get out of them.

Smash Nose Babe opened the door to the office and ushered the copper in. Stevie followed close on his back and flipped on the brass table lamp. The plainclothesman took a chair.

Stevie removed a bottle from the desk drawer and poured himself a drink.

"OK, Swazey," Stevie said gruffly, "what's this all about? I thought you was workin' homicide these days."

Detective Ronald Swazey of the Charles Street Station crinkled up his fighter's nose, flat like a champagne cork. "The captain wanted me along on this one, for old times' sake."

This gumshoe had spent many years working public morals. He preferred it. That was how he'd gottten to know Stevie. "So, don't I get a drink?"

"Thought you didn't drink on duty." Stevie wiped his wire-rimmed spectacles.

"Only when I'm among friends," Swazey replied with a sour smile. His was not a handsome kisser but sort of lovable, like an old bulldog.

"What friends?" Stevie sounded ominous. "Whaddaya mean bustin' in here like this?"

Swazey gulped and loosened the belt of his trench coat. "Hey, let's not go off the deep end. None of this was my idea."

He took a rolled-up late edition of *The Daily Journal* from inside his coat. Hunching forward, he laid it on the desk. "You read the papers?"

Stevie ignored him. Swazey tweaked his mustache and struck a wooden match across the sole of his shoe. He cupped his hand around the flaming tip, lighting his cigarette then Stevie's. "You musta heard about that murder up in Yorkville." Swazey pointed to a headline.

At the word murder, Stevie clenched his teeth. "Whazzat gotta do with us?"

Swazey spat bits of tobacco off his lips. He didn't like working homicide. "It was a real sloppy job. Got the politicians and the commissioner riled up." He spun the paper respectfully like a lazy Susan, then read: "'Groups Back Crime Purge, Demand Action in Ridding City of Sex Fiends and Degenerates.'"

"Eyewash!" Stevie poured Swazey a shot. "Do the kids in the show look like homicidal maniacs to you? They're just a bunch of poor fruits who don't know which john to piss in."

Swazey drank up. The whiskey burned down to his belly. "You don't have to convince me. You know my policy was always live and let live. But John Q. Public's got other ideas." He paused. "And you got a half-dozen SLA violations. Girls sittin' with customers, kids workin' in drag, sellin' drinks to queers. They can crack down on you any time."

Stevie mocked him. "That's just part of doin' business down here."

Swazey pointed to the front page again. "The Village is 'the degenerates' paradise,' it sez here."

Stevie reached for the whiskey bottle. "The *Journal* is milkin' this one for all it's worth."

"Makes good copy with elections comin' up, and the DA runnin' for mayor." Swazey flicked ashes into a souvenir Copacabana ashtray. "The department wants Duggan." He blinked uncomfortably. "And we're supposed to keep the heat on big time. My little visit is a command performance, straight from the top."

"Why don't they give us a break?" Stevie opened another drawer and stoically took out a fat envelope. He tossed it toward Swazey. It landed badly and caved in the crown of the detective's hat.

"Watch it there," Swazey mumbled. He rescued the bribe and balanced it on his palm to assess its weight. It was a lot of money.

"It's good to know you're on the job, Swazey," Stevie smirked. "But that ain't for nothing. You keep your boss and the papers off my back. I depend on you."

Swazey's eyes gleamed like patent leather in the lamp-light. He shuffled his feet, inspecting the scuffed stubby toes of his shoes.

"I'll do my best." He stuffed the envelope deep inside his trench coat.

"It better be good." Stevie rubbed his dead cigarette in the ashtray to end their interview. "That ain't no campaign contribution."

Swazey slunk off back to his squad, and Stevie watched him go. So the heat was on, he thought, and the cops would be wanting bigger payoffs. He hated those crooks as much as he hated the politicians with the gimmes. Their cut of the action was never enough. Sooner or later they'd end up killing off the goose, the golden egg, the whole nine yards. How dumb could you get?

NINE

On the way out of the Candy Box, Swazey told the squad there'd be no charges. They didn't like that one bit.

"Faggot," they cursed Titanic. "We catch you again, you'll do hard time. The guys down at the Tombs'd love you." They gave him a hard shove for good measure before they lowered their nightsticks.

Titanic swayed in his Carmen Miranda outfit, his skirt tapered to the ankles. "Knuckleheads," he mumbled as he lost his balance and caved in backward.

The patrolmen laughed and straggled into the early morning. Blackie and the other entertainers lingered in the middle of the dance floor, where they formed a seething knot with Titanic at its center. He lay with one leg hooked under him, the other thrust out perpendicularly. His skirt was torn, and one shoe had a broken heel that dangled by a flimsy nail.

Blackie went down on her knees on the grubby floorboards. With all the lights on, the club looked less than glamorous. The air was opaque as from a fine dust rising constantly, seeping through the low windows.

"It's all over," she said as she bent over Titanic.

"I couldn't take endin' up in the caboose of a pie wagon tonight!" he said. "Some fat ugly cop tryin' to stick his winkie in my mouth. Degradin'!"

"Slow down." She cradled his skinned elbow. It was streaked with blood. "They're gone."

Titanic sat up. His eyes were oozing sooty streaks of mascara from a rush of tears. "I hate those sadists," he blubbered, hiding his face in Blackie's satin lapels. "For Chrissake, don't let all these people see me cryin'."

She slipped an arm under him. "Can you walk?" she asked.

Titanic sniffed, groaned, and straightened out his legs. "At least I won't have to do time in this outfit—it makes me waddle like a damn mermaid!"

"Relax, you're not onstage anymore," Blackie whispered as she helped him to his feet. Concerned faces surrounded them.

"Give us some room, folks," Blackie said. They squeezed past, Titanic limping on his broken heel.

"Careful of the dress," he said. The dressing room door, where the chintzy paper star twinkled, snapped shut behind them. Inside, Titanic wriggled out of the skirt that had a stranglehold on his knees, then collapsed on the shabby divan. It wobbled under his weight.

"Did it have to be right in the middle of my applause?" He was recovering his composure. "Deafening hurrahs, when here comes Betty Badge swingin' a big black stick."

"The patter of flatfeet." Blackie found a bandage and applied it to his injury.

"Then Stevie takes Miss Lily Law, the detective, off to powwow and leaves us to be shoved around." Titanic patted his elbow. "Of course, there were those two exquisite blond officers built like Tarzan. My eyes, they jump out of the head," he concluded in his Brazilian accent.

"About as mean and nasty as the rest of your bum tricks." Blackie put a cushion under his head. "Do you want anything?"

"You exaggerate. They all seem so sweet at first." Titanic's tone was lighter now. "Break out the brandy."

Blackie fished it from beneath a loose floorboard and poured.

Titanic tossed his back in one gulp and raised himself up on his good elbow. "Carmen is kaput, I fear." He inspected the seams of his damaged costume, then kicked off his shoes. "And I guess my tutti-frutti turban is lyin' trampled out there."

He stood up and went to the mirror. Tilting his head back, he stretched his neck muscles taut. "Look at those chins, those bags under my eyes. I look old enough to be my mother." He plucked two plump homemade falsies—birdseed packed into old nylons—out of a longline bra. "And right now I wouldn't care if I never put on another skirt."

Blackie shrugged whaddaya gonna do, and sipped her brandy. Titanic poured another before he reached under the dressing table for a large hatbox, into which he dumped the falsies, bra, Carmen Miranda blouse, and ripped skirt.

"I'm still takin' actin' classes, you know." He stood, then turned his back to release his penis from the snug cotton cocoon between his legs. "It would be a relief," he sighed, "to play straight roles."

"I can't go down and audition for Broadway either," Blackie said. "That's why I stick with Stevie. He's protection."

"Some protection!" With his back still turned, Titanic stepped into boxer shorts and seersucker trousers. "What if Didi Fletcher-Payne had been sittin' at that table when the cops busted in? Her old man doesn't like scandal. Just ask

Skip! He's always afraid somebody's gonna recognize him."

A high wind whistled around Blackie's ears. This was her chance to say something no holds barred. "More brandy?" She poured Titanic a big jigger.

If she told him her story, he'd be in this thing as deeply as she was, with the same danger staring him in the face. Stevie had a way of finding things out, and Titanic wasn't very good at keeping secrets. As far as letting the Fletcher-Paynes in on the truth, Blackie could do that herself. She had the phone number.

"You know, I never was a 24-hour girl anyway," Titanic went on, buttoning up a white short-sleeve shirt. "Jimmy wanted me to give up drag, remember?"

"The drunk?"

"Don't be a smart ass. Jimmy used to say I was a good-lookin' boy. That I should find myself a decent job, maybe a nice girl, and settle down."

"Like he did."

"And still see him, of course. But I couldn't take the true confessions. His wife, his children, and what we were doin' was a sin."

As she watched him, Titanic took a square tin box that read "Bayer" out of his pants pocket. He shook a little green pill into his hand and popped it down with the brandy.

"That's no aspirin." Blackie looked disgusted. "You told me you were gonna lay off the bennies."

"Oh, you are such a nitpicker, Miss Thing." He didn't give much of a damn what people thought, except for Blackie. "This is my cure for the blues. And it makes me forget my stage fright."

"Some excuse!" She turned away from his glassy eyes. Nobody would be dumb enough to share secrets with a hophead.

Titanic's heart flip-flopped as the amphetamine surge

tightened his jaw. He hated her when she got on her soapbox. He hated her disapproval too.

"Just another sign that I oughta get outta this business," he suggested repentantly. "My nerves are shot." He scanned the photos lining the mirror, then reached over and extracted one.

"Hey, wasn't that Atlantic City?" Blackie thumbed the photo.

"Happier times, dahling," he said. "What I really need is a good man."

"And leave showbiz? You gotta be kiddin'." She paused and fixed him with a look. "Or did somebody make you a better offer?"

"Rahlly, dahling!" Titanic rebounded. "Radio City, the Copa, the Rainbow Room, they all wanted me, but I said no dice."

"C'mon, you know nobody quits the mob." Blackie pulled up a chair next to his. "And besides, you can't run out on the show. I couldn't stand this place without you."

"You always say love's all that matters," he replied with an inscrutable smile.

"Such a smooch!" She leaned toward him, her eyes sparkling green and golden. They posed and hammed it up for the mirror, a family portrait.

In the hallway a voice like a bull moose's bellowed, "Everybody out!" It was Smash Nose Babe. "Stevie's closin' down."

Blackie and Titanic sprang apart like startled deer. Titanic stashed the hatbox under the dressing-room table. Blackie stuck her head out the door in time to catch a glimpse of Stevie puffing toward his office.

"Everything OK?" she asked after him.

He turned around and dropped his tone to sinister. "Sure, sure. It's just we got things to do." His mouth twitched in a little corkscrew smile just for her.

She stepped forward, carefully closing the door behind her. "What did the cops want anyway? Did it have anything to do with..." She paused and lowered her voice to a conspiratorial pitch. "...the stiff?"

Stevie gave Blackie the fisheye. So she still had the dead boy simmering on the back burner. With all the questions she asked, what kind of a future did she think she had in the business?

"The cops don't know nuthin' about that except what you, Tyrone, or the boys tell 'em." He looked at Blackie as though he wanted to fix her in that spot forever.

Blackie shuddered and fumbled with her tie. At that moment Crazy Charlie burst from beneath the red curtain that led to the dance floor. The ragged contours of his head glowed under the lights.

"Whaddaya want?" Stevie took a few steps in that direction.

"It ain't gonna fit," Charlie said in a stage whisper. Sweat ran down his neck and puddled between his shoulder blades.

Stevie slapped Charlie on the side of the head, then grabbed his arm. "For Chrissake, I'm comin'."

Before he blustered off to the kitchen, he turned to Blackie. "You kids head on home."

She backed away toward the dressing room like Stevie was royalty or like she expected a shiv in the back.

Inside, Titanic had finished sprucing up. He looked very proper in a jacket and tie.

"You wanna ride home?" Blackie asked him. Most nights she left her car—the red Ford coupe with white-sidewall tires—around the block where Stevie's goon squad watched over it, safe as Fort Knox. Anybody who touched Stevie's people or their property answered to them.

"No, thanks," Titanic replied and blew a kiss on his way out the door.

Blackie was on her own now in the ramshackle dressing room. Like in those jungle movies, she imagined thick vines grabbing at her arms and legs, and pools of quicksand all around.

TEN

In a couple of hours the sun would be rising over the East River, spread out like an oil slick. Downtown, the Candy Box had closed for the night, and summer showers had petered out to a tepid drizzle. It condensed like tears on sidewalks and windowpanes.

On Eighth Street, Crazy Charlie stepped under a streetlight to look for a taxi. A few seconds ticked away until an empty one crossed Sixth Avenue. Charlie loomed like Frankenstein out of the mist and threw up his hand.

The cabbie slowed down. Pass this one up, said years of experience. The guy looked like he'd showered in that suit. The driver shifted his foot off the brake and edged it over toward the gas pedal.

Charlie kept on coming and blocked the cabbie's way. When the taxi stopped, Charlie stuck his head through the open window. "A couple doors down," he said and got in. The cabbie spun the Checker's tires on the slick street.

"Here." Charlie jabbed an index finger.

"Sure, sure."

They pulled up in front of the Candy Box, and Charlie lurched out. "Be right back."

The door to the club opened a crack, and lights flickered like candles inside a jack-o'-lantern. The cabbie left his meter running. This gin mill no less, he thought. They'd better be big tippers.

The steamer trunk waited in the bar, Stevie on guard. He patted the lock with one hand, then rubbed his fingertips together fastidiously. He'd decided not to use his Hershey-bar-brown limo. He didn't want it to be an ash can for this kind of garbage, or recognized down at the docks. "You take care of everything like I told you?"

Charlie grunted, and Waxy handed Stevie a key, which he pocketed.

"Pier 53, Cunard." Stevie's voice hung suspended in the clammy space. "They'll be there to meet you."

"Sure thing, boss." Charlie grasped one end of the trunk and wrestled it out the door.

"It ain't gonna fit," the cabbie declared.

Charlie and Waxy showed him. They toppled the trunk into the backseat of the Checker. The trunk shifted and ground against their knees as they sat huddled on jump seats that folded down. It was like rooming with a baby hippo. "Step on it!" Charlie yelped.

Maneuvering back west, the taxi headed for the water-front. A sea mist floated between the uprights of the West Side Highway.

"Lousy weather," the cabbie complained, but got no answer from the backseat. Up to no good, he decided. At 14th Street, he turned toward the piers. The horseshoe arches of number 53 stretched downtown.

"Here," Charlie said.

Waxy peered through the back window to make sure they hadn't picked up any unwelcome company. A pale light breaking over the Village silhouetted a low-rise sky-line of warehouses, factories, and waterfront hotels. The two hoods stirred and started to wedge the trunk out the back door.

"Need some help?" the cabbie offered.

"No, no," Charlie answered. Where was that smell coming from? Sticky sweet. He drew back and let his end of the trunk hit the pavement.

Waxy squawked, "Hey, what's the big idea?"

"A buck even," the cabbie said. "The fare's a buck, including the trunk."

Charlie tossed a 50 onto the front seat, then leaned in to examine the cabbie's license displayed on the dash.

"Hey, you, Crumpton, we got your name and ID. We'll always know where to find you."

"I didn't see nuthin'."

"That's right, you didn't see nuthin'."

The back door slammed shut, and the tires squealed as the cabbie lammed it out of there.

"Do we have to carry this thing far?" Waxy wheezed.

"They should be here by now." Charlie looked at his watch. "I'll go have a look."

Waxy watched Charlie melt into the fog like sugar in hot coffee. He kicked at the brass corners of the trunk. Charlie had better hurry it up. A gust of wind sighed down the pier's long colonnade. It blew the foghorn's moan and the clump-clump of hobnail boots Waxy's way.

"That you, Charlie?"

A wide beam of yellow light ripped through the fog and caught the side of the trunk. It stopped there like a blood-hound sniffing the trunk up and down. The beam grew stronger and wider. Waxy slunk back into the shadows.

"Who's there?" came a husky voice. "Answer up."

Waxy heard a whack and saw the night watchman slump. The flashlight rolled helplessly, crazily away, illuminating broad swatches of sidewalk and brick facade. Charlie chased it, a short length of lead pipe in one hand. A whistle sounded at a nearby berth.

"Must be more of 'em. Let's go, Waxy." Charlie tapped the trunk with the lead pipe. "We can't get caught here. We'll leave it, where the guys who're pickin' it up'll spot it."

"Stevie's not gonna like this," Waxy said. "Maybe we should dump it in the river."

Directly behind them, metal scraped ominously against metal.

"You gonna drag it down the pier?" Charlie rasped. "I'm gettin' the hell out of here."

He scampered off at a good clip, Waxy close behind. They didn't stop until they found a phone.

A hazy sun shone down on Pier 53, crowded with baggage and cargo for the ships scheduled to sail on the evening tide. The steamer trunk abandoned by Charlie and Waxy still rested on one end, but its lid gaped open. Brown circles stained the inside.

Two bluecoats on morning watch had seen the trunk sitting there in a little puddle of ooze, all alone on the deserted pier. They put in the call from a nearby box and got stuck with a DOA, brought from God knows where and dumped in their bailiwick. The night watchman was on his way to the emergency room, a concussion. With daytime security's approval, they pried open the trunk but touched nothing. The dead-body dicks would be there soon.

An unmarked, grape-purple sedan skidded to a halt at the pier, and Detective Swazey of Charles Street Station Homicide rolled out of the front seat. Detective Henry Brannan was his driver and partner.

"We'da been here earlier," Swazey said to the uniformed patrolmen. The old station house was only blocks away from the scene. "But this town is full of lunatics."

He lit up a cigarette, and blue smoke trailed out his nostrils. "There was this Brink's truck. Right, Brannan?"

Brannan smiled. Swazey was famous as a friend of the working stiff, for stories that made the job tolerable.

"Stalled in traffic, and this broad comes out of nowheres and climbs up on top before anybody can stop her."

A chuckle spread through the ranks.

"So when she started takin' her clothes off, pedestrians, buses, cab drivers, everybody went wild."

"Nobody could get her down," Brannan said. "It was a friggin' riot, cops pourin' in."

"How far'd she get?" the patrolman wanted to know.

"Down to her garter belt and no undies!" Swazey wrinkled his bent nose and tweaked his mustache. "Before they hauled her off the truck."

Wolf whistles and a horselaugh. "What'll they think of next?"

"So whaddaya got for us?" Swazey asked.

They showed him the body where it lay on its side, the legs gathered up to the chest, the hair matted with blood. It had fallen out of the trunk like that.

Swazey mopped his forehead with his handkerchief and dabbed at his eyes. The naked city was a vicious place. "Just a lad—and a pretty one to boot." The boyish face had an unhealthy flush, like a drunk living rough on the Bowery. At least he wasn't half-eaten by the fish.

They cordoned off the crime scene. Brannan looked at labels in the victim's clothes. "No ID, but he's a nifty dresser." He touched the rib cage and shivered. "Hey, he's colder than Grandma's tit."

"More'an usual?" asked Swazey.

"I got no thermometer, but feel this. It's like he froze to death."

Swazey shuddered. The medical examiner was on his way.

"The night watchman's at St. Vincent's," the patrolman reported. "Here's his name. Foggy night. Somebody slugged him from behind."

"The trunk's clean as a whistle," Brannan said. They would inspect it again, hoping for a few clear prints.

Bernie Levine from the medical examiner's office gave the body a once-over.

"So whaddaya think, doc?" Swazey asked him.

"Blow to the back of the skull. Instant death." Dr. Levine touched Skip's cheek. "But it's like he's been in the deep freeze already. This heat's thawin' him out fast."

"When do you think you'll have an autopsy report?"

"If they're not backed up, and he thaws, I'll try to get somethin' for you tomorrow. Here's the wagon."

"Thanks, doc."

Owen "Skip" Fletcher-Payne went to the city mortuary as John Doe. Swazey returned to the precinct while Brennan looked in on the night watchman.

Between Washington and Greenwich streets, a block from the waterfront, the Charles Street Station had served the precinct proudly since the turn of the century. Twin turrets with fretwork cornices flanked the heart of the edifice, which was approached by wide steps worn smooth by thousands of criminal feet. Real marble columns rose on either side of the stairway. The great seal of the city was carved in stone above the entrance. Stone rosettes adorned the turrets, above horizontal bands incised with Greek crosses.

Midmorning, sunshine sparkled on the river sending waves of light down the narrow Village streets. The station house glowed like an enchanted castle as Swazey started up the steps. Inside, the magic faded.

The front desk was dimly lit, and the daytime crew filed paperwork left over from the night watch. It documented a standard assortment of drunks, petty thieves, pimps, junkies, and hookers sent over to night court. A couple of guys in drag had been apprehended for soliciting, luring men into alleys with the promise of a good time. They waited on a bench in the shadows.

Under the peak of the station-house dome, Swazey tipped his hat to the desk. "Already one DOA this morning," he said.

"Yeah, they told me," the officer on duty replied. "Anybody I know?"

"Nobody nobody knows," Swazey said and went upstairs to the squad room. He hung the tan trench coat on a pair of deer antlers his estranged wife had thrown out of the house. Swazey's IN box had spawned a handful of messages since yesterday. He flipped through a pile of papers that camouflaged scratches on top of the wooden desk, and made one phone call.

"Stevie? Don't worry, no harm done...yeah, it's all taken care of...I'll pick that up later."

Eleven

Everybody said it was news of the raid and summer show-ers that kept some regular customers away from the Candy Box for the next few nights. But Blackie's fans were loyal. When she went out onstage for the first show, a raft of sighs wafted up to her from the audience. At ringside a young woman swaddled in sable let out a moan like an ecstatic bobby-soxer whose toes were curling inside her saddle oxfords. Sinatra had gotten that kind of reception at the Paramount, which reminded Blackie that her career was going great guns.

On the opening bars of her number, she stepped up to the mike. The strings trilled. She swayed dreamily and crooned,

Passion's the rule
And I'm passion's fool.

As the last chords faded, wild applause shook the club like there'd never been a raid. Blackie bowed right and left before she stepped down to take a breather.

As she moved through the room shaking hands, a buxom woman in black shantung silk thrust a single red rose into her hand. Blackie stopped and took it. The woman's other hand held out a calling card, which Blackie also accepted. A glance showed her the name of an actress who'd just finished a long run on Broadway as well as a WIckersham exchange phone number. Blackie raised her eyes to meet those of the star, who looked older than her photographs in the newspaper. Flattered but not swept off her feet, Blackie wasn't in the market for a few laughs and a tumble in the hay.

She explained to the toast of Broadway that she couldn't linger, then turned and headed for the bar, where a public phone hung on the wall a few feet inside the door. She took the Candy Box matchbook out of her pocket. She didn't really need it. She'd studied Didi's phone number until she had it down pat.

Blackie's nickel hit bottom, and she started dialing REgent 7-1968. Her mouth went dry, and her hand shook: the whole ball of wax.

Deep within the cavernous expanse of the Fletcher-Payne apartment, the telephone rang. From the kitchen at the end of a long hall, a slight individual in tailcoat over striped pants hurried to answer.

"Fletcher-Payne residence," he said in a plugged-sinus voice.

Did Blackie think Didi was gonna answer the phone like she was Miss Anybody? "Didi Fletcher-Payne, please."

"Miss Diana is resting," answered the guy with the stuffed-up nose.

The ear Blackie pressed to the receiver sizzled. She felt like a kid who'd been caught with her hand in the cookie jar, some place she had no business being.

"Tell her it's an emergency."

The butler went to call Didi.

While Blackie waited, she noticed Crazy Charlie leaning on the bar. She'd have to keep her voice down. While not long on brains, Charlie had big ears and an even bigger mouth.

Didi Fletcher-Payne's bed was a huge canopied cream-and-gilt affair. A silk-and-lace coverlet lay folded at the foot, and matching scalloped pillows monogrammed *F-P* lay at the head. A pot of hothouse gardenias adorned the Coromandel lacquer bedside table, and a dime novel lay across its rouge griotte marble top. The novel's cover featured two young women cavorting together in their skivvies while a man with a blacksnake whip observed them from a corner. The title read *Forbidden Lust*. Didi had been thinking about Blackie.

There had to be more to sex than the intense fumbling with buttons and zippers she'd experienced with men then a quick push-push. Penises had limited appeal. Her biggest nightmare was ending up pregnant and forced into some silly marriage her family would think suitable. Luckily she didn't need any boring man's money.

Skip had understood. One afternoon they'd sat cross-legged on the Bessarabian rug in his bedroom. "It's passion I'm looking for," he'd murmured. "It's all that matters."

"Passion," she echoed.

No one else had ever talked about love. Didi remembered Mummie's warnings—about men and how they mustn't be allowed to take liberties. Lately it had occurred to her that Mummie hadn't mentioned women.

When the butler knocked at the door, Didi bolted upright on her four-poster bed. Clinging to its sides like Tallulah in the lifeboat, she covered her breasts with the satin sheet.

"Come in," she commanded as the Cupid clock on her drop-front desk chimed midnight.

He leaned in. "A call for you, Miss Diana."

"Who is it, Basil?"

"Sorry, miss, they didn't give a name." Basil had gotten used to odd phone calls in the middle of the night. Master Owen received his share. "They said it was an emergency."

As he closed the door, Didi gasped and reached for the phone. This had to be about Skip. Even if he'd been kidnapped, she knew she'd done the right thing by not going to the police. They would have asked all sorts of uncomfortable questions she couldn't have answered. Now she'd find a way to handle everything discreetly and bring Skip home.

"Hullo," she murmured hoarsely. "It's Diana Fletcher-Payne."

Blackie's pulses fluttered.

"Hullo," Didi repeated.

In the scenario Blackie had been banking on, she had only one line, delivered with a handkerchief over the receiver: "Call missing persons. Your brother is dead." Then she would hang up with a steady hand and go back to work.

But a few words in Didi's Park Avenue drawl sent a rush of heat to Blackie's head. She could see those haunting blue eyes staring straight at her, the alabaster face. In her heart, Blackie had to own up. Even if she would've been safer anywhere, even in a hail of bullets, she wanted to see Didi again. She was finally free of Renee and could feel something for someone again. She cupped her hand around the phone.

"Didi, listen. It's me, Blackie Cole."

Didi's ears buzzed at the sound of that sultry torch-song voice. "Hullo, Blackie."

"I can't talk. I'm at the Candy Box."

"You said it was an emergency?"

"Meet me somewhere."

"Tonight?" Didi was suddenly afraid.

Blackie sensed it. "I know it's late." But it was now or never.

"It's Skip, isn't it?" Didi felt a sliver of pain pierce her heart.

At the bar, Charlie ground out a cigarette. He grinned at Blackie and showed mossy teeth. Her courage ebbed. But she gave him a dynamite smile to throw him off track and cupped her hand tighter over the receiver.

"Yes, it's Skip," she said to Didi, then forged ahead. "We can talk at a place called the Bubble Room. Can you meet me there in half an hour?"

Didi reflected. "Half an hour?"

"The Village, on Sullivan between Bleecker and Houston. You can't miss it."

"You've heard something?"

Blackie saw that Charlie was walking her way. "Yes, in half an hour." She hung up.

"Late date?" Charlie smirked.

"Not me," Blackie joked. "I'm a workin' girl. I just gotta go uptown to the all-night pharmacy, get my mom some medicine. I'll be right back."

"Pills for your old lady?" Charlie looked incredulous. "Stevie said you're not supposed to go out like that. The cops've had complaints."

The Candy Box's neighbors had protested the sight of entertainers coming to work in drag. It made for an atmosphere unhealthy for children, they said.

"So I'll make a run for it," Blackie told Charlie as she passed him in the doorway. She was halfway down the block before he could get his objection out.

Uptown, ruby splotches of light from a Tiffany table lamp festooned Didi's bare arm. Shoeless in her chemise and nylons, she put down the phone and reached for a cigarette, double-puffed while she lit it. From a bottle of champagne that sat in a frosty bucket near the bed, she poured herself another glass to make her forget her fears.

But what was she afraid of? If she behaved like a coward, she was no good to Skip. As a child she'd been brave and defiant, pronounced a holy terror by several New England schools for young ladies that had requested her removal even if her name was Fletcher-Payne. Skip had been well behaved and cooperative at school, and Didi had protected him from abusive nannies and other bullies like their older brother, John Jay IV (or Jay Jay for short).

Jay Jay was now their father's right-hand man at the paper and liked to say Skip was a spoiled brat who hadn't done anything wrong with his life. He just hadn't done anything. Jay Jay wasn't someone Didi would ask for help.

She had to be tough like Ida Lupino, who'd faced down a demented killer in the depths of the North Woods. *She* would've never shied away from a midnight rendezvous, even with a perfect stranger, and Blackie Cole was no stranger. She was gentle, concerned about Skip, and drop-dead gorgeous. Didi felt lightheaded and leaned on the bedpost.

She eyed the dress she'd worn to dinner that night, a heap of gauzy fabric sprawled over a maple-and-rosewood armchair. She thought it didn't really suit her, but she couldn't keep Blackie waiting while she went through her closet. This was serious business, she told herself, not a luncheon date at the Colony Club.

Didi tossed the dress over her head, slipped into her shoes, and reddened her lips with a Max Factor stick. She'd never gotten dressed so quickly. Resting her head against the doorjamb, she considered briefly telling Basil where she was going. There was no one else to tell. She never knew when to expect her father, and Mummie would be sleeping quietly by now. She drank a great deal in her seclusion out on the island.

On second thought, these were delicate matters that Didi didn't want the servants gossiping about. She preferred to be on her own. She turned down the hallway past Skip's bedroom and toward the stairs. Thick walls and 10-foot ceilings soundproofed the apartment, muffling city noises. Didi's heels echoed like gunshots off the gleaming hardwood floor.

Her ancestors squinted down from carved and gilded frames along the walls. Their portrait lights extinguished, they looked more than usually foreboding. The one Mummie's family called Old Pip, governor ages ago, appraised her sternly. Ditto the other one, who had built railroads and founded *The Daily Journal*. Around this prosperous assortment of sagging jowls and paunches, Didi and Skip had always agreed that they felt disapproved of.

A bunch of old fuddy-duddies, she thought, who'd never strayed from the straight and narrow. Her father's family sounded a bit livelier. According to him, they'd fought hostile French and Indians, and established feudal domains on the banks of the Hudson. Was it his fault that the money had run out by the time it got around to him? An old and honorable name was just as good as all the fortune amassed by Mummie's Johnny-come-lately relatives.

Didi ran a finger over the portrait frames. They needed dusting. As she descended the elliptical staircase to the ground floor, the eye of an ormolu toucan twinkled up at her from the oak commode, tulipwood and pearwood veneers with a top of fleur-de-pêche marble. She picked up her evening bag and glanced from the circular foyer into the dim spacious drawing room. Without Skip, the apartment was like a tomb, and all the money in the world couldn't fill the emptiness.

Didi swept out of the elevator and through the paneled lobby. All she knew about passion she'd learned from a lifetime at the movies where suave pirates, gangsters, and private detectives were always waiting to steal your heart away. In real life no adventure had ever come her way to compare with meeting Blackie Cole. She would hear what Blackie had to say.

Ruggles, the doorman, was dozing when she came out. He lurched to his feet.

"Good evening, Miss Diana," he said with a gap-toothed smile. He was surprised to see her going out alone at that hour but never would have questioned anything his tenants did. And Ruggles didn't see why Miss Diana shouldn't have a turn raising a little hell on her own. The rest of the family was way ahead of her.

A cab answered Ruggles's whistle, and he handed Miss Diana into it. He had no way of knowing she was on her way downtown to her first secret rendezvous.

Upstairs at Lucille's all the rooms blushed peach and apple green. A cut-glass decanter of good whiskey sat on each bedside table. Lights shimmered in bronze and crystal sconces.

In the middle of Renee's bed, Old John Jay Fletcher-Payne lay draped facedown over cushions. His skinny shanks and long bare feet protruded from the bottom of an ivory-colored negligee that had mounds of imported lace at neck and tail.

Renee had helped him select it from bureau drawers spilling over with the finest lingerie in large and small sizes, from gowns to the briefest teddies with daring slits. Lucille made good her boast about something for everyone and the best of everything.

"I like it, Jack," Renee said. He was a good tipper. "The color suits you." He needed a little comforting. His streak of luck had faded quickly. He'd just dropped a couple of big ones he couldn't afford to lose at Lucille's poker game downstairs. He should stick to blackjack.

"You worry too much, Jack," Renee had told John Jay before he shucked off his undershirt and shorts and slipped the nightie over his head.

"See," Renee said, fluffing out the skirt. "The length is right. You couldn't have done better at Saks."

"Thank you, Renee," he said as he examined himself in the mirror. "You're really a wonderful girl."

What did she care? Tossing her strawberry-blond curls, she accommodated him in a sort of spread-eagle squat over the pile of pillows. He wished out loud that his wife weren't such an unhappy woman.

"Comfy, Jack?" Renee asked as she fastened a dildo of moderate size and thickness through a hole in the leather harness that encircled her waist and buttocks. Bathroom cabinets at Lucille's housed a wide variety. Five inches, eight inches, 10 inches; rosy or chocolatey; ribbed, veined, and slick.

Attired in scanty knickers and a strapless bra, hard full breasts swelling over the top, Renee took up her position behind John Jay. He relaxed.

"OK, Jack," she said, and squeezed a dollop of jelly lubricant over the dildo. "Here goes."

TWELVE

The Bubble Room was about a half-dozen blocks from the Candy Box. Blackie walked them quickly. She didn't want Didi to get there and find nobody waiting. It was a warm night. She loosened her tie so she could breathe easier. A trickle of sweat overflowed her armpit and ran down her side into the waistband of her trousers.

The Bubble Room's original decor dated back a few decades when it had been an elegant nightclub. Snowy-feathered cranes still danced around the walls, and the proscenium arch dripped faux wisteria framed in bamboo like a Ziegfeld Follies fantasy. But these days the place was a little shopworn, and the crowd considerably less glamorous than in the days of bathtub gin. When they had a night off, Blackie and Renee used to come down and catch the show. Some of the strip acts were friends of Renee's.

The room was long and narrow with a horseshoe of tables around the stage and runway. Near the door, a soft-hearted lug named Kelly Wong, half-Irish half-Chinese, who was missing part of an ear on one side, tended bar. A clump of scar tissue, where the earlobe should've been, shone dead white in the mirror behind his head.

"Hey, Kelly," Blackie greeted him. "How's life treatin' you?"

"Blackie!" He came her way, wiping down swaths of burnished oak bar. "Whaddaya doin' here? They say you've gotten to be a regular little chantootsie over at the Candy Box." He paused. "How's Renee?"

Blackie stared shyly at the floor. "Renee's OK, but I'm not seein' much of her right now."

So Blackie had given Renee the old heave-ho—or vice versa. Kelly was the biggest gossip this side of Kansas City but knew better than to press Blackie for details.

Blackie hesitated. "Yeah, I'm meetin' somebody else. Just for a drink."

Kelly put on a poker face. Blackie wasn't wasting time pining. "What can I get ya?"

"You got champagne, right?"

"You're comin' up in the world."

"You know I always had class, Kelly," Blackie grinned. "Lemme have a bottle over at the table."

She chose one out of earshot as Kelly disappeared under the counter to retrieve two glasses. He raised his head in time to see Didi through the doorway, her silhouette etched against the night sky by a streetlamp.

Didi took a step inside the Bubble Room, and Blackie saw her too. Her evening dress was sapphire-blue chiffon with long wings trailing off her ivory shoulders. Blackie hurried over and touched Didi's arm, as much as anything to make sure she was no mirage generated by the heat. If Didi was afraid, Blackie reflected, it hadn't kept her away. She was a real stand-up broad, the kind you want on your side in a fair fight.

Kelly could only wonder how Blackie did it. She had gorgeous dames coming out of the woodwork.

"Did you have any trouble findin' the place?" Blackie asked Didi.

"Not much," Didi replied. A fragrance by Guerlain enveloped her. She clutched a tiny handbag with gold clasp against her body and seemed smaller than Blackie had remembered.

"I'm glad you could come down." Blackie gallantly drew out a chair for Didi that placed her back to the stage.

Didi's face was a mask of tight control. She seemed deaf to the tinny music blaring from the orchestra, the cheers and guffaws of the audience. But one look at Blackie Cole and her heart thumped wildly. "You said you'd heard something, Blackie." The name felt new and shiny in her mouth.

"Workin' in a place like the Candy Box," Blackie poured champagne, "you hear all kinds of things."

Didi's lips lingered at the edge of her glass. "Titanic used to say the Candy Box was as safe as a mother's arms."

Blackie's eyes rested on Didi's tender naked shoulders, shimmering like the flesh of pale calla lilies. "Titanic was wrong," she said with a hint of foreboding.

Didi took a few long sips of champagne. Added to all the rest she'd drunk that night, they generated a pleasant fog in her brain. "You know, Skip's the warmest, most generous person you'd ever want to meet." She slurred her words a little.

Blackie nodded and drank deeply. She wanted to put something between Didi's feelings and the pain she was about to inflict. More champagne couldn't hurt. She filled their glasses.

Didi drank and grew more familiar. "Titanic used to say Skip wore a flower in his buttonhole," she joked, "because it simply wouldn't stay in his hair!" She rested a hand on Blackie's satin lapel.

"Because of his problem, you know," Didi gulped champagne and turned serious again, "I didn't go right to the police to report him missing."

"You did the right thing." Didi's hand burned over Blackie's heart.

"If Skip's hurt and not able to contact us," Didi continued, her tongue fuzzy, the words cumbersome, "or if the kidnappers ask for a ransom, there's no need to bring anyone else into this." At 21, she'd come into a trust fund set up by her mother. "I have my own money. I can pay."

There was no way to prepare Didi for the truth, Blackie thought. But then she'd known all along that this wasn't something anybody was going to thank her for. "It's not what you think."

"What is it then?" Didi asked.

No more stalling. Blackie spoke the words slowly. "They found a body at the Candy Box."

"A body?" The words seemed to smash into Didi's face. Blackie could almost see it crumble.

"The description fits Skip."

"What description?"

"Blond, blue eyes." Blackie took Didi's hand. "He looked just like you."

Didi had fantasized about Blackie's touch. She found little comfort in it now. "Titanic said I shouldn't worry about Skip. Boys will be boys and all that."

Wrong again, Blackie thought, and refilled Didi's glass. "You don't know how sorry I am."

Didi stared at her with ravaged eyes. "There's a mistake. The police would've gotten in touch with us right away if it was Skip's body." She garbled the last word. "My father's quite prominent," she added as she searched through her bag. She laid a snapshot on the table. "This is my brother."

It was Skip, sure enough, blue-eyed innocence in a dark blazer and cream-colored flannels. "He's dead, Didi," Blackie said simply. "I saw the body in the men's room at the Candy Box. It looked like an accident, maybe a fight. There was blood at the back of his head. Otherwise, he looked like a kid sleeping."

"The Candy Box would've called the police. There would've been an investigation...." Didi's voice trailed off. "What do you mean you saw the body?"

Blackie felt like a heel. The color deepened in her cheeks. "You gotta understand, my boss Stevie didn't know who Skip was. He was just another gay boy to them. I didn't know either until I saw you that night."

Didi raised eyes to Blackie as clear as aquamarine, filled with tears. "Why didn't you tell me then?" She put away the snapshot and took out a cigarette.

Blackie reached for a match. Her knee grazed Didi's, who inhaled.

"You gotta believe me...these people are ruthless. They didn't wanna lose any money. If the cops know you got a body on the premises, they can pull your liquor license and close the place down."

"You knew all along," Didi wailed. The unfiltered tip of her cigarette was taking a mauling. She mashed the whole thing into an ashtray. "What about Titanic? He was supposed to be looking out for Skip."

Blackie looked around at the crowd. All eyes were glued on the show, something with fans and veils. "Don't blame Titanic. He doesn't know anything." Blackie poured them both a last refill. Ice water in a silver-plated bucket sloshed over the empty bottle. "It was too risky to tell anybody."

Didi drained her glass then in search of oblivion. She felt betrayed by all the people she'd just begun to trust. "Risky?" she asked in a hollow tone.

Maybe Didi knew her way around Park Avenue, Blackie thought, but she had a lot to learn about the Village underworld. "Try to understand, sweetheart, Stevie doesn't like it when people tell tales out of school."

Didi's anger tapered off, and her voice softened. "What would he do?"

"Oh, it'll be all right," Blackie bluffed. "He never has to know we talked, you and me."

Didi was one sauced cookie but was beginning to see how far out on a limb Blackie had gone for her. She rose unsteadily to her feet, like a bird dragging one wing. "I'll go to the police. They'll deal with those gangsters."

"Hold on," Blackie said. "I know you don't get it, but Stevie wouldn't like the publicity." Plus he was hand in glove with the police.

"Then I'll go to my father." Didi raised one hand like an avenging angel. "He'll know what to do."

"Siddown," Blackie pleaded. "If your father starts askin' questions, he'll just drive 'em further underground." She imagined the headlines in tomorrow's papers: "Fletcher-Payne Heir Found Dead in Village Toilet."

Didi didn't sit down. "What do you mean 'drive them underground'?"

Blackie hung back. "I didn't wanna tell you." She paused. "Skip's body...it's disappeared. If you start a ruckus, we may never find it."

Now Didi did sit down. "My brother's dead, and his body's missing," she mumbled in a parched voice. Her chin trembled as her debutante drawl unraveled. She put her head down on the table and sobbed.

Several tables around them turned to look. It was a better show than the stripper up front, who was down to her G-string. Kelly shot Blackie a frosty stare.

Blackie got to her feet. "C'mon, sweetheart, let's get outta here," she said in a low wounded voice.

Didi didn't argue. She sagged against Blackie, muttering, "I've got to get home."

"You'll get home all right." Blackie hooked an arm

around Didi's waist. What had she let herself in for? She'd tried to do the right thing, and another sensational tipsy dame had fallen into her arms. But looking down at that golden hair splashed against the black matte fabric of her tux, Blackie felt more alive than she'd felt in a long time, since the day Renee had gone to work for Lucille. She was glad she'd told Didi. She'd see she got home safely, then hurry back to the Candy Box. If she missed the last show, there'd be hell to pay.

"See you later, Kelly," Blackie threw over her shoulder. He didn't volunteer to help with her limp burden. She flexed her shoulders to keep Didi's knees from buckling.

"Hey, Blackie," a gravelly voice spoke up from the bar, "who's your new girlfriend?"

Slinking like a hungry tigress, a hooker and sometime showgirl named Trixie, one of Renee's old crowd, emerged from the shadows. She winked at Blackie and batted her eyes.

"I'll give you a hand," Trixie said as she swung the door open and waved good-bye. Her hair was bleached platinum, and her dress shimmered with black bugle beads.

"Thanks, Trixie," Blackie muttered. Thanks to Trixie, all right, who'd given Lucille Martin's phone number to Renee in the first place, copying it out of a wilted address book.

"Strictly café society and very big tips," she'd droned into Renee's ear.

"Who's that?" Didi asked, straining for a parting glance of Trixie.

"Believe me, you don't want to know." And thanks to Trixie, by noon, every hooker in town, including Renee, would know that Blackie Cole had been seen the night before with someone at the Bubble Room. Blackie hustled Didi into the night. She hadn't counted on that.

Thirteen

Outside, Blackie's curls frizzed in the high humidity. She should've known better than to take Didi to a place like the Bubble Room, where everybody knew everybody. If that blabbermouth Trixie found out who Didi was, it would make her gossip even juicier. The Fletcher-Paynes were an easy target for scandalmongers.

More than the tabloids, Blackie feared Renee, who held grudges. Even if they weren't going together anymore, Renee wasn't likely to forgive and forget. "Here's for messin' around with my dyke," she'd said when she pushed a girl backward over a chair at a party. It didn't pay to underestimate Renee. She'd never believe there was nothing between Blackie and such a gorgeous dish as Didi. Or was there?

"Where's your car?" Blackie asked Didi.

"I don't recall exactly." A lone taxi passed them going uptown. "I came by cab," she remembered, too late to flag it down.

Blackie steered her around the corner onto the cobbled stillness of Bleecker Street. "I'd better take you home." Her Ford was no limousine, but at least it was this year's model, simonized and buffed fire-engine red. She took Didi's arm. She'd have to hurry to make the last show. "Do you feel like walkin' a little?"

"I can walk fine," Didi insisted and stumbled forward.

Blackie shepherded her from doorway to doorway. They weaved another block, then turned up Macdougal where Stevie's goons were on duty. One of them, Nick "The Iceman" Morello, buffed Blackie's car with a length of rag. Didi gave him a zombielike stare as he helped fold her into the passenger seat.

"Howzit by you, Blackie?" Nick asked as he tipped his hat. "Rough night, huh?" He pointed with his bottom lip and a tilt of his head toward Didi.

"Everything's fine, Nick," Blackie replied stoically, and spun off with a roar to a chorus of respectful good-byes. She would make it a quick trip.

A canopy of trees thick with its summer growth of leaves overhung Washington Square. Blackie gunned the engine at Eighth Street. "Park and what?" she asked as she turned east.

"In the 60s just below the Armory," Didi replied. The sparkle had gone out of her like flat champagne. They rode in silence until Blackie stopped for a light.

"I should never have let him go out alone," Didi sobbed. "If I hadn't stayed so long on the island, none of this would've happened."

The man driving the car next to them leaned out his window to listen. Blackie prayed for the light to change. "It's not your fault," she said as she turned up Fourth Avenue. "I'm the one who acted like a coward."

Didi's gown lay in silken pools around her feet. Her hair floated like a golden halo in the balmy night air. "How can we know anything for sure if there's no body? He could be in a hospital with amnesia."

Blackie didn't answer or disagree right away. She stepped on the gas. The car sped along Park Avenue South, then up the traffic viaduct approaching Grand Central Station. A massive limestone Mercury crowned great arched windows, while under the station's star-spangled vault, passengers by the thousands arrived and departed daily.

Blackie wished *she* were going somewhere. She gripped the wheel. "He's not in the hospital, Didi." They plunged around Grand Central on the narrow elevated roadway and curved down onto Park Avenue.

"Skip must be alive." Didi's face shone with a choirgirl innocence. "I can just feel it. We were so close." She paused. "Surely I'd know if anything had happened to him."

"I don't know about that, sweetheart." Blackie swallowed hard. One thing was for sure. Skip's body hadn't disappeared on its own. They had to find it. Tyrone had to know something. He'd stayed behind when Smash Nose Babe had escorted her back to the dressing room. And Stevie, who called all the shots in his little kingdom, would know all the answers.

"It's not that I don't trust you." Didi raised enormous sapphire-blue eyes to Blackie.

"I know." Blackie felt Didi draw closer.

"It's just," Didi's face reflected heartbreak and despair, "I don't know what I'd do without Skip."

Blackie slowed down. Swank residences, their facades broken up by garlands and ornamental balconies, lined both sides of the avenue. "I woulda done anything to help Skip." She paused. "We were too late."

"I'm kidding myself then?"

Blackie wanted to hold Didi, wipe away her tears and sadness. "We'll get to the bottom of this, you'll see."

"What do you mean by that?" Didi sank back into the Ford's upholstery.

"I wantcha to know I saw somethin' else that night," Blackie replied hastily. "A man ran out of the men's room and passed me in the hall. I think he was...the killer."

"The *killer?*" The word stuck in Didi's throat, and her face went pale.

"We'll find him," Blackie promised grimly.

Didi was sinking under a welter of pain. In sight of the Armory, she remembered to point. "Here's the building." Carved festoons hung above windows on the lower floors.

Blackie pulled the Ford over.

Ruggles, the doorman, came out when he saw Miss Diana, her cheeks streaked with tears. He pressed his gray, round face to the window. "Miss Diana," he called out, "are you all right?"

Didi took her time answering. Blackie got out and circled to the other side of the car. "Don't worry," she said to Ruggles, "I'm gonna take her inside where she can lie down."

"You are a friend of Miss Diana's?" He squinted down his nose at Blackie, who figured this would be a good time to beat it. But she wasn't going to let any Park Avenue doorman bully her.

"Just gimme a hand, will ya?" Blackie replied as she hoisted Didi out. Between the two of them, they guided her the rest of the way under the dark green awning and into the elevator.

"Don't leave me," Didi said to Blackie.

"I'm not goin' anywhere." Blackie adjusted an arm around Didi's waist, then turned to Ruggles. "I can manage now if you'll keep an eye on my car.

"Are you sure?" Ruggles asked. A handsome boy, he thought, but very young, slim, and wiry with a delicate air about him. Rather like the young men who visited Master Owen from time to time. That was it, a friend of Master Owen's. Then everything was all right.

Upstairs in the Fletcher-Payne apartment there was nobody stirring. In the gilded bedroom Blackie fingered the zipper on Didi's blue chiffon. Like a bottle cap popping, it fizzed as it opened down her back. The dress dropped around her feet, and Didi kicked it away. She was clad only in a white garter belt and dove-colored nylons with dark seams.

The whirring that had sounded in Blackie's ears when she first met Didi swelled to a roar, like an express train screaming along the tracks. She pulled back the covers.

"Get into bed," she whispered.

"Don't ever leave me," Didi slurred again, and pulled Blackie down over her on the four-poster. Her breasts strained against Blackie's starched white shirt. The bedside lamp threw a thin veil of light around them. Without warning, Didi reached up to Blackie and kissed her long and hard.

Now this is a whole new ball game, Blackie thought. One she could easily lose. Risking your neck was one thing. Risking your heart, she'd have to think twice. Against her better judgment, she let her tongue explore the soft recesses of Didi's mouth, then drew back.

"My pants are gonna get wrinkled," she complained.

The harsh broadcloth grated against Didi's bare thighs. She breathed in sharply and murmured, "Take them off."

It would have been so easy to give Didi what she wanted. Blackie imagined what it would be like to wake up under that gossamer tent with flounces dripping from the bedposts, all creamy and golden. The sticky sweetness of gardenias perfuming the air and the cool satin sheets. No creaking metal springs when she turned over, no ratty pull-down shade flapping above her head. This wasn't Christopher Street. Nobody had to tell her that rich was better.

But Didi had had a lot to drink and a terrible shock. Her head lolled on the pillow.

Instead of crawling into bed, Blackie kissed Didi's upper

lip, where a mist of perspiration clung. "Time for you to get some rest."

"No," Didi protested weakly, her eyes squeezed shut. Her breath already came in deep sighs, the alcohol lulling her into a troubled sleep. A kind of serenity at the eye of a storm.

Disentangling Didi's arms from around her neck, Blackie gently spread the sheet over her and stood up as the Cupid clock chimed. The last show at the Candy Box started in 20 minutes. She imagined Titanic primping, in glossy red satin with high-heel sandals to match. If she didn't come back, he would understand. But Stevie would say her mother had dropped her on her head, and he'd have a point there. Didi wasn't for her. They were worlds apart.

Thinking suddenly of her career, Blackie buttoned her tux on her way down in the elevator. She hurried out to where her Ford waited. "Thanks," she mumbled to Ruggles.

"Not at all." Ruggles gave Blackie another long look. All his years of watching the comings and goings of the wealthy had taught him never to ask questions. But there was something not quite right about this young man. The voice, the smooth cheeks.

Ruggles touched his cap to say good night as Blackie circled the rear end of the Ford over to the driver's side.

Smoldering bluish-black eyes watched her every move, from the rear seat of a taxi parked half a block down the avenue.

"Meter's runnin'," the cabbie said.

"You'll get your fare," replied a voice with metallic edges. The speaker raised the brim of his cap an inch off his forehead for a better look at Blackie. The hands were ropy with blue veins and clammy. He rubbed them down his thighs. Broad shoulders rippled inside his bomber jacket.

If you didn't know, he thought, the dyke from the Candy Box could sure pass for a guy. Pervert, she was probably on her way to the men's room when she saw him. He knew she'd seen him, her eyes as big as saucers. He squirmed like an animal caught in a trap. Her and that colored boy.

Blackie swung her car around and headed downtown, not looking back.

Stupid cunt, he'd been watching her, but so far she hadn't spotted him. He was as graceful as a big cat and stealthy. When he'd seen Blackie hotfoot it out of the Candy Box, he'd followed.

Then the other dame showed up. Under the streetlight, he saw the face and blinked in horror. It was the face he'd tried to forget, along with the sour smell of semen and the crack of the kid's head on the cold unyielding toilet seat. He'd seen too much death. But this broad looked enough like the dead boy to be his twin. Maybe she was.

Breathing so hard his ribs ached, he'd ducked behind a parked car to watch the broad go into the Bubble Room. The dyke was no fool after all. She hadn't wasted her time going to the cops. She'd found out who the kid was and gone straight to the family. He knew those people. They wouldn't rest until they made somebody pay for the kid's death. The colored boy's testimony wouldn't be worth anything without the lezzie's. She'd be their star witness.

He'd go to jail for a long time. He'd been in trouble before, and the cops wouldn't believe he didn't mean to do it. How unlucky could you get?

He paid the cabbie and stepped out onto Park Avenue. *He* was the fool. After what happened—with the boy—he should've disappeared. But at the Greyhound ticket window, Newark, Philadelphia, and Baltimore were just names. He'd had enough traveling to last him a lifetime, during the war, from one rat hole in the Pacific to another. All he wanted to know of geography was the streets of the city, the old neighborhood.

Dark sunken eyes—like those of men torpedoed in shark-infested waters—looked restlessly uptown, then down. He started to walk fast toward the park. He had to think, or he'd be the next candidate for the snake pit or a straitjacket. He took off his cap and stuffed it in his pocket, then ran a hand through his dark hair, sticky with sweat and fear.

Nobody could pin anything on him, except that cuntlapper from the Candy Box. He wasn't about to let a broad like that, who wasn't even a real woman, send him up the river. But if she was in cahoots with the Fletcher-Payne dame, he'd have to watch his step.

Fourteen

Downtown, Stevie was fuming, but he told Smash Nose Babe to hold the curtain for Blackie. "Where the hell were you?" he sputtered when she came barrel-assing into the Candy Box 10 minutes after the last show was supposed to start.

She had her story ready for him, about her mom and the medicine all the way out to Brooklyn. He could fire her on the spot, but that had only happened to two girls who were drunk all the time on the job. And if she was so good for business, Stevie would want to believe her. One thing Blackie had learned was that lies bound people together as the truth never would.

"Gedouddahere!" Stevie blinked behind his glasses. "To Brooklyn and back."

"It was the only way," she argued. "Sue me—I'm sorry." "Don't give me that cornball shit." His lips twisted into a snarl. "You're late again, you'll be out on your ear. Now get onstage."

Over the football forming in her throat, Blackie calmed the restless crowd with the promise of a song and her cupcake smile. As the spotlight mellowed to pale pink, she stepped up to the mike. The orchestra struck up her music, and she dipped into her lower range for a raspy quality.

Even awake, I dream of her.

That song had been about Renee, but not anymore, Blackie thought with a sigh. She was free of her at last. Call it infatuation, but there was a new face, a new smile that made Blackie want to sing, and laugh and make love. She was no two-timer. She and Renee were really through. As the saxophones whined, Blackie sizzled the lyrics into a heap of glowing embers. For Didi's sake she'd be passion's fool.

This was really show business, Blackie thought. Your life was on the rocks, but you went on and sang your heart out. She knew better than anybody that the whole thing with Didi Fletcher-Payne was a crap shoot. It could go either way. But Blackie didn't mind sticking her neck out for a dame in distress. It was second nature.

She spread her arms wide in a big finish, and bowed low to her audience. The applause was tumultuous. Stevie watched from the back, his arms folded over his sunken chest. After Blackie's act, Titanic and the boys, billed as the Village Debutantes, whooped it up. The finale was a swirl of feathers and fluff.

Before closing time, Blackie went back to the kitchen where she expected to find Tyrone. She wanted to have some news for Didi the next time they met. The cooks played dumb like they'd never heard of Tyrone.

"Gone home."

"He'll be right back."

Nobody was taking any chances. Blackie turned toward the dressing room where Titanic sat in front of the mirror taking off his makeup.

"*You* get in here and shut that door," he hissed. "Where were you?"

"It's a long story." Blackie was worn out and still not

ready to talk turkey to him about the things on her mind.

Titanic's ears perked up. "You just drop anchor right here." He pulled out a chair for her.

"Remember, you're not in the navy anymore," she complained, but sat down anyway.

"Where were you? Stevie hit the roof when Waxy told him the story about your mom. He was hollerin' 'dizzy dyke' and 'dumb cluck' at Waxy." Titanic paused. "Actually, I didn't mind so much. They promised I could fill in with my Mae West. Then you showed up."

"Since when are you in charge of castin', Mr. Shubert?" Blackie snickered. "But it's nice to be missed." She stared at the dressing room table. "So you think I'm in Dutch with Stevie?"

"I wouldn't push my luck. Howzabout a little breakfast? Get outta this clip joint for a while?"

She sensed he wanted to tell her something badly, maybe pump her for information too. That would've led her into deeper murky waters where she wasn't ready to venture just yet. "I don't wanna," she finally said. "I'm already sick to my stomach."

"You vant to be alone, Glummy Gus, there's nuthin' I can do." He stripped off his false eyelashes. "But be on time tomorrow. Stevie's called a little meeting of the cast before we open."

"Not another one."

"To tell us how lucky we are to be workin' at the Candy Box."

"To think I used to believe that," Blackie replied.

At Madison and 59th, in the backseat of his low-slung limousine, John Jay Fletcher-Payne waited for the light to change. He reflected that he could've very well accepted the generous offer Mayor LaGuardia had tendered years ago, to install an up-to-date radio-telephone in the family town car.

"Comes in handy," His Honor had said, who loved to make calls from his car while making rounds of the city.

If Diana and Owen were up, John Jay could phone ahead and perhaps take them for breakfast. He was famished and always liked seeing his children. But he wouldn't have felt comfortable calling from Lucille's.

John Jay shook his head and mumbled, "Now, LaGuardia, there was a mayor." Perhaps a bit flamboyant and overbearing, but a man who'd stood up to corruption and double-dealing. John Jay had sat on several blue-ribbon investigating committees.

LaGuardia's sucessor O'Malley wasn't half the man, though John Jay rather liked him personally. Story after story linked him to greedy politicians and gangsters, the kind of publicity that had made him decline to seek a second term. But John Jay was in no hurry to embrace the crusading DA Duggan either.

Judge Valerio had hit the nail on the head the other night. "People who like to play the ponies, Jack," he confided—and Jack was one of those—"that Duggan's gonna be murder on 'em."

John Jay and *The Daily Journal* were withholding an endorsement.

The car roared up Park Avenue through the 500s and into the 600s. When it pulled up in front of the Fletcher-Payne residence, Ruggles, the gap-toothed doorman, rushed out in a gray overcoat. "Good morning, sir," he said, his eyes blank with sleeplessness, and touched his cap obsequiously. He wondered where the old man got the energy to stay out all night.

Through the vestibule, Old John Jay ambled toward the

small elevator. The local papers often carried his image. The tall patrician frame, mouth drawn as thin as a knife blade. Riding up alone, he thought again about Diana and Owen. Pampered and spoiled as they were, he worried about their future.

There'd never been a minute's trouble with the older brother Jay Jay. He'd married young and settled down. But Jay Jay's successes had brought his father little joy. The boy had always seemed more his mother's son, dry and puritanical. In fact, if his wife weren't so fastidious, John Jay might suspect that his eldest was a chip off some other old block.

Upstairs, in the apartment's circular foyer, John Jay flicked a light switch. From a blue-and-white Delft porcelain jar, a half dozen pink hydrangea blossoms raised their ruffled heads. He tossed his hat over the bust of a sad-eyed poet with a wild shock of bronze hair. The old man never had much time for reading.

The walls of the drawing room were green silk brocade. John Jay fetched himself a brandy from a smoky crystal decanter and quickly looked through a pile of yesterday's mail that Basil the butler had left for him on the tea table. Every charity ball in New York was soliciting his presence in exchange for a fat donation, milking him dry. He dumped the invitations back onto the chased silver tray with a sigh.

Not a sound in the apartment. The children would certainly be sleeping. Shoes in hand, John Jay started up to the second floor. He had to walk a gauntlet of ancestral portraits to reach the refuge of the master bedroom where blessed sleep beckoned. A cheerless bunch they were, mostly his wife's relations, and what a lot he'd put up with from them. If marrying for wealth had seemed a solution, John Jay Fletcher-Payne could certainly tell you he'd gotten more than he'd bargained for.

John Jay decided to look in on Owen. He knocked softly at his son's door, then opened it a crack. The bed was empty, not slept in. A faltering smile creased the old man's lips. The boy was a night owl like his father, who loved a good time. Underneath his daughter's door peeked a sliver of light. Diana read a lot. If she'd fallen asleep and left her light on, he'd turn it off. He knocked.

Didi turned lazily on her side. She'd fallen asleep with Blackie's handsome face brooding over her. Didi threw a leg across the bed. Blackie had disappeared, evaporated, and there was that knocking again. It had all been a terrible mistake, she thought suddenly. Skip was at the door. He had come home.

Instead it was Old John Jay who stuck his head in. "Diana, darling, good morning. How's my favorite daughter?"

"Father?" It was both a question and a wail, and afterward, Didi blushed crimson. She tunneled under the sheet and came up with the silk-and-lace coverlet that she wrapped herself in. A blue vein pulsed against its sheen. "What are you doing up so early?"

John Jay lowered his eyes modestly. He hadn't expected to find her so scantily clothed, exuding a sweaty, wine-soaked fragrance. He'd resisted for so long the notion that Diana and Owen were old enough to have bodies with curves, things that dangled and swung. The war years had passed like a dream, and they were all grown up.

"I'm sorry," he said, and sat on the edge of the bed. It was good to sit down. His throat hurt, and he hoped he wasn't coming down with a cold.

Didi peered at her father through a blinding headache that reminded her how hell-bent she'd been on seduction. Blackie had been more reasonable, or maybe, Didi thought with chagrin, she hadn't been interested. A staggering thirst parched her mouth.

"I was going to call the island this morning," she said, "to see if you were out with Mummie."

"You know me, darling." He was composed and carefree.

"Always on the move." He stood up and scanned himself quickly in the mirror above her mahogany Regency dresser. Sandy hair streaked with gray, but still thick and full.

At some craps table, Didi surmised, or with his whores. In deference to her mother, she'd made it her business to know as little as possible about her father's other life. But it was hard. He hadn't always been discreet.

John Jay turned back to his daughter. Like Owen, she had his eyes and looks, but he couldn't remember what she'd asked him. He did notice that she seemed distressed. "What was it you wanted to ask me, dear?"

She leaned into the scalloped, monogrammed pillows behind her and hugged her knees to head off a wave of nausea. She got up to exchange the coverlet for a robe. Her windows overhung the avenue. She slowly hoisted the shirred silk Austrian blinds, then lit a cigarette.

The old man watched her patiently. "So what do you say, Diana?"

"I tried to reach you by phone," she began, "because something's happened." She paused. Her head throbbed. Her voice was hoarse. "It's better for Mummie not to know. It could, you know, set her back."

"What about Mummie?" She'd thrown him off balance.

"This isn't about Mummie or you."

"Who's the culprit then?" If this was some childish secret, he wished she'd get on with it.

Didi got a hold on her voice. "Father, I think you'd better sit down."

"All right," he said, and retreated toward the drop-front desk. He was tired anyway. He pulled up a chair.

"It's Skip. He hasn't been home for days."

Her father assumed a puzzled look, and tented his long tapering fingers under his chin. Diana was a lovely girl, but she'd always worried too much about Owen, babied him. It hadn't been good for the boy. It might've been part of his problem.

"But darling, you've got to realize he's a man now, and probably off on some lark." The idea of Owen out sowing wild oats appealed enormously to Old John Jay, who suddenly remembered he was hungry. "I'm going to call Basil, and we'll have an early breakfast. You'll like that, won't you?"

"No."

"No?" The old man was used to a world under his thumb, where orders were given and people obeyed. "Why not?"

"I think it's time we called the police, Father."

"The police?" he said. "Not because Owen's having a little fling."

Everything Blackie had told her sounded like a bad mystery novel. But Blackie had no reason to lie either, and wouldn't make up stories just to scare her. Didi gulped down a sob. "I'm terribly afraid something may have happened to Skip."

John Jay didn't like the turn the conversation had taken. He dropped his charming robust pose. "What makes you think that?"

At that imperious tone, full of wrath and threats, she cringed. When things didn't go his way, her father could get very angry, shifting gears instantly. She'd seen him so often smiling and generous one minute, furious and unforgiving the next. Almost anything could set him off, from the wrong fork by his dinner plate to a slip in the stock market. He despised the unexpected and had little tolerance for human failings. He railed against them as though it were his right. Those moods had terrorized both Didi and Skip from childhood. She hated that they could still frighten her.

"Diana, I asked you a question," he repeated ominously.

The hard-nosed look on his face put Didi on her guard. She'd seen it when he had something that business associates wanted badly, and he intended to charge full price.

"Father, this isn't simple." She challenged him with a defiant look of her own. "Like the time you asked me about Skip dressing up in women's clothes, in my clothes."

The old man's face went sodden gray like wet newspapers. His collar had wilted and drooped around his neck. "Mrs. Newham said she'd seen him in the lobby," he shot back defensively. The look on his face said someone had plunged a dagger into his heart. "I told her it was a masquerade, one of those madcap affairs." He stood his ground, feet flat down on the Savonnerie carpet. "Why are you bringing all that up now?" he thundered.

"There were other times," Didi said quietly, "that nobody told you about."

"I can't believe you ever encouraged him in that nonsense, loaning him your clothes. "John Jay's voice rose in volume to punish the memory, then subsided. "Owen might be confused," he concluded, "a lost boy." He repeated the phrases like an incantation. "But we can turn all that around."

Didi recognized his need to sound infallible, but none of that mattered now. "I haven't talked to Skip since I went to Mummie's, and I'm afraid he's hurt or worse...." Her voice trailed off. "Please do something."

"You're being ridiculous!" he lashed out again. It was the same irrational fury he usually reserved for his wife when she drank.

"We'll get to the bottom of this right now," Old John Jay announced, and went over to a veneered telephone table. It shook on fragile cabriole legs.

The police commissioner was at home shaving, but he took John Jay's call. They'd served together on several committees.

"Commissioner? I'm sorry to call so early." It was probably nothing, he explained in somber tones, but his son Owen might be missing. The old man's eyes glowed with a pale light. "The rascal hasn't called home, and he's got his mother and sister worried sick."

The commissioner instantly named a chief of detectives and promised somebody would call back within hours. They'd run a check of missing persons and whatever suspicious cases might fit the bill. Had they received any notes or calls asking for ransom?

He questioned Didi briefly about that, then turned back to the commissioner. "No, no, there's been nothing...yes, that's a good sign." His face was drawn and ashen as he hung up the phone.

"Go right to the top," he ranted, and his chest heaved. "That's the way to handle things." He stopped and looked around as though he'd misplaced something.

Didi pulled her robe tighter. She thought he'd forgotten about her.

"Get some clothes on now, Diana," he said abruptly. "I'll tell the servants to expect a call." The cold white light rekindled in his eyes. "The authorities will respond, and everyone must be prepared."

With that, John Jay started down the hall, dreading Basil's stony all-knowing look. He'd been with the family for a long time, and would realize instantly that something was amiss. Basil knew where the bodies were buried.

Hot tears stung Didi's eyes as she threw herself across the four-poster bed. She'd get no comfort from her father, whose shouting had struck her right between the eyes where her head ached.

FIFTEEN

Detective Ronald Swazey slouched into the Charles Street Station early and headed for the sanctity of the squad room. He greeted Brannan, aimed his hat at the deer antlers, and watched it drop like a rock into the wastepaper basket instead.

"Just my luck," he said as the phone on his desk jangled.

The lieutenant wanted a word with him and Brannan. Swazey straightened his tie.

The lieutenant's office was institutional gray-green, with a rear window view of a line of wash. Years of desk duty had puffed his belly like a blowfish. "Whaddaya got on that unidentified DOA from the waterfront?"

Swazey froze. Brannan knew nothing. What did the lieutenant know? He wished instantly that he'd cut them in. Greed, like crime, didn't pay.

"Well, not much, sir," Swazey said apologetically. "We figure it for a dump job. A blow to the back of the head. The fingerprints don't match anything we've got."

"We've been askin' questions along the waterfront," Brannan added. "Trunk's clean, but we've got the night watchman's statement. Body was half frozen when we found it."

"Frozen?" interrupted the lieutenant.

"We're checking out restaurants with freezer lockers," Swazey said. Not the worst duty you could draw on a hot summer afternoon. "But there's a million of 'em."

"Listen, boys, there's somethin' up with that stiff. Chief of detectives called me already this morning, and the commissioner's on his tail."

Swazey knew he had to be careful. "Yeah?" he volunteered weakly.

"Young, right? Good-looking kid?"

Brannan sighed. "Yes, sir, somethin' like that."

"Got a number for you to call." The lieutenant rustled papers on his desk. "REgent 7-1968, ask for a John Fletcher-Payne III. Give him a description of the victim. You know the old man. He's a big shot, and his son's turned up missin'."

The third? Swazey needed time to think. "Ain't it kinda early to be callin'?"

"The chief said now!" The lieutenant waved his hand in dismissal.

As he retreated back to the squad room, Swazey remembered Stevie's slimy hand in his own, poking that fat envelope his way.

"Very generous, Stevie," he'd said, flipping his finger over the wad of bills.

"It's all yours, Swazey."

That was big-hearted Stevie, the clown. He must've known all along who the stiff was. Fear crept up the back of Swazey's neck. Without ID, after a decent interval, they would've buried John Doe over on Hart's Island and forgotten about it. This was a corpse of another color.

As a sallow dawn crept up Sixth Avenue, Blackie had breakfast alone at the all-night greasy-spoon around the corner, a less than glamorous atmosphere. Coffee and eggs side by side with the usual jetsam that had floated out the other end of a long night in the Village, sticky with the city's heat and spent desire.

She imagined Didi still sleeping it off in her gold-and-white Park Avenue sanctuary. Not that Blackie hadn't been in fancy shmancy layouts before, like the night she got shanghaied off to a mansion in Jersey with a lawn the size of Ebbets Field. The morning after, her hostess had been in no hurry to drive her back to town until the husband showed up. Still in her tux, Blackie escaped with a truck driver she flagged down on the highway.

It wouldn't be like that with Didi, Blackie told herself, and longed to call. To hear that voice speaking her name again and not end up with bubkes.

Back in her room, she tried to calm down and get some shut-eye. She pulled out the carpet sweeper and attacked the threadbare rug. Next she shook out the fake serape that covered the armchair and dusted the floor lamp. She did a few dishes in the sink and wiped down the old enamel table, then soaked away what was left of the morning in the claw-foot bathtub. To finish, she scoured the tub with Bon Ami and fell into bed.

Blackie dreamed she opened her mouth to sing, and saw Didi—or was it Skip?—sharing a ringside table with her mom, who was giving Renee warm hugs. Renee hugged Magda Cohen back. They both wore their hair—Magda's mostly gray—piled high. On the downbeat, Blackie's voice came out like rough sandpaper. It was Stevie's voice. She awoke to the wailing of a kid getting a licking somewhere on the courtyard her window overlooked.

She dressed for the Candy Box, but on the way over she reconsidered a call to Didi. Though she had nothing new to report, at least a decent interval had passed. Inside the corner drugstore, a phone booth gave her a little privacy. She shoved her nickel into the slot.

"Fletcher-Payne residence," Basil answered in a pompous tone.

Didi came on the line. "Hullo, Blackie." The voice was weary and distant.

Blackie didn't like the change. "How are you?" she stammered.

Didi's head rested against the sinuous back of the drawing-room sofa, in gilded beechwood and dark amber silk brocade. Her bottom was sunk into the squashy cushions, her eyes swollen with weeping. "My father's here, and he's taken it very badly." She paused. "He phoned the police. Some homicide detectives—one's named Swazey—are meeting us right now to see if it's Skip's body they have at the morgue."

Blackie's stomach heaved. "Swazey?" Stevie's favorite shamus for hire. It couldn't be a coincidence that Swazey was on the case.

"Do you know him?"

"From the local precinct." How was Blackie going to tell Didi that Swazey was on Stevie's payroll? "Why do the police think it's Skip?"

"It's an unidentified body found on the waterfront. Stuffed into a trunk and dumped." Didi sounded remote. "Evidently, it fits Skip's description."

"The waterfront?" Blackie hadn't expected things to move so fast. She was stunned. If the body was Skip's, the Candy Box was in the clear. She had to hand it to Stevie, who'd kept way ahead of the game.

Behind Didi, the Tiffany tall clock knelled the hour. A harsh "We've got to go, Diana" rang out over it.

"Your father?" Blackie asked.

"Yes, give me your phone number."

Blackie heard a catch in Didi's voice like remembered tenderness, then reeled off the Candy Box's number, ORegon 4-0531, and her address on Christopher.

"You can find me there if you need me in a hurry."

"Thank you," Didi murmured, "for everything." This time all the sadness was there, and a fierce longing.

The phone went dead. Out on the sidewalk, heat lightning from the threatening summer storm flashed around Blackie.

Two gurneys in tandem obstructed a hallway at the city mortuary. Outside the lab, attendants were packing more bodies into stainless-steel boxes. "Big fire up in Harlem," one of the morgue detectives explained to Swazey.

A friend of his in missing persons ushered him and Brannan into a white-tiled chamber scrubbed with disinfectant. Better a whiff of formaldehyde than the stench of death, Swazey supposed, and wished for a transfer out of homicide. A body was wheeled out, and an attendant lifted the sheet. Recognizing the boy from the waterfront, Swazey popped another Tums. His ulcer wouldn't allow him to work more cover-ups for Stevie the klutz.

"That's the one," Brannan said.

Swazey brushed at the sleeves of his good suit fresh from the cleaners. He'd picked it up at noon and left off the old one with the mustard stain. "I'll wait for 'em outside."

In search of fresh air, he went back to the steps on First Avenue, one hand Napoleon-style inside his jacket. He walked in a tight little circle, inspecting the toes of shoes in need of a spit-and-polish.

The Fletcher-Payne town car ground to a stop in front of the morgue. John Jay's driver came around and took the old man's arm. Gaunt and stoop-shouldered in pinstripe gray, he stepped out. Behind him, one long lustrous leg stretched over the running board. A black lizard bag followed, then a tailor-fitted sheath with matching felt hat over a mass of golden hair.

Swazey was staggered. Under a breath of veil, the face was the DOA's all over again. She'd dressed sharp for the morgue, he thought, but her eyes were terrible. Doffing his porkpie hat, he extended an unsteady hand and introduced himself in a courtly old-world brogue.

"Detective Ronald Swazey at your service," he wheezed. "And this is my partner, Detective Brannan. Right this way."

They went first to a small chapel. "Hope we're wrong about this," Brannan said. "But from the description, there's a good chance."

Not much of a description, Didi told herself. She followed the detectives along a corridor, with the old man trailing behind. Lots of times in the movies, Didi thought, it wasn't the person they were looking for at all. An older woman would lean in fearfully. "That's not my husband," she'd whisper from behind the corner of the sheet. "Never saw him before," the witness would say. "Not the guy we're lookin' for," the detective would repeat. Every now and then they hit paydirt. "That's her," the husband would say, and turn his head away, eyes streaming tears, or try to throw himself over her body crying her name.

Austere and restrained, Didi's father had withdrawn into his own world. She stumbled, and Swazey hurried back for her.

"Are you sure you feel like going in?"

"We're fine," Old John Jay reassured the detectives.

A woman in white took them through double swinging doors. The body had been brought up by special elevator. A curtain opened for a parting glimpse of Skip behind cold thick glass. Didi flattened out the palms of both hands against it. "Father, it's him," she whimpered, "isn't it?"

The old man's face had gone brittle like ancient parchment. "Yes," he said, eyes glistening. He rested his fists on the window and held his breath.

All vestiges of doubt vanished. Didi beat on the glass. "Skip." She swayed from side to side. "Can't we get any closer? Can I touch him?"

Swazey fished for something to say that didn't betray his jitters. Brannan spoke up, "You'll be able to take him home soon."

"Did my son suffer?" the old man asked sadly, his tall frame quivering.

"No, no, you mustn't think he was in pain," Swazey replied. "It was quick."

"Thank God for that," John Jay said, each word a mouthful of cheap wine turned to vinegar. His eyes lingered on his son's face, unblemished, pure as an angel's. It was the child he'd loved best but hadn't been able to protect. A child always quietly and gently pulling away until there was a gulf between them no one could cross. He should've tried harder, been more straightforward in helping Owen overcome his problem. He'd tried to broach the subject more than once, but finally retreated in confusion. Instead, he'd sent strangers to spy on the boy.

"I wanted him to be happy," John Jay mumbled. "He was so young." He turned back to his daughter. "He didn't understand what it would mean to be a pariah, an unhappy misfit in society." He paused. "I couldn't let Owen think I accepted or approved of...what he was doing."

"Stop it, Father. You're not to blame."

He bowed his head in silence. Didi's absolution consoled him. She pressed against the glass. She knew the next time she saw Skip he would be in a coffin. Clods of earth striking it with a hollow sound, covering him up.

Swazey's hands were square and hard as he eased her away from the window.

"We can't leave him here like this." She tugged at her father's sleeve. "Father?"

Death had stripped Old John Jay bare. He thought he might never move from that linoleum wasteland of a hallway, and didn't care.

Brannan flanked Didi. "Why don't we step outside, miss?"

Didi braced herself, one foot behind the other. "I'm not going anywhere."

"Mr. Fletcher, sir." Swazey appealed for help. "We can talk outside."

John Jay set his jaw in an unforgiving line and reached for his daughter's arm. "Come with me, Diana." She sank into him weeping. Things would never be all right again. They started together for the swinging doors.

Outside on the street, the old man waited straitlaced beside his limousine. The chauffeur had the door open in a jiffy. The Fletcher-Paynes were inside the car, motor running, when John Jay opened his window. Leaning out, he called to Swazey. "Excuse me, detective."

Swazey trotted over.

"My son's possessions? His clothing?" He was having trouble speaking. His breath came in short asthmatic spurts. "There was a ring he always wore. It was a present and had great sentimental value."

"The suit was a mess, sir," Brannan replied. "And we found nothing on him. No money, no ID, no ring. It would've been turned over to you. But I'll put it in my report."

"So my son was robbed?" John Jay asked in a desolate voice.

"Looks that way, sir," Swazey apologized. "What's this ring like?"

"Couldn't we go now, Father?" Didi pleaded.

John Jay's eyes were opaque. "A large diamond," he said. "Originally an earring that belonged to his grandmother."

Swazey jotted something down on a scrap of paper. "I'll put that in my report." He backed away as the old man rolled up his window.

John Jay spoke quietly to his driver. "Park Avenue." The town car roared uptown.

In his backroom office at the Candy Box, Stevie was trying to get off the phone. "I tell you I didn't know!" he repeated, eager to slough the whole thing off.

"You threw me a curveball," Swazey argued, anger and panic welling up, "when you didn't tell me who the faggot in the trunk was."

Stevie was impatient. Even when he told the truth, nobody believed him. "Look, it was just a stiff I had to get rid of," he told Swazey. "The boys bungled the job. Who was I supposed to call? J. Edgar Hoover?"

"I don't like findin' out these things the hard way," Swazey muttered.

"Hey, whaddaya worried about?" Stevie bluffed his way along. "The old man's not gonna want much sleuthin' done. Does he want people to know his son was found dead in a toilet?"

"He don't know that part. Just we found the body on the waterfront."

"Good," Stevie replied, cold as a toad. "If Daddy don't knuckle under, that'll be the clincher. 'Your little boy wears a skirt.' See, Swazey, it ain't the end of the world."

Not one to air his dirty laundry in public, Stevie didn't

remind Swazey what the dead faggot's pedigree meant to the Candy Box. He still had two witnesses, Blackie and Tyrone, who could link the club and the body in the trunk. He had to admit it would've been safer to have had them rubbed out first thing. *Am I a sap?* he asked himself, then flicked a thumbnail against his front teeth and mumbled, "Bleed to death!"

Sixteen

By the time Blackie got to the club, Crazy Charlie and Waxy were pacing the bar like restless apes, hoping for a chance to clobber somebody. They said Stevie was in his office. She passed them by and went on to the dressing room, where Titanic sat swathed in a robe of pastel silk before a circular mirror. His face was awash with light. He furiously brushed shaving lather over his cheeks, then traced neat furrows through the moist foam with his Gillette.

"Stevie's little get-together still on?" Blackie pulled up a chair.

"As far as I know." He wiped his face dry. Sharp yanks of the tweezers thinned his eyebrows and exterminated errant chest hairs. Dipping into the pancake makeup, he coated his skin a creamy biscuit color and reached for the false lashes. He fluttered his eyes seductively as he skimmed the tip of a black wax pencil through his brows.

Blackie tidied up the dressing table by replacing a top or two on jar and tube. "You know, I haven't leveled with you about why I was late last night." She paused uneasily. "And a couple of other things."

"Oh, I'm used to that." Titanic chose an eggplant-colored eye shadow and darkened his lids with bold strokes. "What's the scuttlebutt?"

"No scuttlebutt. I was with Didi."

He suspended a powder puff in midair. "Fletcher-Payne?"

"Are you surprised?" Blackie swept some cotton wads into the wastebasket. "I called her."

"Didn't I tell you she was smitten?" He chattered on. "Did you go to the apartment? What's it like? Lots of Duncan Phyfe, Sèvres, and the family crest on the silver?"

"Slow down." Blackie straightened her tie. "You know I don't know anything about that stuff. I just took Didi home."

Titanic outlined his lips in scarlet. "How romantic, dahling."

"What a gold digger you turned out to be!" Was it bennies or visions of old New York money, Blackie wondered, that had conjured up the gooney bird stare on Titanic's face?

"This is no time for one of your lectures." He blotted his lipstick with a wisp of tissue. "People who live in glass houses..."

"You think everything's about money. I had somethin' I had to tell her," Blackie explained. "That's why I called."

"Rahlly, dahling, don't get yourself in a tizzy." Titanic took a shiny object out of the pocket of his robe. "Was this what you had to tell Didi about?" Right in the middle of the table, he dropped a large blue-white diamond, set in a wide but delicate platinum band.

It glittered, and Blackie raised startled eyes. "Where'd you get that? Is it for real?"

"You oughta know."

"How should I know?"

"Look inside. There's an inscription."

Blackie picked up the ring. "What's so special about it? A gift from one of your admirers?"

"Just read the inscription."

The lights around the mirror blinded her. "How do you expect me to see anything?" But she did see. "*O-F-P.*"

"*F-P?*"

"Fletcher-Payne, and O as in Owen, known to his friends as Skip." Titanic paused. "It seems we all have our little secrets."

She read more. "2/7/49." Skip's birthday? It would've been his last, and this ring the sole survivor. The sadness and terrible guilt were back, beating against her temples.

"Where'd you get this?"

Outside the dressing room, Smash Nose Babe's familiar bullhorn voice interrupted. "All you kids, front and center. Stevie wants you *now.*"

Titanic took the ring. "You can stop beatin' around the bush," he said in a deadpan voice. "I know Skip's dead."

Blackie's throat went dry, and she knew she'd played her cards wrong. Maybe it was too late now, and he'd hate her. But she didn't remember having had much of a choice.

"I tried to tell you," she insisted. "But Stevie told me to keep my mouth shut. I didn't want anybody else to get hurt." She sighed and slouched back in her chair. "Who told you?"

He clammed up and looked betrayed. With a withering glance at her, he took off his robe and threw a lavender gown of organza panels, with one-inch ruffles around the hem, over his head.

"How'd you find out?" she repeated.

Titanic plunked a shoulder-length auburn wig on his head and gave it a few jerks to settle it down. "Go figure," he said at last. "You know Skip was a friend of mine too."

"I wanted to tell you. You gotta believe me. I didn't even know who the kid was until I met Didi." She looked questioningly at Titanic. "And I never saw any ring."

He studied her face for an instant, then shrugged. "No? Well, finders keepers." He dropped the ring into a chasm of cleavage.

"Not so fast." Her shoulders hunched forward. "If that's really Skip's, you gotta give it back."

"Give it back to who?"

"His family, glamour-puss. Didi!"

"You told her what happened to Skip?" The idea seemed to distress Titanic. "How'd she take it?"

"She didn't believe me at first."

Out in the hall, Smash Nose Babe threatened, "On the double. Boss is in a hurry."

"You swear you never saw the ring before?" Titanic asked.

"What's with you and this meshuggeneh ring?" Blackie thought his tiara was definitely slipping. "And who told you about Skip?"

They had shifted into the corridor, Blackie tugging at Titanic's dress, waiting for an answer. A few feet behind them, Stevie's office door opened wide, and he emerged snapping the brim of his fedora. Blackie figured she'd better button her lip.

"Let's get a move on," Stevie growled.

Smash Nose Babe led the way out and under the red velvet curtain, then between tables to ringside. He pulled out a chair for Stevie, who barked "Siddown" at the short-haired girls filing in.

Sully, Larry, Buddy, and Pat Burns, who looked like the young Pat O'Brien, took seats in a semicircle. Titanic, Miss Jackie Mae, and the other boys in wigs and long dresses formed up behind them. Blackie stayed next to Titanic.

Stevie zeroed in on her with a smirk. "Right on time today," he purred like a Mother Superior at a convent school, then removed his hat and dropped a pair of fawn-colored gloves inside.

Everybody looked solemn.

"Couple of things we need to talk over, kids," Stevie

continued. "I don't mind tellin' you it hasn't been easy the last few weeks. With elections comin' up, and that goofball Duggan in the race, the heat's on." He paused. "And that raid sure didn't help business none."

Smash Nose Babe backed him up with a somber scowl.

Blackie's mind wandered. Only a few people had known about Skip, and Titanic wasn't palsy-walsy with any of them.

"The cops are puttin' the squeeze on," Stevie droned and raised a clinched fist in protest. "And they want a fortune in protection."

He sputtered uncontrollably, his face contorted by the injustice, and blinked behind his glasses. "For your own good, I want everything to be legit in case the cops drop in again." He paused. "Especially if I ain't around."

"Where's he's off to?" Titanic whispered to Blackie. "Asbury Park? Sing Sing maybe?"

Blackie's brain hummed. There was Tyrone, but he wouldn't have talked, knowing he could wind up a cold dark pigeon in some back alley.

"For one thing," Stevie lowered his voice, "you girls know you gotta be wearin' some kinda women's clothes."

That got Blackie's attention. They'd hashed this one out before.

"Yeah, otherwise you're trans—" Stevie looked befuddled.

"*Vestites,* Stevie," Titanic shouted from the back.

"Yeah," Stevie assented, "and that ain't legal, tryin' to pass yourself off for a man." He shot Blackie a look like a harpoon.

She squirmed. The other girls in tuxes eyed each other. "Whazzit to you, Stevie?" asked Sully, who had a rebellious streak.

"You gotta be wearing ladies' underdrawers," he answered curtly. "That's what I told the copper, and I'm a man of my word." He smoothed down his crisp mottled hair and looked the girls over. "So howzabout it? I want youse to drop your drawers."

"Clear the decks," Titanic suggested. He didn't like the homicidal gleam in Stevie's eye.

What a setup, Blackie thought. "That's no Sunday school Stevie's runnin' down there," Renee had warned. "You think you're in solid with Stevie, that you got some respect. But to him a skirt's a skirt even if you ain't wearin' one."

"C'mon, you deaf or somethin'?" Stevie grumbled. "On your feet, and make it snappy." He twirled an arm in the air to accelerate the action.

Blackie wheeled around. Forgedaboudit, she thought, and looked for a way out. But Charlie and Waxy had come up to cover the back. She could almost feel their stinking breath on her neck.

"You heard him," Charlie piped.

All the boys were getting off on it, Blackie realized. One of Stevie's little jokes, a real lulu. Well, she wasn't Stevie's whore. She was an entertainer with a great voice. She wasn't dropping her drawers for a bunch of losers. Those scumbags!

"C'mon, girls," Stevie drooled, "you got nuthin' to hide, you get a clean bill of health from me and the cops."

Blackie had plenty to hide. She turned again to make a run for it, but Smash Nose Babe had circled around to intercept her. She bounced off his chest like a rubber ball.

"You heard the boss," Babe barked. The kids exchanged nervous glances.

"You're holdin' me up, Blackie." Stevie's cigarette spiraled to the floor, and he raised one foot to stamp out the butt. "I'm tired of hearin' about how you're shy."

Larry, who danced with Miss Jackie Mae, answered him back. "Lay off, will ya. Customers'll be in before you know it."

"They'll be in when I say so," Stevie replied like a backhanded slap.

A murky silence descended. If Blackie couldn't make a run for it, there were two things she could do. She could drop her drawers, or she could drop her drawers. So she dropped her drawers, letting her suspenders down over her shoulders slowly. Her boxer shorts were baby blue. Her thighs quivered under Stevie's venomous gaze.

There were no more arguments. The other girls looked sheepish as they displayed boxer shorts, white and with stripes, plus a smattering of Jockey shorts and BVDs. Not a single pair of ladies' underpants in the place.

"Now that wasn't so bad, was it?" Stevie's hooded eyes strayed over the lineup. Sure enough, he thought, Blackie had the best pair of legs in the bunch. She would've been a real hit with the johns. If she'd been more cooperative, everybody could've made a bundle. But time was running out.

Blackie was fed up. She pulled up her pants and clutched them around her waist, then gave Smash Nose Babe a shove harder than she would've thought possible a moment ago. "Lemme alone, you shnook!"

"Yipes!" he yowled, and wobbled on his heels.

Blackie made a dash for the closest exit. Stevie bounced in his chair like it was the hot seat. "You think you can just walk out when you feel like it?" he hollered after her. "Wheredaya think you're goin'?"

"The powder room maybe," Sully replied, and started to fasten her pants. The other girls followed suit.

"Get Blackie outta there," Stevie commanded Smash Nose Babe.

"Aw, boss, I can't be goin' in the powder room."

"For Chrissake," Miss Jackie Mae fretted, "so she was late for one show. Don't you think you've made your point?"

Titanic spoke up. "You know Blackie would give you her ass and shit through her elbow. Whaddaya want from her?"

That took some wind out of Stevie's sails. He wasn't in

the market for any advice, and liked to think of the Candy Box as one big happy family. "Time to get to work!" His throat rattled like respiratory failure. "And by tomorrow night, ladies' underwear! No ifs, ands, or buts. Capisce?"

The kids yawned and mumbled among themselves about Stevie the big cheese. "Mr. Personality," somebody whined. They all stretched and shuffled their feet.

No respect, Stevie thought as he blustered back to his office. Just like a bunch of stupid queers to take a swipe at the hand that fed them. And thanks to Blackie Cole, he'd ended up with poached egg on his face.

"Pay no attention, dahlings," Titanic announced to the girls in his best Vivien Leigh. "Don't you worry. I can loan you all the ladies' underwear you'll ever need."

Seventeen

Blackie got as far as the hallway behind the red curtain, then leaned into the doorjamb. She was slow on the uptake, she thought, her eyes stinging with tears she didn't intend to shed. Stevie had knocked the props out from under her. It was the same trick he'd pulled at Ernie's, when he'd called her out from behind the bar—"Drop your drawers. I wanna see your legs"—before he'd put her in the show at the Candy Box. She'd had just about enough of kowtowing to a thug like him, who'd turned her hopes for a career into something low and dirty.

A taste like battery acid flooded her mouth, and she felt sick to her stomach. She hurried along the corridor toward the kitchen, whose back door led to fresh air. An astonished crew kept their eyes on the pots and pans, as Blackie rushed past and down a couple of wooden steps.

The narrow open space behind the Candy Box had once been the entrance to a stable that had long since disappeared. Around the corner, an alleyway led out onto Eighth Street. A tar-paper storage shed was wedged against the wall, under the fire escape. Brick apartment buildings rose all around, their rooftops cutting into the sky.

Blackie sat on the bottom step, her feet spread wide apart, and dropped her head between her knees. She still wanted to throw up. She knew all about humiliation.

When she was a little girl on the Lower East Side, an old man had once tempted her away from the crowded streets with the offer of a penny. Sam Cohen had discovered them in a rotting hulk of basement, his daughter perched on top of a briny black barrel, her dress lifted up to show her panties.

"Degenerate!" her father had thundered at the old man, then started back upstairs with Blanche. "*Kourve*, little whore." All the neighbors watched and listened. Her mother wept like the end of the world. Soon after, when Blanche was five, they moved to Brownsville.

Blackie looked back on her childhood as one long lecture, an extension of her father's political zeal. He was making a better world like all the speakers—socialists, communists, socialist-laborites—who sermonized on every corner of Pitkin Avenue.

"Why do you have to go depressin' everybody?" Magda had shouted at Sam. "You're scarin' the children." What he really needed, Magda said, was a decent job.

Blackie heard Tyrone whistling before she saw him come around the corner of the building, tall with a sassy gait. The splendid white jacket shimmered in the darkness.

He saw her and dug his heels into the dirt. "Blackie," he said with a goofy look on his face, like somebody had conked him on the head.

She knew it was more than surprise. "Tyrone, how's everything? Haven't seen you around."

"I been right here." He scowled.

"Me too." She regarded him suspiciously.

"Gotta get to work," he said, heading up the stairs.

Blackie heard five-alarm bells clanging in her head. "Hey, what's your hurry?" She eyed him squarely. "It's me, Blackie."

He was just posing as a tough guy. He stopped and fidgeted. "You don't look so good." His face softened. "You OK?"

Blackie slicked back her hair. "Oh, Stevie's on the warpath, but ain't he always," she joked. "And how about you? I worried about you, after we found that kid and all. That was a raw deal. He musta been about your age, practically jailbait."

She watched Tyrone's boyish smile fade. How did she know that for days he hadn't been able to shut his eyes without seeing that pretty pink and white face and the freezer closing thud over it? In the silence that followed, through the screen door they heard the kitchen help coming and going, laughing and rattling saucepans.

"You know he turned up over on the waterfront?" Blackie added.

Tyrone feigned nonchalance. "I don't know nuthin'." He started up the stairs again. "I'll see you later."

Blackie gave him a second chance. "You got a cigarette?" To safeguard her voice, she never smoked, but big deal. When Stevie got through with her, she'd probably never sing in this town again anyway.

Tyrone wanted to pull up the drawbridge and keep going. But she had him curious. He stopped and took out his cigarettes. "You oughtn't to be talkin' about that." He drew an index finger across his mouth like a zipper. "Loose lips sink ships." He looked around cautiously.

"Sounds like somethin' Titanic might say." Vintage Titanic, in fact. In Blackie's head, a cog slipped into place. "All that navy talk," she said, and took the cigarette he offered her. He lit it, and she coughed.

Tyrone's face registered apprehension. It had cost him a lot to trust her in the beginning. He didn't feel very trusting now.

Blackie reassured him. "It's OK. Nobody knows how the body got there or where it came from. We're in the clear."

He sat down next to her, his big feet sprawled in the dust, and lit himself a cigarette. "They got nuthin' on me. I'm just the clean-up boy."

She puffed away at her cigarette. "But when I left the Gents, you were still there."

"Not for long." His eyes narrowed.

"You got nuthin' to worry about. I'm no snitch."

Tyrone pivoted around to check for snoopers. "Whaddaya wanna know?" he asked, trying to get off the hook.

"Don't get sore. I just wanna know what happened after I left. I know Stevie. He plays rough."

"You don't know the half of it," Tyrone muttered. His mother had talked to him about people having a lot of goodness, sometimes locked inside. He hadn't seen much of that at the Candy Box. What Stevie had done had eaten away at him ever since, like a tapeworm fastened to his gut.

"You really wanna know what happened?" Tyrone glowered at her and camouflaged his mouth behind his hand. His story began to pour out in whispers, like a hot air balloon deflating. "They put him on ice in that big freezer in the kitchen." He paused, and tears spilled down his face. "Mr. Stevie said clean it out and I did."

"The freezer?" Blackie gasped.

"Yessum." He put out his cigarette in the dirt. "Then it disappeared from there. I guess we know where to now." He stared at the ground. "This is a hateful place."

"Keep an eye on Tyrone for Sundown," Renee had asked. That was before the breakup. "She thinks the club's not the best place for him, but it's a job."

"Sure thing," Blackie had promised, but it hadn't been a

snap playing nursemaid to Tyrone. Sundown was right about the Candy Box being no place for him.

"There's one more thing I gotta ask you," Blackie said.

Tyrone smelled a rat but left his guard down. "Your call," he sighed.

"I understand the kid's family claimed the body. There was a ring they asked about that was missin'. It was worth a lot of money."

Tyrone looked stunned, like somebody had laid him out with a rabbit punch to the back of the neck.

Blackie stuck to her guns. "I didn't see any ring. Did you?"

"Almost show time!" a voice interrupted from the top of the stairs. "Better get a move on." Ankles trembling, Titanic started down in high heels.

Tyrone got up. "I gotta go now."

Titanic blocked his exit with a smile that was comforting and intimate. "Don't rush off." He turned to Blackie. "Are you feelin' OK?"

"I'm glad you happened along," she said to Titanic. "I'm thinkin' of makin' a comeback. But we've got a little unfinished business here."

She stood up and wagged a finger at Tyrone. "The first time you went in alone, is that when you took the ring?"

Tyrone backed up. "You had to go and tell her!" he spat at Titanic.

"You told me she already knew, sweetheart," Titanic replied, with the kind of tender look usually reserved for people who were sleeping together. "You told me she felt sorry for you, wanted you to have it. It wasn't gonna do that white boy any good, you said. Your little pot at the end of the rainbow, you said. That was stupid and unnecessary." He paused. "You know you don't have to lie to me."

"So you lied to both of us." Blackie's eyes blazed like a Broadway marquee.

Tyrone retreated toward Titanic, who answered Blackie. "You can come down off your high horse," Titanic said. "Lying's not a federal offense."

"Y'all don't get it," Tyrone preached to them. "I needed that ring to get some money so I could quit this lousy place, and my mother would think I'd made good." A fearful memory intruded. "I tried to hock the ring uptown, but nobody would take it. They said it must be hot, and where'd I get it? This guy was gonna call the cops. I was out of there like a shot."

"He asked me to help him," Titanic added. " 'White folks can get by with anything,' Tyrone says."

"You were gonna hock the ring?" Blackie's face lit up accusingly.

"And split the money 50–50," Titanic said. "But we can cut you in."

"*Gonif!*" Blackie's voice thundered fire and brimstone. "Thieves, the two of you!"

"You've got some nerve callin' us names," Titanic said and beckoned Tyrone to his side. "C'mere."

"I wanna give that ring back to Didi, to try to make up for her...loss, and everything."

"What everything do you think you're gonna make up for with a ring?" Titanic replied. "The Fletcher-Paynes have got hundreds of 'em as big and splashy as this one."

"You don't even know right from wrong anymore." Blackie took a menacing step toward him. "Gimme that ring."

"Don't lecture me, Miss High and Mighty," Titanic answered. "This is the Village. We don't play by the rules down here. It's live and let live."

That shut her up. Titanic fished the ring out of his bosom. "You think you can hand this over to Didi like some trophy, and she'll reward you with a little nooky maybe?"

Blackie's cheeks burned. "Whaddaya wanna talk like that for in front of the kid? *I* don't usually have to pay for it."

The ring flashed in Titanic's palm like a golden bubble of champagne. "That was a cheap shot," he muttered.

Tyrone looked shy. "You wouldn't tell, would you, Blackie, where you got it and all?"

In her head, one of her father's standard repertory of sermons was echoing. "Everything's bought and sold," she could hear Sam haranguing them over cabbage soup. "There's no justice. You got money, you're A-OK. You're poor, they lock you up and throw away the key." He wasn't wrong about everything.

Blackie didn't reach for the ring. "Get that thing outta my sight," she said instead. "Go hock it, and do whatever."

Tyrone hung back on the stairs. Titanic spoke to him in a soothing honeyed voice. "She's not gonna do anything. You don't have to be afraid. That was just a family squabble."

Blackie started back inside. From the kitchen doorway, she looked down at the two of them, and like a bolt out of the blue, it struck her. There was more than a business deal between Titanic and Tyrone. That would take some getting used to.

Sundown had pleaded with Renee, "Tell Blackie not to let Tyrone take up with any of those fairies. His mama would never forgive me."

Blackie suspected it was too late to worry about that. "Just don't let that ring land you both in the hoosgow," she warned.

Eighteen

The rest of the evening, Blackie sang a few bouncy ballads about a forever kind of love, and Stevie showered her with warped smiles as a bonus. But he hadn't buried the hatchet.

"You keepin' your nose clean?" he growled at her between shows.

"The payin' customers like it," she deadpanned.

Around closing time, Crazy Charlie razzed her. "You still wearin' them BVDs?"

"Whazzit to you, Sherlock? You conductin' another investigation?"

"Who's Sherlock? It's Charlie. Charlie, you dumb broad."

"Who you callin' a dumb broad?" She wanted to take a poke at Charlie, who was reaching for his lead pipe when Titanic danced in between them.

"Only a silver fox, dahling," he ad-libbed, tossing his white feather boa around Blackie's shoulders. "Couldn't you get a gold one? Maybe you could have this one gold-plated."

As Titanic pulled her away, he got a big laugh from Charlie. "You boys are nice," Charlie said, then gave Blackie another threatening look. "But I don't understand these dizzy dykes."

"Must you insist upon cookin' your own goose?" Titanic told Blackie as he hustled her back to the dressing room. "Maybe it's time we all got out of here." He stripped off his fake eyelashes on the way over to the dressing table. "Hopped a slow boat to China or something."

Blackie helped him pull his dress over his head, then hung it up. "Does that mean I can't depend on you and Tyrone?" she asked.

"Depend? For what?" Titanic flicked a switch on the mirror that bathed his face in light.

"I wanna nail Skip's killer."

"What killer?" He examined his makeup and began to slather cold cream over his face.

"There was a guy in the Gents with Skip just before we found the body. He passed us in the hallway runnin' like he'd been shot out of a cannon."

"Tyrone never told me that." A hint of gray shadow on his cheeks emerged from underneath layers of pancake.

"He wouldn't," Blackie insisted, "but I'm tellin' you. I want that guy caught. If I can't bring back Didi's brother," she paused, "maybe I can turn over his killer."

"That's very big of you." Titanic tissued cream off his face. "There's only 10 million guys in New York."

"It's for her...for Didi."

He pulled out his brandy. "And whaddif this killer of yours turns out to be a mobster? Then whadda we do?"

She looked thoughtful. "I'll cross that bridge when I get there."

"Don't expect us all to cross with you." He offered her a drink." Tyrone's already shakin' in his boots."

Blackie refused the brandy. "You coulda told me before what was goin' on between you two."

"Oh, you do carry on." Titanic sipped. "Tyrone and I are just friends."

"And I'm a monkey's uncle," Blackie said.

"Aye, aye, sir." He gave her a mock salute.

"I gotta go," she said, and got up from the rickety chair she'd sat astride. "You waitin' for him?"

"Whaddaya mean?"

"Tyrone, you chump, Tyrone."

Titanic blushed.

"And don't forget to ask him about the guy we saw outside the Gents," Blackie said. "He can help ID him."

"We'll see." Titanic drained his glass. "Even Didi Fletcher-Payne's pretty little titties ain't worth gettin' yourself killed over."

"It's not like she asked me for anything." Blackie stood by the dressing room door. "But you know, I gotta ask myself whadduz a dame like that want with somebody like me."

"Whadduz anybody want with anybody?" Titanic spoke with an air of great wisdom. "You don't have to be a hero. Isn't it obvious she's not lookin' down her nose at you?"

"Yeah, yeah, but once this is over, I'd like to see her again, you know?"

"Everybody wants that, dahling. But you always have to be ready to let go."

"Like it's that cut and dried." Blackie waved good-bye.

The front door of the Candy Box opened a smidge, and she slipped out onto Eighth Street. It was a couple of hours before dawn. The rain had stopped, and the sky shimmered blue-black like a fresh bruise. A lamppost threw its long quiet shadow across her path. The air was soft on her cheek; the only sound, her heels striking the pavement. She imagined she could hear people snoring through their open windows.

Didi would be sleeping too, a fairy-tale princess in her gilt-and-white bedroom, if she could sleep after her visit to the morgue. Blackie imagined Didi looking down at Skip's body with only that con artist Swazey to comfort her. But she'd make it all up to Didi, no matter what it cost her—even if it meant turning in the whole Candy Box operation, including Stevie the Frenchman.

To watch Blackie cross Sixth Avenue, the guy in the bomber jacket fell back into a darkened doorway, squat garbage pails on either side. He'd waited for her with the patience of a death-row inmate, the way he'd been watching the rooming house on West 47th that he shared with other drifters and grifters. When the story of the Fletcher-Payne kid's death didn't hit the front page and no cops showed up looking for him, he took heart. Maybe there was nothing to worry about. Maybe he'd dreamed it all. Sometimes he still had nightmares of kids dying—torn to pieces by bullets, drowning. He lit a cigarette and exhaled an angry stream of smoke.

The dyke was the key. He kept her in his sights, tailing her until she turned onto Christopher.

Trees crisscrossed above the street to form a rain-soaked bower, cooling the air. Almost home, Blackie sang softly to herself and thought of Didi's lips that would open again just for her, and those big indigo eyes. She was Didi's, heart and soul. She bounded up the stoop and into the entrance hall of her building.

Blackie never heard the door slam shut behind her. Instead a rush of footsteps made her turn around. The man looked broad as a battleship. He wasn't from the building.

"You lookin' for somebody?" Blackie asked. It was late to be visiting.

He stared back at her with searing eyes. "This number 30?"

"Other side of the street." She was tired, her eyes playing tricks on her. The entrance hall seemed to stretch out long and narrow, the man fading into the distance. Panes of glass in the door framed his face.

"You work at the Candy Box, don't you, girlie?" he asked, taking a step forward, sounding friendly.

Blackie didn't buy it. She was used to dealing with smart alecks at the club. "Who wants to know?"

"I seen you before," he replied, "up onstage. You really know how to put over a song."

"A fan, huh?" She wanted to put an end to this conversation. She stared as her eyes grew accustomed to the light.

He glowered back, a hunter's eyes, dark and piercing. Stupid dyke, he thought. She didn't even recognize him. Nothing to worry about.

Then their eyes met, like that night in the hallway of the club, and she knew. She told her legs to move.

He saw her surprise, her fear, and stepped forward. "Hold on a minute."

Blackie stood paralyzed. It was true what they said about murderers returning to the scene of the crime. He had her cornered. She wanted to scream, to wake somebody up.

"The kid at the club," he began, "I didn't mean to hurt him."

"I didn't tell." Her voice was barely audible.

"I seen you at the Fletcher-Paynes'."

She had to get away. She feigned left, then right, and tried to circle around him.

But he sprang straight for her. The back of her head hit the wall, stunning her. "Whaddid you tell 'em?" his voice pounded.

"Nuthin', I swear."

He aimed an open-handed slap at her head. "You're a lyin' cunt."

Blackie jerked sideways under the impact of the blow, blackness and shooting stars behind her eyelids. He hadn't followed her there to apologize. As she slid to the floor, the pale sweet face of the boy he killed swam up before him, startled blue eyes. Other faces joined that one, gaping wounds at the throat.

They were a few feet from the first-floor apartments. In the split second her assailant hesitated, Blackie crawled for the nearest door. She focused on something she'd seen before—a large black umbrella, the handle made of heavy dark wood. Left to dry, her brain said. She grabbed the handle.

He was back, dragging her by one leg. "You ain't goin' nowhere," he hissed. His hands closed around her throat.

Blackie gasped for breath and flailed at him with her makeshift weapon.

"Whaddaya doin'?" His grip relaxed a little.

She lashed his shoulders with the umbrella shaft.

He faltered. She wasn't easy prey.

On the second-floor landing, the stairway creaked to the sound of heavy feet coming down. Some working stiff on his way to the early shift of a thankless job.

Blackie's assailant cursed his luck. The man in blue work-shirt and carpenter's overalls was halfway down the stairs.

"I'll be back," he whispered, then clattered his way out of the building.

Blackie lay in a heap on the floor, still clutching the umbrella. It was bent, metal stays popping out like stilettos. The broad ruddy face she saw above her, hair graying at the temples, spun around a few times before she recognized her neighbor. Ed McLaurin had lived in the building a lot longer than Blackie. He knew nothing about her life.

"Say, who the hell was that?" He leaned over her. "You need to go to the hospital?"

"I don't know."

He put out a hand to help her get to her feet. "You want me to call a cop?"

"No, no," Blackie protested. She knew she was on her own. "But thanks." She rested on the wooden banister painted brown.

"Want me to help you upstairs?"

She refused again. She would climb slowly, stopping on the landings.

"I gotta get to work, kid," Ed McLaurin said, "but when you're feelin' better, go on over to Charles Street and report this to the precinct." He paused. "They gotta do somethin' about all the thugs hangin' around this neighborhood. Lock 'em up, like the DA says. Duggan's got my vote."

She nodded weakly.

"You need a witness, give 'em my name."

"Sure thing," Blackie replied, as though she had the same rights as everybody else.

Once inside her room, she turned quickly and locked the door. In the bathroom, she sank down on the toilet seat and crossed her arms over her chest for protection. She leaned forward, her head between her knees. She'd never really been afraid before.

Not that being Jewish had always been easy. When she was a kid, toughs from other neighborhoods called her names. But this was America, not Nazi Germany—those horrible films that everybody had seen by now, the pitiful starved bodies, the yellow star. Hugging herself, Blackie squeezed her eyes shut so as not to see them, and tears ran down her cheeks.

She just wanted to be an entertainer, and now a man had tried to kill her. This was more serious than she'd ever imagined. Nobody would protect her from this lunatic, now that she'd ratted out Stevie to the Fletcher-Paynes. All for Didi's pretty little titties. Titanic didn't mince words.

"I'll be back," he'd whispered. But he wouldn't catch her napping again.

Blackie got up to look in the mirror. An angry welt spread from her temple to her cheekbone. She traced the outline of the blow and recalled its staggering force, heard the thwack of her assailant's hand against her head. She had to sit down again. She felt she was swimming underwater, unable to breathe. Her throat ached.

Blackie didn't know how long she sat cowering in the bathroom. Finally, next to the old armchair, she removed her tux. Her tie had come loose, and the perfect creases in her pants were spoiled.

Sunrise seeped into the room from the dingy courtyard. Blackie lay down gratefully. A pleasant numbness spread through her limbs. The mattress quivered on its springs. When she closed her eyes, that malevolent face flashed across her consciousness. She heard the panting, and those strange words came back to her: "I seen you at the Fletcher-Paynes'." Exhaustion and confusion overtook her, and she only wanted to sleep.

The Albert Hotel was a no-star Village establishment on the corner of University Place and 10th Street that catered to transients and theatricals. Titanic's tiny room was bare except for the bed, a few cobwebs, a chair, and a bureau whose mirror had lost its sheen in big round spots like a tropical skin disease.

A pigeon sat cooing on the windowsill. Against the snow-white sheet, Tyrone's body was the color of cinnamon bark.

Titanic's tongue caressed it, lingering over the nipples. He kissed his way down the belly. The bed smelled of ginger, cloves, and sassafras.

"Relax," Titanic whispered. He bent over to cup Tyrone's penis and balls in both hands like a chalice of fine wine.

By the time the sky had cleared to a dismal gray, Tyrone sat looking out the window. His naked buttocks rested close to the edge of the chair, legs spread and one foot resting on the front rung. His penis dangled in space, thick and pendulous.

A fresh breeze stirred the early morning silence. Squeals and giggles filtered through the wall, punctuated by slapping noises like someone swatting at flies.

"What's goin' on over there?" Tyrone asked without turning around.

Titanic sat up in bed and stuffed a pillow down behind his back. "It's that pervert next door. He's always draggin' girls in. Says he only wants 'em to hit him with wet towels, then he gets fresh."

The tender expanse of Tyrone's back glowed in the half-light. He laughed a slow deep laugh. "Look who's callin' who a pervert!"

"Careful you don't get a splinter in your butt, dahling."

Tyrone turned to face the bed. "I was just kiddin'," he said. "You know I don't care if you like to dress up like a woman."

"Drag is a costume," Titanic explained. "It's part of my act—people love it."

"You don't mind 'em laughin' at you?"

"Not as long as they're payin' through the nose." He stroked the inside of Tyrone's thigh with a touch as light as falling leaves. "Why don't you come back to bed?"

"It's hot, and I guess I oughta get on up to my aunt's."

"It's not that hot, for Chrissake, and your aunt's not there anyway."

But Tyrone was pulling on his trousers, silvery droplets of sweat sparkling on his chest. "I really gotta go."

"Suit yourself...you will anyway." Titanic paused deliberately. "I have to ask you something, though."

"Yeah?" Tyrone was immediately suspicious.

"Blackie says you saw a man run out of the men's room the night Skip got killed."

"She's got a big mouth," Tyrone snapped.

"C'mon. She doesn't wanna get you in any trouble."

"I'll bet." Tyrone buttoned up his shirt.

"Don't be that way. Blackie just wants the guy nailed because she's carrying a big torch for Skip's sister." Titanic smiled knowingly. "I think she's in love."

"I don't care who's in love," Tyrone muttered from under the bed where he was looking for a missing shoe. "You can count me out."

He found the shoe and sat back down on the chair by the window. "That whole business is the worst thing ever happened to me." He paused. "And I'm not havin' anything else to do with it."

"But you want the money," Titanic reminded him.

"I took too many risks already for that money." He honed his words to a fine edge. "And so far I haven't seen a dime."

"Soon, I promise you."

Tyrone crossed his legs Indian-style. "You better not be playin' me for a sucker," he said with youthful swagger.

"And what are you playin' me for?" Titanic replied.

Nineteen

Far out on the island, where the Fletcher-Paynes had their estate home, they buried Skip quickly in sight of the sea, a restless grave. A blustery breeze sprang up. Gulls spiraled on the horizon, and the sky exploded upward in ballooning clouds.

Skip had loved unspoiled beaches, the pleasant bays and harbors safe for small craft. His obituary in the New York dailies was brief. A local island newspaper sent a reporter to the gravesite, but he was dismissed without a story. The family drove back in silence through marshlands, tall grass blowing on either side. An abundant fresh water table fed a small lake.

Later that somber morning, Old John Jay sat on the screened porch that enclosed one end of the family's white clapboard house. It overlooked a thick carpet of lawn, bushy white azaleas, and weeping willows. In the near distance, beyond the other side of the privet hedge, the ocean swelled.

"Have you heard anything more from the police?" Didi asked him. She wore a simple bias-cut sheath in black. A tray of stiff drinks in frosted highball glasses separated them. Mummie was having her drinks alone, in the paisley stillness of an upstairs bedroom. Jay Jay had already returned to the city.

"They have no leads," John Jay said, studying the dappled landscape before him.

"No suspects?"

"These things take time, I suppose." He'd requested a confidential investigation from the police commissioner. Any new information would go right up the chain of command. A word to the press could win you a transfer to a remote precinct in Queens or Staten Island.

Helplessness didn't suit Didi. "Father, I don't want this to be like that poor girl on the East Side whose story was all over the front page, then they never found a trace of her killer."

She crossed and uncrossed her legs in quick succession. Her heels were perfectly round and smooth in sling-back pumps. "We can't let whoever's responsible for Skip's death go scot-free."

Bursts of shallow light broke through the jagged leaves of a holly tree that shaded the porch on the north. Deep furrows creased John Jay's brow. "They'll pay all right. I'll spare no expense."

"What are you going to do?" Didi asked.

"Why don't you go up and see how your mummie's doing?" he replied in his inscrutable way.

"Don't dismiss me like that, Father." She slapped both feet to the floor. "I want to know what's going on."

He drew up short. Like Owen, she was a sensitive child, easily wounded. "Of course, it's natural. You've been under a terrible strain." He puffed himself up by pushing down on the arms of his chair. "There's nothing to tell right now. You should really check on your mother."

"All right." She rose.

"Will you be leaving tonight?" he asked.

She lingered a moment and shared his pain. "I'll take the train in the morning."

"Don't be silly," he replied. "That's what we have the car for."

"I'll take the train," she repeated, then headed for the door. Beside it, a bouquet of red zinnias, yellow marigolds, and blue delphiniums filled a Japanese sang de boeuf vase. "Will you be all right?"

"Of course." John Jay sat bleary-eyed, his suit and tie dark against a perfect white shirt. He'd spoken to Detective Swazey and his partner a few times about bringing the ones responsible for Owen's death to justice. The detectives wrote squiggles all the while in a small notebook. The old man had told them the boy had no enemies, but he didn't know who his friends were either. Owen had nothing to do with the paper or other Fletcher-Payne enterprises. He'd finished school, then traveled a bit.

"Any old grudges?" Swazey had asked. "Anyone who mighta wanted to hurt you through Owen?"

John Jay had enemies, of course, like all men of power and prestige. And his gambling debts could've made him a target, he thought uncomfortably, except that his creditors knew he was good for all of them, that they'd get their money. Hadn't he made good before?

"It's possible," he'd said, denying any emotion in front of Swazey and Brannan, lackeys whose competence he regarded as questionable. "When you have a certain position, some people—envious, greedy people—may want to see you brought down."

Swazey had scrawled something else and confirmed that they had little to go on. No tracing the trunk. There were a thousand of them just alike.

The old man looked out across the flawless green carpet of his estate grounds and sipped his highball. He picked up the phone next to him and dialed the number of *The Daily Journal*. The police seemed hopelessly stalled, their investigation a sham.

"This is Jack Fletcher," he said. "Get me the loading dock."

An oldtimer named Moe came on the line, newsstand trucks backed up behind him. "Yeah, boss."

John Jay had often gone down to chat, believing it was good business to keep your finger on the pulse of the operation at all levels. Jay Jay said that was nonsense and a waste of time.

He asked Moe about one of the swampers who loaded the trucks.

"Vic? He ain't been around for a while now."

John Jay was staggered by the emotions that swept over him. He'd counted on Victor to have some answers to the questions that were torturing him.

"That so?" he said to Moe.

"Yeah, I figure he musta done somethin' really stupid this time, got hisself fired for good...OK, boss, I'll try to find him for you." Moe hung up.

John Jay held the phone until it went dead and wailed in his ear like a lonesome coyote. He'd kept Victor on, a handsome sloe-eyed fellow and a veteran. But a petty thief who'd stolen money from another man and newspapers off the trucks to sell on his own. Jay Jay had been determined to fire him.

"If they pull my sheet and read back," Victor had confessed to the old man, "they'll see I got a record. I'll do hard time." He paused. "You keep me on, I'll pay you back every cent I owe."

John Jay didn't want his money, didn't want to involve the police. The young man promised to do whatever he was told and keep his mouth shut. That suited John Jay.

Victor hadn't had sex with anybody since the kid—that awful night. A few days later he'd gone with a small, sallow-faced man to a hotel room near Times Square. The man reached for him, and he recoiled. The fumbling fingers, the apologetic grin made him want to bash the man's face.

"It's just money," he repeated what he'd told himself a hundred times before. But it wasn't working. His cock hung limply between his thighs. He was being punished for what happened to the boy.

"Maybe we should just talk," the little man said, soft eyes pleading. "I don't mind."

"Why the hell would I wanna talk to you?" Victor replied contemptuously.

"My name's Dave."

"I told you. I don't wanna know."

Victor never gave his name to any of them, except for one regular, and only after they'd known each other a while. The guy was a big shot, and he'd been good to Victor. Bought him clothes, took him to fancy restaurants, got him the job at the paper when there were no jobs to be had.

In the park there would be no names and no talking.

Victor's eyes shone like black satin as he passed a row of stone benches at Columbus Circle on his way into Central Park. Other eyes searched his for a flicker of interest or acqui-escence. Instead he acknowledged a few familiar faces with a friendly nod, not to be mistaken for an invitation, and resumed his quest. It led him across the darkening plain of the Sheep Meadow and down the broad sloping steps to the fountain, its guardian angel outlined above the tree line.

Evening shadows percolated from the lagoon. Rounding the far corner of the boathouse, Victor chose a narrow path that wound up a small hill and into dense woods, not routinely trimmed and manicured. In this area, called the Ramble by the park's original designers, tall trees cut off the sky, generating a shady twilight during the day up among the large boulders. At night the retreat was plunged into total darkness. That didn't bother Victor, who'd stalked Japs in the jungle where you couldn't keep a straight line of march.

After all that, he'd been stupid enough to get caught stealing on the job. He knew he couldn't stand being locked up. When he told the boss, the old man, he'd do whatever he had to do to stay out of stir, he didn't know he'd be getting in over his head.

Deeper into the secluded thicket, Victor followed the twisting moonless path. A breeze hummed in the treetops. The underbrush smelled of summer green and heat. Snapping twigs punctuated the restless silence. In the veiled heart of the city, the woods were on fire with lust.

He needed time to think, to beat this rap. Now that the lezzie had had a second good long look at him, he had to get her. She had a big mouth and could pick him out of a lineup. Next time she wouldn't know what hit her. He knew where to get a gun and how to use it.

The path abruptly opened out into a woodland glade and a rustic bench banked by brambles. Victor sat on one end. A brief rustling brought someone to his side. An eager hand stroked his knee. Without a word he rose and followed the shadowy form.

Out in the darkness a deft hand loosened Victor's belt and unzipped his pants. Instantly, a host of other hands converged on his body, gliding, rubbing, grasping. One took out his penis and squeezed it. Others stripped off his shirt, pinching at his nipples. A tongue, rough like a cat's, licked his belly while voices murmured seductively, "I want your big fat cock, all of it. I want your ass." Someone was sucking at his fingers, one by one.

Relief flooded Victor's body. He'd been granted forgiveness

for all his sins, for what had happened to the kid. His body was redeemed, and a wail of thanksgiving swelled his throat.

WEEK THREE

TWENTY

Sunshine filtered through skylights in the coffered ceiling of Penn Station, 100 feet above Didi's black-straw cartwheel hat. She was tired and impatient after the long ride in from the island, the train groaning and banging like a stagecoach. Her pumps clicked on granite and marble as she traversed the concourse, then climbed the broad stairs between towering Doric columns up to street level.

She hailed a cab, and without thinking, rattled off the Park Avenue address. While the cabbie slashed through traffic on 34th Street bound east, Didi settled back to light a cigarette. But what was she rushing back to the apartment for? Skip wouldn't be there. Just endless reminders that he was gone and that nobody was going to do anything about it.

Only Blackie had cared enough to show any courage, and it was Blackie she wanted to see. Even if she'd made a fool of herself the last time, Didi could apologize. An entertainer like Blackie was probably accustomed to girls throwing themselves at her. Didi hadn't expected to be one of them. They'd left so much unsaid.

"Wait a minute," she commanded impulsively. "I want to go to the Village."

The cabbie glanced in the rearview mirror. The lady wasn't kidding. Fifth Avenue was handy. The taxi rounded the corner in the shadow of the Empire State and forged its way downtown, past Madison Square Park and the narrow graceful prow of the Flatiron building.

"Where to, miss?"

He left Didi in front of Blackie's brownstone, its stoop swarming with curious neighborhood children. Dusky from playing in the streets, they pressed around her.

"Wow, will ya get a load of her!"

"Oh, boy! Oh, boy! Are you a movie star?"

Confidence and words seldom failed Didi the way they did now. The kids were worse than opening night at the opera, popping flashbulbs and reporters. But she was the great-great-granddaughter of men who had tamed the American wilderness and waded into the crowd.

"You movin' in?" piped a small boy, crusty nose and bruised cheek.

Now wouldn't that be something! thought Didi. She smiled and strode into the building.

Blackie had slept fitfully after her ordeal, and lay soaking in the claw-foot tub. When a string of leaden blows sounded on the door of her furnished room, she sprang out of the tub. Dripping a trail to the closet, she snatched a shirt and slacks off a hanger. The fire escape was her only chance. But if it was that murdering scum, would he bother to knock?

One foot into her trouser leg, she heard a voice, muffled but recognizable. "Are you home? It's me."

Blackie did a double-take, then quickly slipped into a white terry cloth robe. She would never have expected to hear that voice outside her door.

She threw it open to find Didi standing there, framed by

the hall's mildewed wallpaper. In her little black dress, dark glasses, and ropes of real pearls, she looked like the Hope Diamond left in a hock shop.

"How'd you get here?" And what did this visit mean? At least the place was clean. "Are you OK?"

"I had to come," Didi replied, and not just because of Skip. She was sick of lies and death. A little unsteady on her feet, she crossed the floor to the drooping armchair. Blackie was as handsome as she'd remembered. "This is where you live?"

She pivoted slowly to scan the tiny kitchen and old enamel table. The whole apartment was smaller than her bedroom, but she hardly noticed. Her big turquoise eyes lingered on the unmade double bed under the window. With no breeze stirring, the cloth pull-down shade hung lifeless. A pale sun reflected off the walls of the courtyard, lighting the room.

Blackie watched Didi and wondered how much she recalled about that night in the Park Avenue apartment. If Blackie got a second chance to lie down beside Didi, she wouldn't be so honorable. After her run-in with the killer, she figured she deserved at least another kiss.

"Yeah, this is my place," Blackie answered shyly. "Siddown." She motioned Didi into the armchair.

The room held the afternoon heat like a soup bowl. Humidity mingled with the warmth from Blackie's bath. She balanced sweating on the edge of the bed, and pulled up the covers to tidy it.

Didi sat in the armchair, leaning away from the sagging back, and watched the pillows disappear under the bed-spread. Shame wasn't part of her emotional repertory, and she wouldn't deny that she wanted Blackie Cole. At school she'd had a terrible crush on the pitcher for the softball team—a whiplash underhand fastball. But Didi was young. Nothing happened.

A photograph, a frame with rounded edges, on Blackie's

bedside table caught Didi's attention. A full serious face, dark hair pulled back above an iridescent print dress, looked out, a skinny boy in knee pants at her side. An older matron, with lined face and hair piled on top of her head, held the hand of a small girl with round eyes and a plump toddler in a sailor suit on her lap. The man beside her had unruly dark hair.

"Is this your family?" Didi asked. A safe topic.

Blackie felt suddenly ashamed. She imagined Mom and Pop, sister Doris and her kids against the backdrop of gray and dirty red Brooklyn tenements. "Yeah." She paused to study Didi's flawless complexion, milk-white like fine porcelain. "They don't live around here."

"I haven't been home," Didi said in a grainy voice. "I came right from the island." She paused, her spine rigidly perpendicular. "Skip's funeral was yesterday."

"Oh." Blackie swallowed hard. "I didn't know about the funeral."

"It was just a few people." Didi took off her dark glasses. Grief had drawn inky circles under her eyes. "Father didn't want any publicity."

"Under the circumstances, I guess..."

"Under any circumstances." Didi took out a cigarette. "He lived in fear that somebody would find out about Skip."

Blackie reached for a match, and Didi caught a glimpse of lean damp legs between the folds of Blackie's robe. She also noticed the cheekbones soared higher, and the jawline was more delicately chiseled than she'd remembered. She shifted around in her chair.

"If it hadn't been for you, we'd probably never have known anything. Skip would've just vanished."

Blackie went down on her knees beside Didi's chair and hovered over the cigarette.

"I can't thank you enough," Didi murmured as the match flared. She touched Blackie's cheek and saw the bruise, and there were dark purple shadows on Blackie's neck. "What's happened to you?"

Blackie blew out the match and pulled away. "It's OK." She wouldn't let on just yet. "I ran into a door."

Didi's lips brushed Blackie's cheek. "Does it hurt?"

"Not a bit." Blackie felt another one of those tremors like the wind booming past her, coming over the crest on the Cyclone at Coney Island. She knew she'd risk everything for the soft curves under Didi's dress. She lit another match.

Blue smoke trailed out of Didi's nostrils. "Where did you find the courage to tell me about Skip?"

"I didn't like the way the whole thing was handled. And I guess..." Blackie paused, her eyes heavy with longing. She took Didi's cigarette and ground it out in the ashtray. "I like the way you kiss."

"Passion," Didi murmured, "makes people do all sorts of things."

Blackie's mouth closed over Didi's. Her hands burned to caress Didi's flesh. It was only a few steps to the bed. Didi sloughed off her dress, then touched the knot on the sash of Blackie's robe to untie it. Her arms slid around Blackie's naked back.

The springs creaked under them. Didi lay back on the pillow, a sleek Park Avenue odalisque, her black lacy slip hiked up around her hips. Her body shimmered in the encroaching twilight.

Their lips met again with mounting intensity. They shared the same breath as they sank toward some dark forgetful place. Blackie's slender thigh slid between Didi's legs.

"I don't know much about women," Didi whispered. "Will you be my teacher?"

With one hand, Blackie quested for Didi's bra under the slip. Hooks fell away from metal eyes, releasing their stranglehold, and Didi's nipples popped up big as a baby's thumbs.

"I'll be whatever you want me to be," Blackie said. Small, pointed nails skittered across her back. In the near distance, thunder rumbled over the steamy city, promising showers and nighttime cool.

In the quiet depths of the Fletcher-Paynes' island home, sunlight drifted into the study through windowpanes of leaded opalescent glass. Floor-to-ceiling bookcases filled with bound embossed volumes lined the walls alongside a couple of old masters sketches.

His back to the window, Old John Jay sat at a Sheraton-style mahogany writing desk, in a chair upholstered in leather the color of dried blood. He bent over the desk and slapped the last red deuce down hard on a black three. Even if he had to cheat sometimes at solitaire, it felt good to win.

A photograph in a silver oval, of the children when they were small, rested on the desk. Diana held Owen on her lap, while Jay Jay stood protectively by. The big brother.

"Shattered lives," the old man whispered, and wished earnestly for a second chance.

If he had it to do over again, he would have gone to Owen, reasoned with him. The boy might have been persuaded to seek rehabilitation. There were doctors and clinics in the city—John Jay had looked into it—where results were guaranteed. Owen would've untangled a web of confused feelings.

It was too late. Out of his shame and cowardice, he'd hired private investigators to tail the boy. They'd brought back detailed statements of where he went, the people he met, pictures of elaborate costume balls. John Jay had a thick file.

"More feathers and frills than a whorehouse," one private eye had written. "Out of several clubs, favors one called the Candy Box, which caters to what we call the twisted trade. Men dressed like women, women dressed like men, often make illicit sexual advances to customers."

John Jay thought of Mabel, that freakish colored woman who performed at Lucille's dressed as a man. That was the society Owen had chosen. Blackmail waiting to happen.

Before anyone smelled scandal, Old John Jay had conceived what seemed to him a subtle plan. Owen was brazen but delicate. A carefully staged threat would make him think twice.

That's where Victor came in.

A discreet knock ushered in a maid with a fine old silver coffee service.

"On the table," John Jay said as he stood up. The leather made a soft slurping sound. He moved over to a modest club chair upholstered in chintz, for his money the only comfortable chair in the whole place, and sat down again.

She poured, curtsied, and was gone.

He crossed his legs, scrubbing one knee across the other, then stirred in two sugars. He sipped his coffee.

"I know you don't want to go to jail," John Jay had admonished Victor. "A word about this to anyone," he paused ominously, "and I'll have to reconsider your situation."

But something had gone terribly wrong. Victor had disappeared. Gone from the rooming house on 47th Street, Moe called back to say. The dipsomaniac landlord had already let the room to another ne'er-do-well.

John Jay's hand shook so that the coffee cup rattled in its saucer. He put both down. Pretend to recognize Owen, he'd told Victor, threaten to expose his disgrace to the family. Victor would've had no reason to harm Owen, would never have dared.

John Jay tugged with one finger at the thin white band of his shirt collar. But a thousand other creatures from that shadow world his son moved in...

It burst upon John Jay with sickening clarity. Like any normal boy, Owen had been curious. Just the sort degenerates preyed upon, took advantage of. He imagined Owen taken by surprise in some sinkhole of depravity, by fiends capable of horrible crimes.

That had a familiar ring. John Jay reached for *The Daily Journal*, open on the coffee table, rosewood inlaid with Chinoiserie designs. He flipped a few pages and read, " 'When fiendish and horrible sex crimes are committed against men, women, and even small children, oftentimes the person who commits such an act is found to be a deviant. Sometimes the bodies of these victims are horribly mutilated.' "

It was the latest piece in the wake of that young girl's murder uptown. The police were rounding up the usual suspects, it said, a mile-long list of sex offenders. John Jay glanced at the byline.

An elaborate clock, in gilded bronze and red marble, ticked loudly on the mantelpiece. The old man rose briskly and walked over to the fireplace. He rested one foot on a brass andiron, then turned and picked up the phone.

"Get me Lee Morris."

Morris, a columnist for *The Daily Journal*, came on the line.

"I'm calling about your series," John Jay began. "Degenerates on the rampage, the collapse of law and order..." Morris's brassy style sold newspapers.

"No, no complaints." As John Jay talked, his plan took on more precise contours. The words felt like action.

"I want you to go deeper into the city's seamy side...yes, Sodom and Gomorrah, exactly."

Morris was anxious to share ideas. The war had upended things, he said, and some people thought they could do whatever they pleased. The public was sick and tired of it.

The rhetoric filled John Jay's head, keeping his pain at bay. "Spare no one, Morris. You know the situation. SLA violations galore, violence and crimes that go unreported. Lewdness and dissipation in Greenwich Village."

"The Village!" Morris replied eagerly. He'd spilled a lot of ink crusading against female monstrosities, fairies, pouting queens, fags, skirted women-hunters, male magdalens, congenital abnormals, and nature's mishaps.

"We'll back you all the way," John Jay said.

Turned loose to hunt a favorite prey, Lee Morris said he had plenty of material. If they'd save space for him, he'd have an article ready for tomorrow's final edition.

They would save space, Old John Jay assured him. "And Morris," he added, "see what you can find out about a place called the Candy Box."

No sooner did he hang up the phone, than it rang again, and he answered without thinking, "Hullo."

"Jack?" a voice like a judo chop replied. "It's me, Pete. I been tryin' to getcha."

"Yes, Pete." That's what he'd hired a house full of servants for, to keep himself out of reach. He could kiss that good-bye. "How've you been?"

"Good, Jack, but a little short."

John Jay knew what was coming. Pete was his bookie.

"It's Joey, you know," Pete explained. "He's pushin' me hard."

John Jay got to his feet and walked to the window. "I've had a run of bad luck, Pete."

He rested his head on the window sash. Outside a lone gardener was trimming the perfect hedge.

"Yeah, but your luck'll change, Jack." Pete hesitated. "Actually, Joey'd like to see you. Give you a chance to settle up."

"He said that? He knows I'm good for it."

"Sure thing, Jack. It's just that Joey's got a big overhead."

"At Costa's?" A slick gambling operation in New Jersey, close enough to welcome fleets of Cadillacs from the city at all hours of the night. John Jay was no stranger there.

"Yeah, Costa's. He'll be lookin' for you."

John Jay wanted to slam the phone down. "I've had some family problems, Pete."

"Joey's a family man too, Jack. But make it as soon as you can."

That felt like the old one-two punch in a velvet glove. John Jay said nothing.

"Would you rather someplace else, Jack? We could send a guy over."

"No, no," John Jay answered, his head spinning. He would go to Costa's. He thought he didn't have much more to lose.

Twenty-One

Didi stirred and opened her eyes. Overhead a jagged crack in the plaster split the ceiling from the window to the light fixture. A siren wailed with painful intensity down a nearby street. It wasn't Park Avenue, but she could turn over and smile at Blackie's profile silhouetted against the bedclothes. Didi dragged her fingertips along the nape of Blackie's neck, then cuddled close.

Blackie woke up to a dull ache at the base of her skull, a reminder of her struggle with the killer. But the pain, her fear, none of that mattered right now. She rolled over and kissed Didi, who succumbed with a languorous sigh.

Didi had never been much for kissing before, but Blackie's mouth tantalized her, shifting from rough and playful to soft and yielding. Blackie was working her way toward Didi's belly when she saw the clock and sat up.

"I've gotta get dressed for the club," she stammered. "It's late."

"Don't go," Didi entreated. "We're so happy here, and you said yourself, it's dangerous."

"I'll be fine."

Didi covered herself with the sheet to disguise her disappointment. She didn't know what she'd expected. The books she'd read talked about whips and knives—and a lust for pain. But with Blackie, reality was an inconceivable tenderness. She only wanted to sink back into Blackie's arms and forget the world.

"Then come away with me." Didi's mind raced as she clung to Blackie. "There's absolutely nobody at the Palm Beach house in the summer. We can do whatever we please."

Palm Beach? thought Blackie. *Like in the movies?*

"You know, we could live very well on my allowance."

"C'mon, Didi, I'm no gigolo." She pretended to be hurt, then pulled Didi closer. "Besides, we can't let Skip's killer get away with it. I'd never forgive myself."

"But, darling..." Fear crept into Didi's voice. "That's a job for the police."

"They'll never find him, sweetheart. You oughta know coppers don't go out of their way investigatin' the deaths of gay boys." Blackie shrugged. "Like they don't go all out for dykes who get all beat the hell up either."

"Father's been on the phone prodding the detectives. He won't rest—"

Blackie pressed two fingers to Didi's lips. "Just a minute, baby. I know you believe that, but down at the Candy Box everybody knows your Detective Swazey because he's always comin' by to pick up his payoffs." She paused to let that sink in. "He's not gonna make trouble for Stevie."

"Oh, Blackie," Didi cried. "Don't tell me any more."

Blackie only wanted to wake up every morning to Didi in her bed. They were in this together now, until the end. "We don't have to depend on the police," she boasted, "'cause I got a plan."

Despite her fears, the promise of action excited Didi. She reached for a cigarette. "What do you mean you have a plan?"

"To get the killer dead to rights."

Didi trembled. Blackie's voice was like a lifeline. "What do you have in mind?"

"We'll set up our own stakeout at the club," Blackie improvised, "and when the killer shows up, we'll nab him." It was risky. She would be the bait, and she'd need help.

"How can you be so brave?" Didi touched the short-cropped hair that curled across the tender nape of Blackie's neck.

"It's not just that, Didi. I'm mad now." Blackie's voice thickened. "I saw our man again...just last night."

"He came to the club?"

"He followed me home."

Didi reached up to Blackie's burning cheek. "And what happened?"

"I didn't run into any door. I ran into him."

Didi examined Blackie's bruises at closer range. "The monster! He could've killed you." She paused. "He knows you saw him that night."

"He knows all right." Blackie glanced again at the clock and got up. In the bathroom she studied her face and neck. "Titanic's gonna have to help me cover up this shiner," she called out.

Didi got out of bed too and stood naked in the doorway. "Please don't go!"

Blackie grasped her by the shoulders. "I've gotta go, sweetheart. We're gonna string Stevie along for a while, until we get our man." She paused. "But meantime, I wantcha to go back uptown where it's safe."

"You don't really think I'd leave you down here to face the killer alone?"

"Be reasonable. I know my way around."

Didi melted against Blackie. "How can you be sure he'll show up again at the club?"

"Oh, everybody gets back to the Candy Box sooner or later," Blackie laughed.

Didi shook her head. "I'll be worried sick until this is over."

Blackie stroked the golden flood of Didi's hair that fell across her shoulder. "I have to tell you this. Don't let it scare you, but the killer said the strangest thing to me."

"What was that?" Didi hugged her tighter.

"I told him I hadn't ratted on him, that I hadn't told anybody." Blackie looked puzzled.

"And he said he knew I was lying, that he'd seen me at the Fletcher-Paynes'."

"The night you drove me home?" Didi couldn't hide her alarm.

"He knows where I live. He knows where you live." Blackie lowered her voice. "And maybe he knew who Skip was too."

She said it and marveled that the possibility hadn't crossed her mind before. Good detective work, putting all the pieces together, took time.

"Your family must have enemies," Blackie prodded, suspecting they were on a hot trail.

"Do you mean you think Skip's death wasn't a random act?" Didi caught her breath.

"Is there anyone...a guy with a grudge, who would've done somethin' like this?"

"A man like my father..." Didi began. Ambitious and power hungry, she wanted to say, who'd locked horns with hundreds of associates, dismissed scores of underlings without a second thought. Her eyes filled with tears. "I'm sure many people would like to harm my father." Plus there was the cast of desperate characters who frequented his whorehouses and gambling dens.

"Don't cry, sweetheart." Blackie brushed tears from

Didi's cheek. "When we nab the killer—and we'll nab him—he'll give us all the answers."

When Blackie stepped out of the building on her way to work, an oily humid haze hung over Christopher Street. It dimmed the yellow glow of streetlights, and seemed to change every doorway into a sooty hole where stickup and strong-arm men might hide. She looked back over her shoulder.

"You can't go gettin' the jitters now," she advised herself. But as she descended the three steps into the Candy Box, she wished she were back in Didi's arms.

In the dressing room, Titanic and Miss Jackie Mae faced each other across a table strewn with jars, rhinestone sprays, and makeup tubes.

"It's the weekends that pack 'em in," Titanic said smugly. "Eat your heart out, Beulah Bondi."

He took the eyebrow pencil, arched his brows, and fattened them with a dark brown line.

"Joan Crawford," he whispered lovingly into the mirror.

"Ethel Merman," quipped Blackie from the open doorway. Miss Jackie Mae dissolved into giggles.

"And some people will never be as old as they look tonight," Titanic fussed at him, then turned to Blackie. "What happened to your eye?"

Jackie Mae left off teasing his wig and listened for an answer.

Blackie looked at herself in the mirror. "Does it look that bad?"

Titanic's eyebrows went up in a rush of amphetamine. "Bad enough," he said, then turned on Jackie Mae. "And do you know that cheap wig makes *you* look like a horse's rear end?"

"Nobody asked for your opinion, Mary!" Jackie Mae paused. "As you can see," he confided to Blackie, "the Dragon Lady is havin' a bad night."

Titanic grabbed for Jackie Mae's chair. "Maybe you should stay out of my way then, Miss Chickenshit."

"Cut it out, will ya!" Blackie intervened, glad she'd never felt the sharp edge of that tongue.

Miss Jackie Mae had a thicker skin. "We do *not* touch the chairs other people are sitting on!"

"It's not the worst thing *you* ever sat on," Titanic screeched back. He struggled for the chair with Jackie Mae, who retreated back under the eaves.

"And you, sir, are no lady," Jackie Mae complained. "It's all that rough trade she hangs out with," he explained to Blackie. "But pay no attention. I was leavin' anyway."

Titanic ignored him. "Siddown," he said to Blackie, "and tell me, now that we're alone, what happened to you?" He mimicked astonishment. "Did the fabulous Miss Four Hundred slug you already? That doesn't bode well for the future."

Blackie counted three like they did in the movies, then replied coolly, "If you mean Didi, she had nuthin' to do with my black eye."

She paused. "But she did come to my place today, and...well, I'm in love."

"The delectable Didi?" Titanic was enraptured. "On Christopher Street? How did you entice her?"

"I wasn't even expectin' her." Blackie stood up and paced the room. "She just showed up."

"I'll drink to that," Titanic said, reaching for his brandy bottle.

"My eye, on the other hand, that's not such a pretty story."

Titanic's face registered surprise. "What happened?"

"Somebody jumped me last night on my way home from the club."

"Was he after your money?"

"He wanted to shut me up. It was Skip's killer."

"Killer?" Titanic glanced at her nervously. "The guy from the Gents?"

Without missing a beat, he reached under the table to pull out the old hatbox, and began removing his Gene Tierney and Dotty Lamour look-alike photos from the mirror.

"It's definitely time to start packin'."

"Wait a minute." Blackie laid a hand over Titanic's. "I'm not runnin' scared. I wanna see this thing through, give Didi the satisfaction of seein' justice done."

"What justice?" He tossed the photos into the hatbox, then moved down the table raking in other paraphernalia." "You think you're gonna give Didi this guy's head on a platter and she'll love you forever?" He paused. "Nuthin' lasts forever, except Didi's fortune, of course. Lotsa dough she will always have." He lapsed into a gloomy silence.

"Hey, what's eatin' you tonight?" Blackie's eyes were hard like thumbtacks. "I come in here to tell you I'm in love, and that some hoodlum's after my ass. And whadda I get from you? Zero, zip, zilch."

Titanic slumped in front of the mirror like a stumblebum in a waterfront dive.

"C'mon, let's have it," she said. "Is it Tyrone?"

"Go away." Titanic buried his head in his hands.

"It is Tyrone. Did somethin' happen to him?"

"He's leavin'."

"Ohhh," Blackie commiserated.

"I know it's stupid." Titanic raised his head. "He's so young, still wet behind the ears, and not even my type."

"Where's he goin'?"

"As soon as we get the money for the ring, he wants to quit the Candy Box."

"Smart kid."

"Well, I told him I wouldn't do it." There was a heart-broken catch in his voice. "That I won't hock the ring."

"So he can't get away."

"And now he hates me." Titanic collapsed again over the dressing table.

"OK, OK, so you're not Donna Reed." Blackie pulled out the brandy and poured Titanic a double. "But he don't hate you."

Titanic took a long swig. "He said he did."

"Lemme talk to him."

"Whaddaya gonna say?" The brandy and the possibility that Tyrone's departure wasn't imminent revived Titanic. He passed his glass for a refill.

Blackie poured herself a short one too. "Leave that to me. I got a plan."

Titanic was a magician. Under a thick layer of pancake, Blackie's eye and the bruises on her throat were invisible. Maybe it was just a thin and shoddy whitewash for gloomy secrets, but it did the trick. Her audience drooled while she sang and flashed her famous come-hither smile.

Between shows, as part of her plan, Blackie called Tyrone out back.

"I gotta finish cleanin' up," he sulked.

"If you'll give me a few minutes," she tempted him, "you can forget about cleanin' for a while."

"How do you figure that?"

Blackie had explained to the bartender that Tyrone was on the outs with the chief cook. "Howzabout lettin' the kid work behind the bar?"

"The colored boy?" The bartender wasn't keen on the idea.

"He can wash glasses," Blackie had parried, "just till things cool down."

"You can help out up front behind the bar," she told Tyrone.

"Who said?" He was reluctant.

"It's all set."

Tyrone hesitated. "I bet Mr. Stevie don't know nuthin' about it."

"Aw, c'mon. This ain't got nuthin' to do with Stevie." Blackie paused. "You remember what that guy in the Gents with the dead boy looked like?"

"Oh, no you don't." He backed away. "That was a mean-lookin' white man."

"You're not in any danger. If he shows up at the bar, you come tell me or Titanic. That's all you have to do. I'll handle the rest."

"No, thanks," he said, and started up the steps to the kitchen.

"OK, OK," she called after him. "I know Titanic's holdin' out on you."

Tyrone stopped. "Whaddid he tell you?" he asked in an abrasive voice, eyes blazing like somebody had struck a match to a short fuse.

"Does that matter?" She took a step toward him. "But if you'll do this favor for me, I'll get you your ring back." She paused. "I'll even help you hock it."

"No law says I gotta help you," he said. "How come you can't just let go a' that boy? He's dead, and you're gettin' in way over your head."

"I gotta do what I can," she replied. "Otherwise, he'll haunt me for the rest of my life."

"Ain't nobody hauntin' me," Tyrone said, even as that phantom face, pretty and blond like the angels in the Sunday school book, swam up before him.

"You'll hock the ring for me? You won't back out?"

"You got a deal," Blackie swore.

"What makes you think that man's gonna show up here again? He can't be that bigga fool."

"You know how they all return to the scene of the crime," Blackie said confidently. "You just wash a few glasses and keep your eyes open."

Twenty-Two

The dove gray town car fishtailed up the rain-soaked ramp and onto the George Washington Bridge. Below it, the west side of Manhattan, Harlem to the Battery, sparkled like a colossal Christmas tree. The car glided toward Jersey, while in the backseat, by a low-watt overhead bulb, John Jay read "Dick Tracy" in *The Daily Journal*. The detective was finally closing in on Influence, the one who'd hypnotized Vitamin Flintheart with those special glasses. At least in the funny papers the police apprehended criminals.

John Jay turned back to the front-page story. A banner headline announced that businessmen and clergy pledged to join forces to rid the city of deviants and degenerates. Lee Morris hadn't wasted any time.

"Good for circulation," Jay Jay had said. But somehow screaming headlines didn't help to assuage the crippling sadness Old John Jay felt. He watched the city lights fade as the car veered west into a rural countryside dotted with small towns and farms. His eyes wandered down the page to Morris's warning about "potential Jack the Rippers, in little neighborhood nests and a few bars and nightclubs famous for sex deviants."

The police commissioner loved the series. He'd phoned John Jay personally to express his thanks, as had the Manhattan DA. "It's good to know we're on the same team," said Duggan.

John Jay made no commitments. He had more important things on his mind than politics. Morris had dredged up a wealth of damning information about the city's deviant haunts, and in his next paragraph called for "the closing of taverns and restaurants like the Candy Box in Greenwich Village, which stages provocative and lewd shows, and harbors sex offenders and degenerates."

We've got everything but a picture of the place, thought John Jay. "The manager's one Steve Francioso," Morris had told him. "Just some thug, plays second banana to Fred Capotello and his boys."

Heavy black lines at the bottom of the page framed the titles of articles still to come: "Sex Offenders Wiggle Through Legal Loopholes," "Apathy of City Agencies Attracts Sex Fiends."

If that didn't get the police moving, John Jay didn't know what would. And he'd put a private eye on the recreant Victor's trail, who might provide some clue to Owen's tragic end. Nobody walked out on John Jay. Revenge would be sweet. But first he had to make peace with Joey.

At Costa's Hideaway, set in the middle of a cow pasture, Joey Apollo poked the carpet with the toe of a bench-made, high-gloss shoe. He'd selected the deep pile and color, and supervised the installation of the new wall-to-wall to spruce up the joint. From outside, Costa's looked like an ordinary Quonset hut with a rounded metal roof.

But inside it was the swankiest layout in Jersey. Good food, fine wines, and liquor flowing like Niagara Falls—all on the house—kept the customers coming back and close to the tables.

They could gamble the night away, and the next day too. Costa's never closed. The local hick-town cops steered clear, and nobody ever thought to question how the chief and his deputies amassed small fortunes in their bank accounts on salaries of a few thousand a year.

"A smart move," Joey had convinced his boss Fred Capotello. "Take the operation out of New York, where we ain't got no flimflammin' DA on our back." At the same time Costa's opened, Joey brought 2600 phones over to Jersey to accommodate layoff betting. Business was booming.

As soon as he spotted Jack Fletcher-Payne, Joey started across the room in his direction. *Not bad-looking for an old codger,* thought Joey, himself a fancy Dan whose real name was Joey Diodato. The moniker Joey Apollo suited his princely good looks. "Just like George Raft," said the zaftig blonds he favored. Joey said George Raft looked like him.

"Jack." Joey waved to John Jay.

John Jay turned, flashing his aristocratic profile. As much as he hated the idea of being summoned to Costa's, a visit from Joey or one of his boys to the Fletcher-Payne residence would've been more distasteful, and on the heels of Owen's death, intolerable.

"Joey." John Jay willed his palms not to sweat. He couldn't blame Joey or Pete, who'd both been patient about the money.

"Howzabout a drink, Jack?" Joey's dark brown hair gleamed with amber highlights. He gave John Jay the glad hand, and pulled out a chair for him at a table near the bar.

"Yes, thanks. Scotch on the rocks." It was after that big loss at Belmont that his luck had flown right out the window.

"Glad you could make it, Jack. Last time was with Judge Valerio, right?"

Over Joey's shoulder, John Jay glimpsed the roulette wheel. One tantalizing spin, 20 red his lucky number. If Joey would stake him to a few chips, he could win it all back.

"Joey..." he began. He was good for it. Joey knew that.

"Yeah, Jack. How was the traffic comin' over?"

"Quite smooth, Joey. No delays."

"That's what we like to hear." Costa's couldn't survive without the suckers from New York, and a lot of people looking the other way. Joey snapped his fingers at the bartender for a round of drinks.

"Jack, we don't have a lotta time. I'll get down to business."

Behind the deep-set blue eyes, the Scotch hammered at John Jay's brain. Even partial restitution would be expensive. Last year he'd deeded a large tract of his wife's family property—in the middle of the island, a few scattered farms—to a corporation named by Joey, to cancel his debt. John Jay's lawyers were baffled. "Skyrocketing in value," they told him. Another sale like that and they would cry skullduggery.

"Your marker's always been good, Jack, but you've had a run of real bad luck." Joey paused. "There's a couple of ways we can go with this."

John Jay stopped guessing and listened.

Joey leaned his elbows on the table to get closer. "With elections comin' up in the city, we got a interest, see?"

A long way off, John Jay heard the crack of the dice, a call of "seven." "Elections?" The last thing he'd expected.

"Yeah, you know, Duggan's not our kinda guy."

The crusading DA? John Jay waffled. "I'd have to agree with you there, Joey."

"Attaboy, Jack." Joey straightened up in his chair. "You wanna back a winner."

John Jay hazarded a smile. Joey talked as though the mayoral elections were just another horse race. "I'm not backing anyone right now."

"But you're a guy with a lotta pull, Jack." Joey's eyes were black with long lashes. "You gotta take a stand."

"Personally, I don't think any of the candidates have much to offer," John Jay stammered. "I'm sure the paper will endorse someone, but..."

Joey leaned forward again, deadly in earnest. "It's O'Malley we want, Jack, for a second term."

"O'Malley? He's not running."

"You can say you heard it here first, Jack. Hot off the presses, so to speak." Joey laughed. "O'Malley's back in the race. But he's gonna need some backin'."

"I didn't realize New York politics would be so important to you."

Joey shrugged. "In business, Jack, you gotta cover all the bases."

"You want me to come out for O'Malley?"

"You and the *Journal*, and any of your rich friends who've got interests." Joey's eyes were hard. "And you'll be off the hook for the money you owe us."

His son Jay Jay wouldn't stand for an endorsement of O'Malley. A man with a reputation for double-dealing, corruption in government, mob connections.

"You'd cancel...my indebtedness?"

"It's a sweetheart deal, Jack. You play ball with us, we'll wipe your slate clean."

Of course, that's why they wanted O'Malley back. He was soft on crime, on gambling and gamblers.

"And if I can't do it, Joey? Back O'Malley, I mean?" He fished around for an angle. "Where the paper's concerned, it's not just my decision."

"You're a good customer, Jack. I'll give you 48 hours."

Joey's words were like a switchblade pressed to John Jay's throat. He pushed back his chair. "Why don't we cut for it?" John Jay asked. He had an even chance, the odds 50–50. "High card, double or nothing."

"You're way over your limit, Jack."

"One cut, Joey." With a shaky hand, John Jay grabbed a waiter by the sleeve. "A new deck here, please."

Snoozing in Stevie's backroom office, Waxy saw a doll baby stacked like Ava Gardner coming toward him. He put out his hand, and she faded away. When he reached out farther, his chair slipped out from under him just as Stevie stormed in.

"Now what?" Stevie screamed at Waxy, sprawled half-asleep on the floor at his feet.

"Hi, boss." Waxy scurried crablike out of Stevie's path. "I dropped somethin'."

Stevie snatched the phone. "Just keep outta my way, and get Charlie in here. I wanna see the botha youse."

Waxy retreated.

"Get me Capotello," Stevie grunted into the receiver, fumbling in his coat pocket. He sat down and tossed *The Daily Journal* on the desk.

"Fred? How are ya, Fred?" Stevie only paused a second. "Have you seen the papers?...Yeah...Are they still lookin' for a patsy to pin that murder on up in Yorkville?" He read aloud, " '...homosexuals who practice drug addiction and sadism.' "

Rollicking laughter echoed back from the phone.

"Yeah, well," Stevie answered, "I say, fine, if a guy don't wanna have nuthin' to do with pansies, but especially in our line of work, Fred, it's live and let live."

"Take it easy, Stevie my boy," a gravelly, fishmonger's voice replied. "They been warned to stop harpin' on the queers."

"But Fred." Stevie's sagging cheeks swelled with rage. "They're goin' after *me*. It sez, blah, blah, '...taverns and restaurants...'" He stumbled over the words. "'...like the Candy Box in Greenwich Village.' Buncha sleazeballs!"

"Yeah, yeah," came back the voice. "But I'm tellin' you, it's all taken care of. They ain't printin' no more stuff like that."

"You sure, Fred?" Stevie patted his graying hair. "I already got the bulls knockin' on my door."

"Relax, Stevie. I'll see you at the Sons of Loyola. It's the Waldorf this year, so get out your best bib and tucker." The voice paused. "And I'll have a little surprise for you and the boys."

"Nuthin' to do with degenerates, I hope, Fred."

"I'll let you decide that, Stevie."

Stevie put the phone down. Maybe Fred didn't know as much as he thought he did. He didn't know about the faggot son, dead in the Candy Box's toilet. Stevie would wager somebody had leaked the story to Old John Jay. Why else all this name-calling in *The Daily Journal*?

The old man would hang Stevie out to dry if he could, for not playing nursemaid to his limp-wrist son. If he needed witnesses, here was Blackie and Tyrone still walking around loose, waiting to tell their stories, if they hadn't already. If they hadn't already! He saw now how stupid he'd been to trust that dyke and the colored boy. He had to act fast.

"Dirty squealers," Stevie mumbled. "I'll have 'em pushin' up daisies."

He threw open his door and thundered down the hallway, "Charlie! Waxy!"

They rolled into his office like a pair of tumbleweeds. "Yeah, boss."

"Listen to me," he said through clenched teeth, "I want Blackie and that colored kid Tyrone out of the way."

Waxy rubbed his eyes. "Bump off a dame?" He liked Blackie, liked her voice. Tyrone was another matter.

"She's a dyke," Charlie explained. "It ain't the same."

"Dyke or no dyke," Stevie commanded. "Take care of her, permanent. The sooner, the better."

"I don't like it," Waxy murmured.

"You ain't gettin' paid to like it." Stevie pushed Charlie and Waxy out the office door.

Twenty-Three

On Christopher Street the heat wave continued unbroken. The sheets were damp with sweat under Didi, who'd taken to dropping by every afternoon.

"What's wrong, darling?" she asked Blackie.

"Aw, nuthin'." Propped on one elbow, Blackie brooded. "Our stakeout's in place, but no sign of that son of a bitch. Maybe I was wrong."

"I'd almost rather he didn't show up."

"We can't just leave him out there till he kills somebody else." Blackie spoke in a parched voice.

"I understand that," Didi paused, "but something else is bothering you, I just know it."

"I guess it's Stevie. He's been skulkin' around the club like Bela Lugosi, and never speaks to anybody." Blackie rolled over toward Didi. "Then there's Charlie and Waxy, bird-dogging me all the time like I'm their long-lost sister. A double whammy."

"Oh, Blackie, you've got to get away from there." Didi kissed her forehead.

Blackie feared she was right. The glamour had faded from

the club, from the whole shebang. But she couldn't imagine who she would be without it. She could go back to tending bar, but there wasn't much in that for a girl like Didi, who liked a little excitement, the bright lights.

"You can be free of them right now," Didi insisted. "Tell Stevie tonight's your last night, or don't tell him anything."

"Not yet, sweetheart." Enough talking. Blackie stretched herself out over Didi, pinning Didi's bare arms above her head.

Didi felt suddenly and deliciously unsafe. "Whatever you say," she murmured.

After a while, Blackie reached up to the drawer of the bedside table where she kept a smooth pink dildo. The strap fit around her waist and hips.

Without a word, Didi shifted around to straddle Blackie's stomach. The dildo reached for the deepest wettest spot between Didi's legs as she rocked forward, her mind drifting.

"I'll never let you go," she said, and swung her nipples over Blackie's lips.

"Where'd you learn to do that?" Oblivion tasted good to Blackie.

"Wouldn't you like to know?" Didi whispered back, then arched forward to cover Blackie's face with kisses.

Darkness was seeping into the room. Didi nestled into Blackie's arms. Their bodies fit easily.

"Do you ever think about other women when you're with me?" Didi asked.

"Nope," Blackie mumbled.

"But you've had lots of other women."

"None like you."

"What does that mean?"

"My first girlfriend seduced me with Cokes at the neighborhood candy store." That was Lily, who'd lived over on Bristol Street, and the frosty red ice chest was at Mr. Holman's candy store on Pitkin. "Then there was the nurse at this camp where I worked." In the Catskills, the Jewish Alps. "We smooched in the infirmary if no patients showed up."

"Was that all?" Didi laughed.

"No," Blackie said, and nuzzled Didi's breast.

"But what if one of your old girlfriends showed up?" Didi challenged her. "What would you do?"

"You mean would I go back to her? Don't be silly!" Since Didi had come into her life, the memory of Renee had faded. It was a relief.

"Who were your old girlfriends?"

"Nobody you'll ever meet."

"But *you* could run into them anywhere," Didi objected. "On the street, at the club."

"But playin' around's not my style. I'm no two-timer," Blackie reassured her. "You can relax." She kissed her way down Didi's neck. "I'm the one takin' the chances, you know."

"Why is that?"

"You're the straight girl just out for a good time and a few laughs."

"Don't be so sure." Didi lifted Blackie's mouth to hers, and they kissed for a long time.

"Can't you ditch your father tonight and come back here?" Blackie complained. She couldn't face the prospect of rumpled sheets and no Didi.

"That shouldn't be hard," Didi replied. "He won't be concerned with my whereabouts." A wry smile lifted one corner of her mouth. "He has his political future to think about. All of a sudden he and the mayor are like blood brothers."

She still marveled at their conversation yesterday when her father had asked her to the Waldorf for the annual Sons of Loyola awards banquet. "But we're not Catholic," she'd reminded him.

John Jay had oozed old Knickerbocker finesse. "This is really a political gathering, my dear, in honor of my old friend Mayor O'Malley. I've been asked to make a presentation."

"But you've always opposed O'Malley," she'd reminded him again.

"We've decided to let bygones be bygones, for the good of the city."

That was a sham, but the truth about Costa's and Joey Apollo was worse. Joey had cut the deck first, an eight. John Jay's hand trembled, like taking candy from a baby, he thought. He drew. Three. He stared at the card for a long time. A deal was a deal.

Didi said she didn't want to go to the banquet. "Don't be difficult, Diana," he pleaded. "You know your mother's not up to anything like this." He paused. "You'll have a lovely new gown."

Didi had given him a chalky smile. He'd always been quick with a bribe, to win the children's loyalty or their silence.

Now, in the middle of the rickety bed, Blackie snuggled between Didi's ample breasts. "So I'll see you back here later?"

Didi nodded. "For sure."

"Swell," Blackie grinned "And if the killer shows up tonight, we'll give him a medium shellacking, and then he's all yours."

Uptown at Lucille's on East 55th Street, the drapes were drawn over the tall French windows. If she could get through tonight, Lucille thought, she'd make a bundle and rest up tomorrow, which was Sunday. A family time, when mobsters and swells took their wives out to dinner and whores got a break.

With her hair bobby-pinned in the fat round curls she often napped on, Lucille descended the staircase into the entrance hall with its rock-crystal chandelier. Pushing her way through the swinging door into the kitchen, Lucille noticed Sundown had everything shipshape and spotless.

Bending down, Lucille rescued a bottle of whiskey, her private stock, from under the sink. Her backside had grown the last few years to stick out like a loading platform so that her robe hiked up in the rear. The seams of her nylons were crooked, like the spindly, knock-kneed limbs of wading birds.

She poured herself a shot and sat down to read *The Daily Journal*. Soon she was deep into an editorial titled "Sex Fiends Roam City. Laxity in Laws Blamed." Degenerates were lurking on rooftops, in dimly lit parks, subways, and public washrooms.

The vacuum cleaner caterwauled through the living room like a bull elephant on the rampage. It stopped as suddenly as it had begun, and Sundown shuffled her way into the kitchen, eyes on the broken knotted laces of her work shoes.

"Sorry, Miss Lucille," she said, wiping sweat off her face with a thick brown hand. Her dress was faded blue cotton, shapeless and scoop neck. "It's Mr. Stevie on the phone."

Lucille followed Sundown into the living room and took the call in her pink peignoir. "What's up, handsome?"

"You takin' a breather before the crowd gets in?" Stevie had stopped in early at his backroom office. There was nobody at the club but the bartender and the kitchen crew.

Lucille preened the satin bodice of her robe over her bosom. "Somethin' like that. Can we expect you?"

"When you see me comin'." He stroked the lapels of his

hand-tailored tux and adjusted his spectacles. "I got a big affair tonight."

"Is that so?"

"Yeah, I'm on my way to the Waldorf to pay my respects and make a nice contribution to the party's hope chest."

"Rubbin' elbows with high society, are you?"

"Just a bunch of politicians with the gimmes."

"Yeah, word's out that O'Malley's back in the race." Lucille paused to sip her whiskey. "After all that boondogglin'."

"He's Fred's choice," Stevie replied, then shifted gears smoothly. "That's what I'm callin' for, Lucille. I need a girl to take along to the Waldorf, make it a party."

"Your old lady ain't up to it?" Lucille quipped.

"She don't like parties," Stevie replied dryly.

So that was the story. Lucille's brain churned like an adding machine, calculating how much dough she stood to lose if one of the girls went out for the evening. On the busiest night of the week, there'd be a zillion customers. She took out a cigarette and stuck a match under it.

"Strictly business, you understand," Stevie continued. "I want the redhead."

Lucille poured herself more whiskey. "Renee?"

"That's the one."

Her most popular girl, of course. "You know she's nobody's idea of a little doll." Lucille suggested they wouldn't make a pretty pair, Renee towering a good half a head above Stevie.

"I ain't askin' to marry her," Stevie snarled.

"She's got a temper, that Renee. Comes out when she's had a couple of drinks."

"All redheads got a temper," Stevie said confidently.

Lucille rolled shifty eyes. "Howzabout I loan you Flo, my brunette? Or the blond Marie instead?"

Stevie's patience was waning. "I'm tellin' you I need a

knockout dame who'll make the boys sit up and take notice."

"A real feather in your cap," Lucille replied with conspicuous sarcasm.

"Around 8." Stevie hung up.

Lucille shrugged as the kitchen door swung open.

Sundown had changed into her black dress with white apron and cap. "I'm through."

"Is Renee in her room?" Lucille asked. Renee wasn't going to like the idea of spending an evening with Stevie, but she'd have to make the best of it.

"Yessum."

"Get her for me, will ya?" Lucille said.

Sundown stiffened her back and sucked her teeth. If she went up and down those stairs one time, she went up and down them 86,000 times a day.

"Yessum," she sighed, and reminded herself she owed Lucille a lot.

Upstairs, Renee was sprawled across her bed, eyes swollen from weeping.

"Whazzamatta, Renee?"

Sundown hurried back to the kitchen. "Miss Lucille," she announced, breathless and frazzled, "you better come upstairs."

As soon as Lucille saw Renee, she took her in her arms.

"It's Blackie," Renee sobbed.

"Not again," Lucille replied. "Nobody's worth all this. I thought you were gettin' over her."

Renee told her about a call she'd had that same afternoon from Trixie: "You might as well forgedabout Blackie...yeah, cootchie-cooin' with a society dame at a back table in the Bubble Room...whaddaya gonna do?"

"For Chrissake," Lucille exclaimed, "you oughta know better than to believe Trixie!" But she was curious. "Who'd she say the broad was?"

"Trixie swears she saw 'em," Renee said, her hair a glittering, red-gold mass. "Blackie and ol' Jack Fletcher's daughter, no less!"

"Trixie needs glasses. And how would she know who Jack's daughter is?"

"The papers, she says she's in the papers all the time," Renee bawled. "I was hopin' me and Blackie, you know, we'd get back together."

"I know, I know," Lucille commiserated. Nobody understood these things better than Lucille, whose "men are for business and girls are for pleasure" policy had been the talk of the town. If Lucilee was more than a little AC/DC, it had never been bad for business. But to get where she was in whoring, she'd left love on the back burner for too many years.

She feathered Renee's cheek with her fingers. "Even if Blackie's goin' with somebody else, it ain't the end of the world."

Sundown hovered in the doorway.

"Go get Renee some coffee, will ya, Sundown?" A night out would do the kid good. Things had a way of working out.

"Yessum," Sundown muttered.

Twenty-Four

"What a dump!" Renee put on her best Bette Davis telling off Joseph Cotten in their latest hit film, when she and Stevie alighted at the streamlined Park Avenue entrance to the Waldorf-Astoria.

"Watch your mouth." Stevie hadn't seen a movie since *G-Men*, and didn't smile. "This ain't the Copa."

He clamped down on Renee's elbow like a vise and whisked her inside, looking like a million dollars in slinky strapless green moiré with elbow-length gloves, and a real diamond bracelet on loan for the night from Lucille.

"OK, OK," Renee hissed back. Stevie had fewer brains than Heinz had pickles.

They negotiated the wide stairway up to the foyer, classic lines with gold-and-silver leaf overhead. As she sailed regally across the hand-tufted carpet, Renee's graceful silhouette turned heads. Stevie gave her the fisheye.

The air-conditioned lobby, with massive columns of black marble from floor to ceiling, overflowed with the dress-for-dinner set. Tuxs and tailcoats, white ties and starched collars beside satins and lace, ranch mink spilling off shoulders. Renee caressed the diamond clip that held the upsweep of her copper-colored curls in place, as an elevator took her and Stevie to the third-floor Grand Ballroom. The gallery sparkled with crystal pendants, cascading over silver chandeliers.

"This place is lit up like high mass," Renee muttered to Stevie, wishing she had a drink.

As they approached the doorway, Stevie looked stern and gave his name to a guy in a tux who bowed. He'd RSVP'd.

"This way, sir." A thousand Sons of Loyola and their wives were already bent over Rock Cornish hen, pommes au gratin, and haricots verts. Stevie and Renee were ushered to a table in a far corner under the two-tiered balcony.

"Howzabout somethin' closer to ringside?" Stevie asked, and cupped a C note into the man's palm.

"This is *your* table, sir," he replied in a refined tone, pocketing the bill.

Stevie sulked. Renee settled in. The ruddy-faced individual next to her introduced himself as a pharmacist from Queens, a family man with his wife.

"Come here often?" he asked.

"Uh-uh, first time." Renee wasn't much for polite conversation. "I can't see anything from here," she complained to Stevie.

"So what's to see? That's O'Malley and the other high rollers up there." He gestured toward the stately dais. "Eat up."

Instead, Renee skipped the entree and gulped her first glass of champagne, with Beluga caviar from a crystal swan dish. By the time the chocolate mousse and demitasses were served, she was feeling mellow.

"Ladies and gentlemen...ladies and gentlemen." The festivities had begun. "It's my pleasure to introduce..." The chairman of the annual dinner committee continued, and the crowd stirred. "A man of unquestioned integrity and longtime friend of our honoree."

Clutching a sheaf of neatly typed bond, Old John Jay rose on a crescendo of loyal applause.

"Ladies and gentlemen," the chairman quieted the audience, "I give you that courageous leader of our city's fourth estate, and distinguished philanthropist, John Jay Fletcher-Payne."

More applause. Renee guzzled champagne. Stevie's jaw went slack. If the old man Fletcher-Payne was the surprise Frank had promised, it was a doozie. What was *he* doing working this side of the street?

"Ladies and gentlemen," John Jay repeated, deep-set eyes gazing out over the audience. A rehash of O'Malley's political career, prepared by the mayor's staff, extolled his common touch and progressive vision.

"That rascal Jack!" Renee exclaimed. "In like Flynn with City Hall."

"You know Fletcher-Payne?" Stevie responded with a razor-sharp look.

Renee was no snitch, and could be very discreet about the customers. But the booze had gone to her head, and she figured with Stevie what difference did it make? "He's one of Lucille's regulars," she disclosed behind a white-gloved hand.

Now there was a juicy piece of gossip, thought Stevie, that gave him one up on the millionaire stooge. He was getting to like Renee. "One of Lucille's broad-A crowd, eh?"

"Yeah, but the girls say he's strictly from Mortimer Snerd."

"What else is new?" Stevie smirked.

On the dais, John Jay rambled on. "His commitment to the struggle for those values we all hold dear," he reached down to his right for a bronze plaque, "has inspired public confidence in his administration."

He read from the inscription, "To Reform and to Serve." A flurry of applause swept through the great hall. "A motto worthy of the recipient of this year's Annual Sons of Loyola Leadership Award...His Honor James Patrick O'Malley, Mayor of the City of New York."

The audience stood up and roared its approval, as did the dignitaries to the right and left of John Jay. Wheeling around, a mitered hat atop his snow-white hair, New York's reigning Cardinal shook the mayor's hand as O'Malley made his way to the podium. Carmine De Mauro, an Italian brave from the Tammany Wigwam, gave him a burly slap between the shoulder blades. From under bushy eyebrows, O'Malley sized up John Jay as they came together under an enormous American flag. John Jay handed over the plaque and set off a firestorm of flashbulbs from the press. An orchestra under the eaves struck up the party fight song.

Stevie wasn't singing along. Instead he watched Fletcher-Payne drift down the table, back to his seat next to creamy white shoulders above silver lamé. Peering over the heads of the couple from Queens, Stevie saw Fletcher-Payne's arm encircle the young woman, whose face... Stevie blinked and wiped his glasses. She was a real looker, all right, tits out to there, and... Stevie gagged on a reflux of bearnaise sauce. A dead ringer for the stiff.

Renee scrambled to her feet. "Who's the broad with Jack Fletcher?" She craned her neck for a better look. But Trixie's description of her rival left little room for doubt.

"Little Orphan Annie! How should I know?" Stevie popped off. The Fletcher-Paynes were trouble, and he already had enough of their family secrets to last him a while.

O'Malley had launched into his acceptance speech. "And we stand ready to defend our administration's record," the mayor insisted, "on crime and public morals, against all comers."

Then, presto change-o, the Fletcher-Payne babe was on the move, not sticking around to cheer. Stevie and Renee watched her leave her seat on the dais and scoot across the Grand Ballroom like a base runner stealing second.

"Wheredaya think she's goin'?" Stevie asked.

Renee certainly intended to find out. She started after the blond, upsetting a bowl of apricot-colored tea roses in the middle of their table.

"Hey, what's your hurry?" Stevie grabbed for Renee's arm. "Gimme a break." Renee snaked out of his reach. "I gotta go to the powder room."

What was it with dames always going to the powder room? "OK, take this." Stevie fished out a 10-spot for Renee to tip the attendant.

She took the money, while behind her O'Malley announced, "With the support of many loyal friends, I've decided once again to throw my hat into the ring." And mild pandemonium erupted.

Dodging well-wishers coming and going, Renee kept Miss Rich Bitch in her crosshairs—only to discover that *she* was also on her way to powder her whatever.

The door sighed like a woman in love as Renee pushed through it. She pulled up short, heart pounding, dazzled by glowing mirrored walls, concealed lights set high in the corners. A flight of glossy metal birds swooped around the room. Draped nudes bent over baskets of flowers at the entrance to the toilets, from whence emerged Didi, dabbing at her eyes.

Renee had to admit the Fletcher-Payne brat was some tomato even if she wasn't exactly her type. Mouth dry, Renee pulled out a cigarette as Didi sat on a black velvet pouf in front of a small vanity with glass top and polished chrome tubular legs.

With just enough Dutch courage under her belt to risk it, Renee approached. "Got a light?"

Didi sniffed into her hanky, then scrutinized Renee's image in the mirror. The face and figure were star quality, not exactly what she would've expected from the Sons of Loyola. She took out a blue enamel cigarette case with *F-P* in pavé diamonds and a matching blue enamel matchbook cover.

"Here you are," she said, striking a match across it.

Renee hung the cigarette off her lip, eyes flinty. "You're Jack Fletcher-Payne's daughter, aren't you?" she asked, careful not to say "ain't" like some dumb Dora.

Didi wadded her hanky into a ball. The question was a reminder of how much she despised the notoriety to which her father had chosen to expose them both.

"Yes, John Jay Fletcher-Payne's my father," she admitted. "Are you interested in politics?"

"No, no." Renee tried to sound confident. "I'm in the theater. You know, Broadway."

"How nice. I really should be getting back to the party."

Enough schmaltz, thought Renee. She looked around. Two women were exiting the powder room, a black lace Balenciaga, an elaborately draped Fath creation, and jewels by Harry Winston.

"OK, I'm gonna level with you."

"That's not necessary," Didi said as she drew back. She'd caught a whiff of the Broadway chorine's breath, smelling like a still.

"Hold on," Renee insisted. "I know more about you than you think." She paused. "I know your family's been in so many messes, you should have a mop on that coat of arms you're so proud of."

Didi couldn't argue with that. Was this about Skip? Her

father's baser habits, or even poor Mummie? But Didi was schooled in the social graces, including extricating herself from unpleasant situations, and rose to go.

"I really must be getting back." She tried to sidestep Renee, who didn't back off.

"OK, I'm just gonna ask you one thing." Renee dropped her voice. "You been goin' with Blackie Cole, haven't ya?"

At that, everything came to a halt. Renee had stomped Didi's heart dead center. "What do you mean?" Didi murmured.

"Goin' with her, sleepin' with her."

Didi's shoulders drooped like bruised blossoms. She thought she'd pooh-poohed all the lessons in propriety that had been drummed into her from childhood. But here she was feeling bewildered, embarrassed by this crude woman's accusations.

"C'mon," Renee snickered. "I don't give a damn if you like women. Under the mink, we're all sisters."

Didi stalled. Was that what they called it—*liking* women? "Who do you think you are?"

Renee saw her chance to put the kibosh on the whole affair. "Never mind who I am, but I can make it plenty hot for you." Bigger names than Fletcher-Payne cringed in terror at being called queer.

"I could plaster you all over the front page." Renee savored the notion. "The tabloids'll love it."

"Nobody would print such garbage," Didi countered, suspecting they might.

"Don't kid yourself, sugar." Renee was going to put the screws to her. "And why wouldya wanna go out on a limb for Blackie Cole?"

"What are you talking about?"

"Blackie and me, we go back a long way." Renee paused to admire herself in the mirror. "So I know she musta given you her line about love and forever."

Didi didn't deny it. She had little experience with schemers and double-dealers.

Renee pressed her advantage. "But whaddif she's just stringin' you along for laughs?"

"What do you mean, you and Blackie go back a long way?" Didi asked, not to be reduced to tears.

"Do you have to ask?"

A searing anger took hold of Didi. "You were...more than a friend of Blackie's?"

"What makes you think that's past tense, sister?"

Didi couldn't consider the possibility of betrayal. "I don't believe you."

"Just try me." Renee stood her ground, though she felt woozy and needed a drink badly. "If you don't stay away from my dyke, I'll expose you all over town."

"And how much money would you want to leave us alone?" Didi waxed defiant. The woman fairly reeked of liquor.

"I don't want your dirty money," Renee replied smugly. "I can get plenty of that myself." She paused. "You just stay away from Blackie Cole, or I'll give you a scandal you'll never forget."

So this was what fear felt like. Didi didn't like it. "Get out of my way," she said, and gave Renee a shove toward the door. She had to talk to Blackie. There would be a good explanation for this woman's behavior.

Renee shoved back. "I'll scratch your eyes out."

Just then, the door sighed again when an elderly woman, dripping diamonds and emeralds like a jewel rack, pitter-pattered her way inside the powder room.

The old woman slipped absentmindedly between Didi and Renee. "Diana, dahling," she fussed, her lips grazing Didi's cheek. "Do tell your father how we've been moved by his support of the mayor."

"Thank you so much, Mrs. Van der Hoop." By the time Didi disentangled herself, Renee was gone, looking for Stevie. She'd found out all she needed to know.

Twenty-Five

Stevie had worked his way over to the speakers' platform where Mayor O'Malley dispensed promises and handshakes. Fred Capotello stood in front, talking to one of the party's go-getters.

"Carmine..." Uncle Fred was saying. "Stevie, my boy," he interrupted himself and introduced Stevie. "Mr. Francioso is an old business associate."

Carmine shook hands and moved on.

Uncle Fred drifted in the opposite direction with Stevie by the arm. "Did ya see *The Daily Journal* today? Things are coolin' down already." He paused. "They always do."

"The *Journal*'s comin' out for O'Malley?"

"Bet your bottom dollar." Capotello chuckled, and scanned the table. "Get a load of Old John Jay over there with Judge Valerio."

Not without trepidation, Stevie turned to look. He'd already seen enough of the Fletcher-Paynes. But instead of the two old campaigners, he caught a glimpse of Renee back from the powder room—buxom and lusty, her ice-blue eyes flashing fire. His stomach lurched. Without so much as a howdy-do, she passed him by.

"Wheredaya think you're goin'?" he began.

Her nose in the air, she went right for the dignitaries. "Jack," she gushed at John Jay Fletcher-Payne, whose vacant eyes bulged. His sunken cheeks blushed.

"You're lookin' very handsome tonight," Renee went on. "You too, Judge."

Judge Valerio's knees buckled like he'd taken a jab to the stomach. "Renee, dear."

"In person. Howzabout a little drink, boys? When you're done speechmakin', of course."

Jack rebounded. "I didn't know you came to this sort of affair."

Stevie was fast on his feet too. He didn't want any trouble with Fletcher-Payne. He reached for Renee. "That's enough, sweetheart. These men have important things to talk about, and it's past your bedtime."

Renee tried to shake Stevie off. "C'mon, Jack." She tugged at his sleeve and tossed her long strawberry curls. She had a much juicier story to tell him. Whether it got her Blackie back or not, Renee would give the daughter, who thought she was such hot shit, a little taste of heartache. "Let's have that drink now."

Judge Valerio mumbled a warning about photographers. A flashbulb popped. Renee posed. If Old John Jay knew anything about the newspaper business, it was how much it would cost him to keep those pictures off the front page and buy up all the negatives. He winced and took cover.

"Noodle dicks," Renee muttered.

"C'mon, kid," Stevie said to Renee, blinking behind his glasses. Not quite the way he'd planned it, but she'd been a big hit with the swells. "I'll take you home."

From a distance Didi had watched Renee sidle up to her father in a disgustingly familiar way. As Renee edged closer, Didi's anger mingled with panic. A shameless hussy like

Renee, it occurred to Didi, would be as good as her word, and stop at nothing to get what she wanted.

Didi came alongside her father. "Tramp," she hissed at Renee.

John Jay's brow showed a couple of new furrows. Diana couldn't know anything about Renee. He'd always been discreet.

Renee cocked a fist. "Keep your distance, sister," she threatened Didi, then added in a low smooth voice, "Your little secret is safe with me, as long as you stay away from you know who."

With two gorgeous dames spitting insults at each other, the photographers went crazy.

"Blackie Cole's not for sale," Renee yelled as Stevie grabbed her around the waist.

"Excuse us, gentlemen," John Jay said to the photographers. "Diana, I think it's time we were getting home." He'd planned to drop by Lucille's for a nightcap and a game of cards. But maybe some other time.

Didi, on the other hand, decided she was suddenly tired and that she would rest easier at the Park Avenue apartment than in the Village. She would explain later to Blackie why she hadn't shown up. "Yes, Father, let's go home."

At the Waldorf's exit, Smash Nose Babe took charge of Renee. He settled her beside Stevie in the backseat of the big brown limousine and climbed in.

"Whadda mouth you got on you!" Stevie snarled at Renee. "You got some beef with the Fletcher-Paynes?"

"None of your business."

"I'm makin' it my business. You wanna be a hooker with a busted wing?"

At a nod from Stevie, Smash Nose Babe twisted Renee's sylphlike arm behind her.

"And whadduz the old man's daughter have to do with Blackie Cole?"

Babe twisted harder.

"She's tryin' to steal Blackie," Renee gasped, "when everybody knows Blackie belongs to me."

"Your main squeeze, huh?" Stevie shrugged and signaled for Babe to let go of Renee. He should've known. It wasn't like Lucille hadn't warned him Renee wasn't exactly his type. "Whazzit to a big man like you anyway," Lucille had consoled him, "what the girls do on their own time?"

Stevie blinked behind his glasses. "Since when has Blackie Cole been steppin' out with Little Miss Moneybags?"

"I dunno," Renee mumbled.

So he'd been right all along. Blackie had talked, and to who else but the dead boy's sister. Stevie had to hand it to Blackie. She had great taste in dames, but they weren't gonna do her much good. Charlie and Waxy had their orders, and this time they'd get the job done, or he'd know the reason why.

"Don't worry, kid. I'm laying odds you'll get her back." In a pine box, thought Stevie as his car sped back to Lucille's. Maybe he could spend a couple of hours after all with Flo, Lucille's brunette, or Marie, the blond with the powder-blue eyes. He'd had enough redheads to last him a long time.

Downtown, Victor cradled the snub-nosed pistol in the palm of his big hand. The dark barrel gleamed like polished obsidian. He was going to shut the dyke up, even if she'd already spilled her guts to the Fletcher-Payne dame, bamboozled and lured her to the Christopher Street apartment. He'd seen her, more than once. Two broads like that, not a dick between them, teamed up against him—he had to take chances.

As Victor came up Macdougal, past the park on his right,

wrought iron curlicues blossomed on streetlamps. Lights flickered behind the little square windows of a Bohemian afterhours eatery. An alley behind it lay steeped in shadow. He had to get close enough and shoot straight, he told himself, and thrust the gun into the pocket of his bomber jacket.

Turning onto Eighth Street and a block of low brick storefronts, he drifted into the bar at the Candy Box as the show was beginning, and ordered a beer. He'd timed it right. The lezzie was up onstage. She would've made a good-looking guy.

He measured the distance that separated them, from the end of the bar, under the archway, and across the narrow performance space. He was patient. After the show, on her way home, he'd catch up with her, and this time he wouldn't miss.

The footlights glowed. Blackie flashed the paying customers her extravagant smile. "Whatever the papers have been sayin' about us..." she began.

The audience snickered while Victor nursed his beer.

"The Candy Box has a fabulous show for you tonight, with lotsa laughs."

To soft music, a line led by Titanic and Miss Jackie Mae emerged gracefully from the wings. In dresses of frothy pink chiffon, necklines punctuated by rhinestone clips, the boys ranged themselves on benches.

"Faggots," Victor chuckled to himself and squeezed the glass between his hands.

A chorus line of tuxedos, featuring Sully, Larry (Jackie Mae's dancing partner), and Pat Burns, who looked like the young Pat O'Brien, stood behind the boys.

Hard to believe those are women, Victor thought, and caressed the pistol, cold and solid inside his jacket pocket. His mother had been some dish too, scraggly hair hanging limp over the stoop while she puked her brains out. Screaming his name down the street.

"We're here every night for your pleasure." Blackie was

winding down. "So just drink up, relax, and let me present to you, our very special audience, our very special entertainers in the High Hat Revue."

The spotlight shifted from her to centerstage where the girls sang with punch and swagger.

Life is such a drag...

They gave the boys a big hug from behind.

When I'm not with you.

Red and blue lights twinkled above. Victor's hand closed around the butt of his gun. Pansies and cuntlappers. If he shot them all, right up onstage, they ought to give him a medal.

While the other kids were taking a bow, Blackie stepped back into the spotlight. "Ladies and gentlemen, we've got a surprise for you."

The boys and girls pranced out into the audience. Victor straightened up, his pistol hand trembling. He didn't like surprises.

Blackie doffed her top hat. "On this next song, we want you to join in. It's one you all know."

Amidst guffaws and giggles, Titanic coaxed the customers around him. He took a matronly lady by the hand while Sully persuaded a rawboned man with a long face to be her partner.

The orchestra struck up the music.

"Our entertainers will help you out with the steps," Blackie promised. This was no torchy lamentation. She belted out,

All together now

Knees together now.

Victor leaned on the bar and watched the dance begin, flabby fannies shim-sham-shimmying in the darkness.

Back in the bar, Tryone scrubbed glasses, one eye on the crowd. He felt the heft of the big diamond ring against his thigh, deep inside his pants pocket. He'd taken to wearing it on his finger sometimes too, alone up at Sundown's, where he could watch it glow in the sunlight like a thing alive. Blackie had been on the level, and soon he'd have his money. It wasn't a bad deal, considering that white man was never going to show his face around there again.

"Don't bet your life on it," Blackie had said.

Tyrone didn't like the sound of that, and bent lower over the dishwater. It was a warm night, beads of sweat popping out on his forehead. Then a cold rush of air swept across the back of his neck. He shivered and raised his eyes. At the far end of the bar, a profile, craggy and dark, stood out for an instant in the swirl of smoke. Like the polestar, it held Tyrone's gaze. He gulped and gasped for breath. The man turned to order and scanned the bar with burning eyes. Tyrone looked down.

This had to be a ghost, right out of Tyrone's worst nightmare. But if he turned out to be real, Tyrone had to move fast before he was noticed, his brown skin a dead giveaway. The moment he'd dreaded was upon him, and he had to keep up his end of the bargain. He prayed for stealth as he eased under the bar at his end. The bartender was busy with customers.

Tyrone dared another furtive glance, praying not to meet the killer's eyes. They were glued to the dance floor anyway, looking for somebody or something. Heavy blue veins crisscrossed his hands. Tyrone wasn't breathing at all.

The kids from the show gaily flounced arms and swayed knees from side to side. Their partners from the audience tried to keep up with the razzle-dazzle music. Titanic tripped from one couple to another, babbling encouragement.

Tyrone spotted him and took heart. From a shadowy corner of the room, he signaled to Titanic with a frantic wave of his hand.

High as a kite, Titanic turned to dance Tyrone's way. He whirled nonchalantly, trailing his feather boa behind him.

"He's back there in the bar," Tyrone whispered.

"Who, dahling?" Tall and slender as a reed, an unthinking reed, Titanic dipped one shoulder toward the floor and reversed directions laughing, a short bell-like burst.

"The man, our man." Tyrone drew closer. "The killer, he's here. Do something!"

Titanic swung the boa over his head and down his smoothly gyrating body. He sang along with Blackie, who had left the stand-up mike. A single spot followed her across the stage.

Step and glide, step and glide...

Tyrone came out of the shadows. "You hear what I'm sayin'?"

Customers clapped to the rhythm of the song. Everybody chimed in.

And twist around and twist around.

Onstage, Blackie swiveled her narrow hips. The crowd responded with bawdy laughter, writhing in their own shameless hootchy-cootchy dance.

"Stop actin' a fool," Tyrone pleaded with Titanic. "He's here."

Suddenly a hullabaloo like a 21-gun salute erupted at the entrance to the Candy Box. When a rush of policemen poured in, the carefree merrymakers dropped their arms or stiffened them out in space at odd angles. The orchestra faded away to the shocked whine of a single saxophone.

As a first line of defense, Miss Freddi threw up her hands. "What can I do for you, gentlemen?" she demanded in a shrill voice, as she imagined Stevie would've done.

But Stevie wasn't there. Officers and men paid Freddi no mind. They spilled right past onto the floor of the club, spreading out like thick molasses, entrapping audience and entertainers. The din was terrific.

Nightsticks rose and fell at random while the cops established their dominance on the dance floor. The musicians crouched against the onslaught, covering their heads and their horns. Tyrone slunk into the shadows.

Blackie ducked as a chunk of the bandstand flew past her head and struck the wall. She saw the other kids scatter like tenpins, thwacks and curses pursuing them. They clawed and shoved their way through the paying customers to get at the exits, only to be met by stick-wielding reinforcements.

Tyrone edged his way along the wall toward the kitchen.

A plainclothesman in a tan trench coat and porkpie hat headed the relief column of officers. His was not a handsome kisser, the nose plastered flat like a fighter's or a champagne cork.

"Swazey," Blackie muttered. The dirty copper and master sleuth. He had some nerve. In the middle of the dance floor, his cordon of bluecoats had the entertainers surrounded.

"Get movin', toots." A patrolman approached Blackie. "Show's over."

Before the dragnet closed around her, she picked up the microphone and swung it across her body. It whirled through the air at the officer's head. He sidestepped, and she barreled off in the opposite direction, shifty as a halfback. She burst through the kitchen door. Frightened black faces observed her flight over tables, pots, and pans.

"It's a raid," she told them. "Cops all over the place." She saw Tyrone and asked, "You stayin'?"

He hesitated. The cops had nothing on him. He was just the hired help. But that never stopped them from busting heads. He followed her down the steps and into the back alley.

Rounding the corner, they pulled up short. Paddy wagons, which the police had backed up to the entrance of the Candy Box, blocked their escape. Their doors yawned menacingly. Down at the station house, Tyrone knew his life wouldn't be worth a plug nickel.

"C'mon," he said to Blackie, clambering to the roof of the shed in the alley. She followed.

"Up here." Tyrone pushed her in front of him, then lifted her up to snag the bottom rung of the fire escape. As a kid in Brooklyn, Blackie had learned her way around fire escapes and rooftops. Nimble as a trapeze artist, she swung in a tight arch, hoisting herself up. On the landing, she unhooked the ladder and let it slide down to Tyrone. He began his ascent, his foot on the second rung.

"That's as far as you go, boy," a voice growled, as powerful arms jerked Tyrone back. A wallop to the side of the head knocked him into the alley. Victor paused long enough to crank a live shell into the chamber of his automatic.

The last thing Tyrone saw were two piercing eyes. "You think I wouldn't recognize *you?*"

"No!" Tyrone shouted. The melee inside the club drowned him out, and the shot.

Twenty-Six

Blackie bent over the fire-escape railing to watch Tyrone sprawl lifeless in the dirt, blood gushing out of his heart. She recoiled in horror as the killer turned his searing eyes to meet hers. All massive head and shoulders, he'd returned, just like she'd predicted. But this wasn't the way she'd planned it. She'd gotten Tyrone killed, and now it was her turn. She couldn't go another round with this lunatic. All she could do was flee for her life, upward into the darkness.

Victor rose swiftly up the ladder behind her. One more bullet would erase the Fletcher-Payne kid's death forever.

Blackie climbed past the flickering neon sign next door that spelled out RENO BAR. Its garish lights flashed red and green across her face. Below, the raid spilled out of doors. She heard the whack of a nightstick like a baseball bat on cowhide and someone crying in pain. She looked down. He was gaining on her. She flung herself over the roof's ledge.

Across the pitch-black surface she ran, past treetops, to the opposite edge, and looked down at the roof of the adjacent building—the squat storefronts along Eighth Street. It was a 50-foot drop, a costly mistake for her.

Fear, she thought, confused you, made you forget the obvious. She pulled herself together and ran for the triangular lean-to, in the middle of the roof, whose door led downstairs. She pulled at the handle. It was stuck, or locked from inside. She pulled harder, then tried to kick it in. Nothing budged.

"It's all over, sister," came that terrible voice out of the darkness. She heard the tread of heavy shoes. The killer was on the roof.

She stooped out of sight, her heart beating so hard she thought he must hear it too. Her fingers found an empty bottle, and she tossed it away like a live grenade. It crashed against the wall behind her and broke. In the tense silence that followed, she knew she'd bought a little time.

Victor turned toward the sound, then walked over and peered down at the roof next door. Nobody was going down there, he thought. He knew his way around rooftops too.

Blackie stood against the sky at the front of the building. The police were loading the kids into the paddy wagons. She thought she saw Titanic, plumage drooping. As she opened her mouth to scream, a bullet whizzed past her ear.

Someone looked up, and she waved her arms. She'd had enough. She'd take her chances with the cops.

"Hold it right there," the voice threatened, and Blackie dove back onto the roof for safety. A second bullet crashed into the wall.

Below, the mesh door of the paddy wagon hung open. Detective Swazey ducked behind it. "What the fuck was that?" he cursed. "Some asshole shootin' at us?"

A broad beam of light rose up the facade of the building.

"Somebody's up on that roof," an officer said.

"Get up there on the double, and get 'em down," Swazey ordered, and a squad raced into the building. "I told you I heard a shot before. And whaddabout the dead colored boy in the alley?"

"No ID, sir," a patrolman explained, "but we found this on him." He held up Skip's ring for Swazey to see.

Swazey examined the ring, his eyes like flickering torches. This had to be the ring, a diamond the size of a goose egg. And there was an inscription inside. "The dead man had this on him?"

"In his pants pocket."

Swazey grunted and turned up the collar of his trench coat. He'd welcomed the raid on the Candy Box, to put distance between him and Stevie. If they reopened the investigation of the Fletcher-Payne kid's death, he had to come out smelling like a rose.

But Swazey hadn't counted on this kind of a break. They could give Old John Jay back his ring and this boy, who worked at the Candy Box, as his son's killer. One murder solved. Maybe they could link the perp up to the murder of that girl in Yorkville, get both cases off the books. Swazey might get a departmental citation.

On the roof, Blackie lost Victor in the shadows. He found her, stood over her, and pressed the gun barrel hard into her neck. "I guess this is the end of the line, girlie."

She didn't struggle. With his face tilted crazily above her, he seemed at least seven feet tall. Tyrone lay dead in the alley, and she was sinking into nothingness. She forced the words out. "I know you didn't mean to kill the Fletcher-Payne kid."

"Stupid dyke!" he swore, and buried a hand in her short curls. Like a pile driver, it forced her down. But she was still alive. She kept talking.

"You knew he was rich?" she asked.

"Whadda you care?"

"Rich people are trouble. They get all the breaks."

"Don't try to con me, you cunt." He fixed her with those searing eyes. "You being so palsy-walsy with the Fletcher-Payne dame."

Blackie's shoulders quivered. Stevie was right. Blackie should've kept her mouth shut.

"She don't know nuthin' about you."

Victor smirked. "The hell you say!" He hunched down beside Blackie. "The society dame, she queer too?"

"Who wants to know?"

"A whole family of freaks," he mumbled. The cold steel bit into her neck.

"If you hate queers so much," she blurted out, "what were you doin' in the bathroom with that kid?"

He brought the gun up to her temple. "You think you got all the answers."

"You got me wrong." Blackie kept her voice steady. "I know what it's like to be in a jam."

"So now you're on my side?" He jerked her head back.

Blackie searched for words and stammered, "You say you didn't mean to hurt him."

Victor paused, measured how it would feel to make somebody understand, that it wasn't his fault, not even his idea. And the lezzie wouldn't be doing any more talking.

"The whole scene in the bathroom," he muttered, "it was just part of the deal."

"The deal?" She held her breath.

"With the kid's old man."

Blackie's head was spinning. "His father?"

Victor lowered the gun barrel. "You think I don't know people like that, stupid? You'd be surprised. And he ain't the only one."

"Sure, sure, I believe you. What kinda deal you talkin' about?"

Victor seemed to reflect. "The old man worried about the kid hangin' around with a gay crowd." He paused. "I was supposed to throw a scare into him so he'd straighten up."

"You scared him?" Blackie spoke in a whisper.

"Penny ante stuff," Victor insisted. " 'Pay me hush money, or I'll expose you...tell the family.' That was the deal." He shook his head. "But the kid started a fight."

Up so high, no street noise penetrated. A breeze stirred the treetops in the courtyard.

"A fight?"

"Yeah, he fell backwards, just laid there."

Blackie studied Victor's face. He already had two corpses to his credit, and Tyrone's was no accident. She was dying in slow motion, frame by frame. She spoke. "His father never found out?"

"You crazy or somethin'? Not from me, he didn't." Victor flashed the gun again, in front of her eyes. "A man like Fletcher-Payne don't like slip-ups." His voice dropped to sinister. "And now there'll be nobody around to say I was ever there."

A rumble shook the roof, like it was being torn apart by a battering ram. A few feet away the slanting door that led from inside the building creaked and shimmied, then sprang open. A patrolman leapt out, his .38 scanning the rooftop. Another followed quickly, then another. Victor gasped. They spun toward him.

"Freeze, buddy."

"Hold it right there."

Victor dropped Blackie and scrambled to his feet, wigwagging with his pistol. When the Japs had come screaming out of the jungle, his company had been up to their waists in the river. His buddy took a bullet in the throat and one to his chest. Victor screamed, "You're not gettin' me."

As Blackie rolled away, a barrage of bullets cut him down. She saw him whirl under the impact. One sleeve of his bomber jacket was torn off his arm. His face smashed into the roof.

Victor lay still, blood leaking from the side of his mouth. Blackie pulled her knees to her chest and sobbed. It hurt to breathe.

"You all right, fellow?" The cops approached her.

One knelt down. "Hey, Mac, it's a girl."

The officer came closer. "Whaddaya doin' up here dressed like that?" He hesitated. "You one of the kids from the Candy Box?"

She shrank back, afraid to speak.

The officer shrugged. "Some joint! We already got one body down in the alley." He pointed to Victor. "And who's this?"

Blackie realized she didn't even know his name. She stared up at them and shook her head. "I dunno."

"You better ride over to the station house with us."

She didn't move.

"C'mon, don't be a tough guy. You don't want us to cuff you."

Blackie struggled to her feet, and they cuffed her anyway.

When they brought her down from the roof, Swazey recognized her instantly. He'd seen her act plenty of times. A great little entertainer, great voice. His philosophy was live and let live. He didn't want to see anybody get hurt.

"The guy up on the roof, the one doin' all the shootin'," he said, "we got his name." He looked down at a battered wallet and faded discharge papers. "It's Victor Callahan. That mean anything to you?"

So that was the killer's name. She clammed up. Whatever she had to say was for Didi's ears only, if she could believe any of this Victor's half-baked story. "Never saw him before in my life." Nobody could prove different.

She wasn't going to be helpful. "What were *you* doin' on the roof?" Swazey asked.

"I ran up there. I was scared...." Her voice trailed off.

"So why was he after you?"

"You know, this town is full of lunatics."

That was his line. He couldn't disagree.

"We found another body in the alley, a colored boy."

"Yeah? I didn't see nuthin'." Blackie wanted to play dumb, but her nonchalance lacked conviction. A couple of tears spilled over her eyelids and onto her shirt.

She knows plenty, thought Swazey. But he wasn't sure he wanted to dig too deeply. What mattered was that he had the colored boy dead to rights, so to speak, with the diamond ring on him. A keepsake the Fletcher-Payne family would be glad to have back, along with somebody to pin the kid's murder on. Case closed. And the punk on the roof could've been hopped up on dope and bad liquor, thinking he was King of the Cowboys, just shooting up the joint. The autopsy would tell the tale. Maybe nobody would claim either of the bodies.

"Bring her along, boys," Swazey ordered.

"Whaddaya gonna do with me?" Blackie's voice rose and cracked. She dug her heels into the sidewalk.

An officer pushed her from behind. "She thinks she's a big man."

"A night in the slammer oughta loosen your tongue, toots," another patrolman remarked.

Two pairs of hands seized her and hauled her toward the prowl car. Swazey frowned. He wasn't much for rough stuff, no brass knuckles. But he seldom let on. The boys didn't like queers and were always spoiling for a showdown. He tweaked his mustache.

"Easy does it, boys," he reminded them gently. "Remember, she's just a dame."

Uptown, Sundown put down the tray of drinks she was carrying to answer the telephone in the hall. "Lucille Martin's residence."

"That you, Sundown?" One of the cooks from the club, an ebony face under a puffy chef's hat, was on the phone at the Candy Box.

"Yeah." As she listened, an alarming pallor, yellow like almond paste, suffused her face. She slid to her knees, keening her despair.

Her screams brought Lucille on the run, who snatched the phone dangling from Sundown's hand. Stevie followed Lucille out of the living room, and on his heels was Renee in slinky green silk and elbow-length gloves, just the way she'd come home from the Waldorf. "What the hell's goin' on here?" Stevie complained.

Lucille covered the mouthpiece. "It's her nephew, Tyrone. He's been shot."

Sundown slumped against the wall, a dark disheveled heap with shiny white apron. Her eyes rolled back, saffron-colored and vacant. Renee caught her under the arms to keep her head from striking the floor. "Sundown!"

Lucille hung up and spoke quietly to Stevie. "It's a double whammy. The cops raided the Candy Box, took everybody in. And Tyrone's dead."

"Chiselin', low-down cops," Stevie replied, then wondered if Tyrone had talked to them before he cashed in his chips. But why would the bulls shoot a colored boy? Maybe Charlie and Waxy had done their job for a change, instead of letting somebody else beat them to it. "They hauled the kids off to jail?"

"That's what the man said."

"Blackie too?" Stevie cursed his luck. The dyke canary could be singing to the cops—any song they wanted to hear—while Charlie and Waxy stood around twiddling their thumbs.

"Not Blackie!" Renee sobbed.

"C'mon now," Lucille pleaded, "let's get Sundown on the sofa." Renee helped Sundown up, while Flo the brunette and Marie the blond fluttered around like angels of mercy. Lucille pushed her way through the swinging door into the kitchen. Then she was back, with a glass of water and a damp dishcloth.

Stevie blinked behind his glasses. "We gotta get those kids outta the pokey quick."

"Yeah?" Bighearted Stevie? That was a new one on Lucille. She moistened Sundown's forehead, who was coming around.

"He's my sister's boy," Sundown murmured. "Whaddam I gonna tell my sister?"

While the women comforted Sundown, Stevie slunk away, back to the telephone in the hallway. Did Blackie think he'd take it up the ass like some faggot? He'd teach her to rat out Stevie the Frenchman. He dialed the number of a pool hall downtown on Thompson Street where some of the boys hung out.

"Yeah, gimme Crazy Charlie." Charlie came on the line.

"You rub out the colored boy?" Stevie didn't waste time.

"No, boss, the cops were all over the place. We never knew what hit us."

"Well, he's out of the way." He heard balls cracking on

the pool table. "That just leaves Blackie. She'll be back on the street in a couple of hours, the dirty squealer. You got your orders. I want the job done *now*."

Charlie knew Stevie meant business. He looked over at Waxy, leaning on his cue stick. "Sure thing, boss. You can count on us."

Stevie raised his eyes to heaven. "I want the lezzie," he muttered low into the receiver, then slammed it down.

Twenty-Seven

Long after midnight, silence enveloped the block of Charles between Greenwich and Washington Streets like a summer blanket. A breeze blew mist up from the river that settled around the turrets of the Charles Street Station. The rounded arches of windows on each of its upper floors blazed with light, welcoming those apprehended at the Candy Box.

Wrapped in his feather boa, Titanic led the parade down from the paddy wagons. His foot on the bottom step, a flash-bulb popped, and a round gnomish face grinned up at the kids. "Thanks, boys."

"What was that?" Jackie Mae asked, gaudy and defiant.

"You've seen him around," Titanic replied, "that runty photographer who chases fire trucks and loves all kindsa freaks. Maybe we'll make the front page."

He took Jackie Mae's arm, and they advanced in lock step, up the wide stone steps to the station house. "No matter, dahling," Titanic confided in falsetto. "Still better to be Spanish than mannish."

Their arrival was big news. A young patrolman, his jutting

chin clouded by a dense 5 o'clock shadow, stopped to watch. The drunks he was herding inside were dazzled.

More cops, their jaws set at a righteous angle, shoved the other kids from the Candy Box into single file. They shambled along as though they were already in leg irons.

A prowl car screeched up to the curb, and Detective Swazey got out. At his command, Blackie's captors lifted her out of the backseat headfirst. Her weight sagged from her shoulders in the sweaty night air.

Sully was the first to spot her. "What happened to you?"

Blackie shook her head. "Titanic inside?" He would blame her, she thought, for what had happened to Tyrone, and he would be right. She'd stuck her neck out for Didi, soft and sleek, a cloud of golden hair around her shoulders, and dragged Tyrone along too. Only he wouldn't be around to collect his payoff.

At the station house desk, the officer was booking two unlucky youths. One twisted his grimy cap into a bow. His accomplice rocked on the balls of his feet, lanky wrists protruding a few inches from the sleeves of a flannel shirt.

"Attempted robbery, the liquor store over on Hudson," the arresting officer told the desk.

As the young men were led away, a patrolman took the cuffs off Blackie. She slumped onto a bench beside Titanic. One look told her he knew nothing about Tyrone.

"Where were you?" he asked.

"The roof," she replied, eyes sunken and glazed. If she was going to have to tell him the boy was dead, she didn't want an audience.

"Good try." Titanic patted her knee. "They got everybody."

"Whadda they gonna do with us?" She'd heard stories.

Titanic looked around nervously. He'd seen the inside of a few police stations. "Keep us for a while, till they get tired of razzin' us."

"And Stevie?"

"He'll pull some strings." He paused. "Just pipe down and sit tight."

The booking of the queers began. Pushed up against the oak railing, the kids from the show who'd already invented stage names for themselves fabricated new aliases for the police blotter.

"Sigmund Freud," replied one of the boys before they hauled him away to a cell.

"Greer Garson," said Pat Burns, "traveling incognito."

It was Blackie's turn to stand in front of the desk.

"Easy does it," Titanic whispered.

"Name?"

Blackie focused on the thick wad of tobacco that rose and fell in a noxious ball inside the officer's cheek.

"Name?" he repeated.

"I wanna make a phone call." To Lucille's, to tell Sundown about Tyrone. She'd find the right words.

"In a pig's eye."

Like a punch-drunk prizefighter, Blackie didn't know when to quit. "I got my rights," she said, loud enough to rattle cobwebs high up on the ceiling.

"Michaels," the desk summoned an officer, "get her outta here and lock her up."

The patrolman poked Blackie's ribs with his nightstick. "Let's go, lezzie, and shut your ratty-ass mouth."

Blackie froze at the hatred in his voice.

"She's got a nasty temper, boys," a passing patrolman remarked. "Maybe she's on the rag."

"We could have a look," said another, cold as death. He hitched up his pants with one hand.

"You leave her alone," Titanic yelled, then came up off the bench and head-on into a rampart of nightsticks. Coldcocked by one of them, he slid to the floor. Chiffon shredded like tissue paper. They dragged him down a hallway deeper into the belly of the station, right behind Blackie.

In the detention cell, like a giant birdcage, one of the robbery suspects was pissing. The splashing triggered another wave of the stench that permeated everything. Fresh urine on top of stale. When Titanic opened his eyes, the distant ceiling swam into focus, pitted in a few spots by water stains from some leaky pipe. His lip drooped where blood had dried on it.

"Hey, pretty boy, your lipstick's smeared," an officer said through the bars. "Here's some more playmates for you."

He nudged a couple of stinking drunks inside. "Be nice to 'em, boys. They're ladies."

Titanic sat up and folded his tattered skirts around his knees. Edward G. Robinson and Jimmy Cagney were in and out of jail all the time, he thought. Of course, they weren't wearing a dress and stiletto heels.

Blackie leaned her back against the cold steel of the bars. "You OK?"

"I could use a stiff drink."

If he knew about Tyrone, he'd make that a double. She didn't know how to tell him. Things weren't supposed to turn out the way they did. "How long they gonna keep us?" she asked instead.

"Overnight, all weekend," he said, who'd been down this road before. Outside, a rising sun had just begun to gild rooftops. The first glimpses of a forlorn leaden sky filtered through the barred window.

"Do we get charged?" Blackie asked again.

"If they take a notion."

Just then a patrolman sauntered up to the cell, the shadow of his cap brim low over his face. "All right, you beauties," he said, and smacked his thigh with his nightstick, "geddup."

Blackie was rigid with fear.

"Don't make me come in there and getcha." He spat on the floor.

They rose slowly, then backed away.

The officer reached for Titanic. "C'mon, sucker. All of youse made bail."

His fingers bit into Titanic's arm, who twisted away. This could be a trap.

"No, thanks," Blackie said.

The patrolman grabbed her with the other hand and thrust an outsized foot into her rear end. Blackie's pretty teeth missed the floor by inches. "I said, let's go. Everybody up front."

"For Chrissake, stop leadin' with your chin, dahling," Titanic said. He prayed it would be OK, that they weren't dragging them out to work them over.

Blackie raised servile eyes and swallowed her tears. Her brain was churning. If Didi went back to the Village, she could've found out about the raid. If she came through in a pinch like this, she really did care. But would Didi show her face in a police station? Blackie's confidence flagged. She dared to hope.

Beyond the next door, the troops of the daywatch were arriving. "Hey, butch," one of them snorted, "looks like you had a rough night. Next time, save some for me."

Blackie looked down at her clothes. The tux, the natty black pants she'd kept brushed and pressed were pure skid row. No cleaning job would save them. She slicked her hair back. A little dirt wouldn't faze Didi.

The blue-coated phalanx jeered. One cop put out his foot

to trip Blackie. "This is how we handle tough guys. Right, boys?" he taunted. She stumbled, and he pushed her into the arms of the next man in line. "Flat-chested bitch!" he muttered, and squeezed her breasts so hard she cried out. Another boot sent Titanic reeling to the desk, where the officer leaned down, drooling tobacco juice.

"C'mon, you degenerates, this is your lucky day." His teeth were brown. "In the old days you'da got six months in the workhouse instead of a few hours in the tank."

"You're not old enough to remember that, handsome," came a sultry voice out of the shadows.

All the cops followed the voice with their eyes, mesmerized. A tall shapely redhead flipped her hair off her shoulders and flashed them a profile shot. She was stuffing a sizeable bankroll into her clutch bag.

"You've had your fun, boys." The voice was husky, like Lizabeth Scott's, with unfiltered cigarettes and too much whiskey. "We'll be goin' now." She advanced toward Blackie, swaying deliciously the way she used to do on the runway.

Blackie rubbed the back of her head. She was dizzy, confused, and suddenly exhausted. Not Didi, but... "Renee?" she murmured, listing to one side. Her heart rose into her throat. That was Renee—all rough edges, nail-tough, with moxie to spare.

Renee slipped an arm around her. "I thought I could trust you to stay outta trouble."

"Hey," wisecracked one of the veterans in their wake, "even the hookers are turnin' queer."

"Sorry, sweetheart," Renee threw back and cut her eyes at him. "When you're not on duty, you know, you can do what you please."

The patrolmen laughed cautiously. Sully, Buddy, Pat Burns, Larry, Miss Jackie Mae, and the other boys from the Candy Box converged on the desk to thank Renee. They were sitting pretty because of her. Even Titanic admitted he might've given her a bum shake before. "I guess I had you figured wrong."

"No more deadbeat hooker?" she replied with a brittle laugh.

"Just kiddin'." Titanic looked repentant.

Larry, the dyke who danced with Miss Jackie Mae, joined them. "You'd better cover up those shoulders," she said, and threw her jacket around Titanic. "You'll catch your death."

"So much for the big time," Blackie said to him. "Can you make it home?" He looked fragile and innocent, like the boy next door only prettier. She couldn't bring herself to mention Tyrone. He'd know by evening anyway, through the grapevine, and come looking for her. He would have her shoulder to cry on, if he wanted it.

"C'mon, sweetheart," Renee reminded her. "I've got a cab waitin'."

"Good-bye," Blackie whispered as Titanic faded into the background. She let herself be led away to where Renee opened the taxi door.

Blackie slid across the backseat. She had so many questions, like they'd parted long ago. "How'd you know we were here?"

"Bad news travels fast, honey. Somebody from the club called Sundown."

"Then she knows about Tyrone?" Blackie fought back tears. Sundown would never know the whole truth.

"Lucille and Sundown are on their way to the morgue." Renee paused and took Blackie's face gently in her hands. "Strong-armed you, didn't they, the bastards? Somebody oughta..."

The Checker cab hit the West Side Highway and accelerated uptown. Blackie sat forward. "Hey, I gotta get off at Christopher." Didi was probably at the apartment, sleeping in the big bed under the window, or searching the streets for Blackie, who suddenly felt like a heel and a low-down two-timer.

"Tell the lady," the cabby mumbled.

"I thought you was takin' me home." Blackie didn't know what Renee wanted or expected from her. "I'm a mess."

"No reason to get your feathers ruffled, sweetheart," Renee parried. "Get off at 23rd," she said to the cabbie, "and go back downtown. Christopher." She took Blackie's hand. "I just wanted a little time with you."

Blackie felt guilty. "Any other time, tomorrow." But not at the apartment. "You were always good to me." She was almost past talking. "And I shouldn't have left you flat."

"I wanted to square things with you too." Renee paused. "Before I left town."

"You're leavin' town, leavin' Lucille's?" Blackie stammered. She didn't like the way this was going, or the sadness she felt.

"Sure, just like I told ya I would." Renee brushed a kiss across Blackie's cheek. "I know you didn't understand it was all about makin' lotsa money fast."

Blackie looked remorseful. "Where ya goin'?"

Renee smiled. "You know what my mother used to say, 'A good-lookin' girl like you, Hollywood's the place.' "

Blackie had stood beside Renee at her mother's funeral, and held her those long, desolate nights she woke up crying. "Hollywood?" Blackie murmured. A million miles away.

"I wrote to Phil." Renee's eyes sparkled. "You remember Phil?" Phil Howe was a handsome boy and former chorine at the Club 181, who'd been shanghaied off to California a couple of years back by a rich old man. "Phil's already been in a couple of movies. He knows somebody who can get me a screen test just like that." Renee's fingers clicked like castanets.

"Lucille's lettin' you go?"

"She said, 'I'll miss you, baby doll, but this ain't white slavery,' and wished me good luck." She paused. "Phil sez in Hollywood all you need is to stick way out in front and back, that I'm just the kind of talent they're looking for."

"I never doubted you got what it takes," Blackie said in a hollow voice, her lips remembering every inch of that amazing body.

"This is Christopher," the cabbie said.

"Just down here," Blackie droned, "the middle of the block."

Renee lowered her voice. "I know you been with other dames."

Blackie nodded woodenly. But it wasn't other dames, just Didi, doe-eyed and trusting. Her curves warm and familiar too.

"And I don't care," Renee hurried on. There wasn't much time. "I wanna take you with me. Get out of this lousy town and make a fresh start. Phil sez California smells like orange blossoms and all that sunshine. You'll never wanna go back East again."

"This it?" the cabbie asked.

Blackie gulped. "Yeah." But she didn't move. "I can't go way out to Hollywood. There's my folks." And there was Didi. Weren't they bound together now, by good times and bad? "Howya gonna get there?"

"I got money saved up, plenty a' money." Renee laughed. "I can have two seats reserved anytime, on the 20th Century to Chicago, then the Santa Fe Chief to Los Angeles, everything first class." She paused. "And I'm cleanin' up my act for the movies. No more booze."

Blackie had heard that one before, but people changed. She'd seen it happen. She'd changed herself. "I dunno," she began.

"Phil sez there's plenty of work for you in clubs. It's the same operation, and you've got good connections."

"Phil sez, Phil sez." Blackie's ears buzzed. "Don't forget, the mob don't like people runnin' out."

"Lady, the meter's runnin'."

"Sour grapes," said Renee. "What's left to run out on at the Candy Box?"

"I'll let you know," Blackie answered, and opened the taxi door.

Renee reached over and kissed her, long and deep. "I'll always love you, baby," she said in a honeyed whisper that bewitched Blackie. "But don't wait too long. I gotta get outta this crummy town."

Twenty-Eight

Uptown, John Jay made greedy smacking noises as he sipped his third or fourth cup of coffee. He wore a herringbone tweed jacket and tie with regimental stripes. The New York morning dailies lay piled around him on the drawing room sofa, in gilded beechwood with green silk brocade.

Didi came in smoking her cigarette through a three-inch amber filter. Pale blue Chantilly lace swirled around her calves, and her hat was pure Lilly Daché.

"Just look at this," the old man said, pointing to one front-page spread. "All the papers are full of O'Malley...and yours truly." He paused and sipped. "Duggan's out of the race. Party solidarity, you know."

She glanced at a two-column photo of the mayor and her father, shaking hands in front of the American flag. It recalled a torturous nightmare she'd awakened from that morning, pursued by faceless reporters and that redheaded vixen screaming, "Blackmail!"

"I'm planning to go out and see Mummie," Didi announced tentatively. She'd call Blackie from the island. She needed time to think, away from the glare of city lights. She'd never in her life questioned anything she did, never cared what people said. That was before she'd come face to face with shame and fear at the Waldorf.

"That's fine, darling. You'll be wanting the car." John Jay put down his coffee. "Sit down. I've got some more good news."

"I'd much rather the train, Father." It occurred to her that, swinging by Christopher Street first, she could explain to Blackie in person how she'd been held up last night. Blackie would be hurt, angry, probably sleeping late. Didi could almost feel those lean strong arms enfolding her. But what if someone was watching the apartment? To entrap her? Didi sank into the squashy sofa cushions, next to her father. "What's the news?"

John Jay sat up straighter. "The mayor has made me a handsome offer."

Didi gave him a wide blue-eyed stare.

His chest swelled. "To place my years of experience in the private sector at the service of the public." He paused. "After the election, I'll receive an appointment to his administration."

Her jaw dropped several inches. "Aren't you taking this O'Malley business a bit far?" Every schoolchild, she thought, knew the mayor was a crook.

He looked wounded. "Commissioner of the Department of Finance is a very important post, dear."

"Finance, Father?" She ground out her cigarette in a gold and onyx ashtray on the tea table. "That *is* remarkable." Mummie would certainly be amazed, dumbfounded. City funds at the disposal of the husband whose gambling debts and shady dealings over the years only her family's reputation, and ready cash, had managed to cover up.

John Jay returned to his papers. "It's a civic duty, darling. You'll understand about that when you're older."

Didi walked over to the window and raised the shirred

silk Austrian blinds. Light streamed in like vice cops. She understood far too much and was feeling foolhardy. "Did you know the redhead at the Waldorf, Father? She seemed to know you."

He raised icy blue eyes. "No, dear. The strangest people pretend to know you when you are in public life." Two could play this game. "What was she shouting about? Some character called Blackstone or Blackburn?"

The Tiffany tall clock in the hallway knelled the hour. Didi lit another cigarette. "That was a lot of drunken foolishness. I have no idea who she was talking about."

"Discretion, my dear, discretion," he mumbled in reply. "That's all that matters."

Didi flopped back on the sofa. Maybe this wasn't the time to go down to the Village. She'd go out to Skip's grave instead, leave flowers, and cry for a long time.

In striped pants and cutaway coat, Basil, the butler, appeared at the drawing room door. "Sir, someone to see you."

John Jay looked disapproving. "We're not expecting anyone."

Basil nodded, talking through his nose. "A detective, sir. His name is Swazey."

Didi and her father exchanged anxious glances. John Jay pushed the papers aside and waved Swazey in. "Good morning, detective."

Swazey clutched his hat in front of his belly, his head round like a rubber ball and his thinning hair the color of tobacco. He had a little mustache to match. "Sorry to bother you so early, sir." He made a courtly bow in Didi's direction. "I wanted to rush right over. I have important news."

"Not at all, detective." John Jay didn't offer him a seat. "What is it?"

Swazey fished in the pocket of his trench coat. "I wanted

to come myself," he took out Skip's ring and held it up for them to see, "because we think we've got our man."

Didi reached for the ring. Her eyes filled with tears. "Where did you get this?"

It was warm. Swazey shucked off his trench coat and folded it over a small chair with cane seat and claw front feet. "We took it off a colored boy who worked at the Candy Box Club in Greenwich Village."

John Jay bit his lip. "A colored boy?"

"Yes, sir. His name is Tyrone Miller. We believe he may be responsible for other homicides. A dangerous character."

"Is he in custody?" John Jay wanted the whole story. "Have you questioned him?"

"Unfortunately, sir," Swazey looked down at the square well-worn toes of his shoes, "he was killed in a shootout last night during a raid on the club." He paused. "We found the ring in his pants pocket."

Didi listened with ravaged eyes. "A raid?"

"Yes, ma'am. It's part of a clean-up of the Village." Swazey laid it on thick. "The kind of action those articles in *The Daily Journal*, sir, have been callin' for."

"Yes, of course." John Jay murmured. "So are we to suppose my son frequented such a place?"

Swazey backpedalled. "No offense, sir. All kinds of people go to places like the Candy Box, out of curiosity." He tweaked his mustache. "They don't know what they're gettin' into."

John Jay took Skip's ring from Didi and held it in his palm. "And some meet with foul play." His shoulders drooped.

Swazey was finding it hard to swallow. "You can count on the department's discretion, sir. This whole thing'll be kept hush-hush." He paused. "Enough harm's been done already."

"Indeed, detective."

"I think you can rest easy, sir, that our killer has paid with his own life."

John Jay got to his feet, sensing he would never rest easy again. But for fear that more tawdry details might come to light, he wouldn't press further, risk leaks to the press. "It's settled then?"

Didi felt feverish. Detective Swazey was a smooth talker, but Blackie hadn't said anything about a colored boy. She would've mentioned that. And a raid on the Candy Box? Didi had to get down to the Village.

The two men shook hands. John Jay's eyes were sunken, shadows multiplying around them. "Thank you for coming by, detective."

Basil stepped forward to usher Swazey to the elevator. At the other end of the hall the phone was ringing.

Blackie soaked for a while in the tub. No sign of Didi, who could've come and gone last night before Blackie's release. Even if she'd heard about the raid, she wouldn't have known what to do. Renee was more savvy, that was all.

Blackie's stomach reminded her that it had been hours since she'd tasted food. But she had news, too, that was eating away at her. She didn't know where to begin. Victor Callahan was a good place. Since she couldn't wear her tux from the club out in broad daylight, she dressed inconspicuously in dark slacks and a short-sleeve shirt. She didn't slick her short hair back, so that it curled almost like a girl's. In a Dodgers cap, its bill pulled down, she cut a sympathetic androgynous figure.

Out on the street, she turned toward Sixth Avenue and the neighborhood diner where they knew her and didn't ask questions. Inside the corner pharmacy, she slipped into the phone booth and dialed Didi's number.

The phone was ringing off the hook, nobody answering. Blackie thought she should hang up and try again, when Basil came on the line, nasal and out of breath. "Fletcher-Payne residence."

Didi got to the phone on the double. "Blackie, are you all right?" Guilt and fear mingled with curiosity. She turned her back to the drawing room and shaded the receiver with one hand. "We just heard there was a raid on the Candy Box."

"Who told you that?"

"The police were here." Didi's voice was faint and cautious. "They have the killer."

"Swazey was there?" Blackie barked.

"Yes, Detective Swazey." Didi lowered her voice again. "He says the man...a colored man...had Skip's ring on him."

"Colored?"

"Yes, you never said—"

"Who are they tryin' to kid? Skip's killer wasn't colored."

"No? They even had a name, Tyrone something."

"Tyrone? He's just a kid, and he's dead!" Blackie's voice splintered and broke. "He didn't kill anybody." Customers in the pharmacy gave her the fisheye. She fought for control of herself. "That low-down four-flusher Swazey."

"My father believed him, the whole story." Didi strained to make herself understood. "Case closed."

"Your father?" Blackie scoffed. "Ask *him* if he knows a Victor Callahan. That's the guy who killed Skip. He almost killed me last night, but the cops gunned him down." She paused. "Otherwise, we wouldn't be talkin'."

"Slow down, Blackie." Didi couldn't take it all in. "Who's this Victor Callahan?"

"Ask your father, I dare you. He hired this Victor to spy on Skip, scare him into givin' up the gay life." Out of the corner of her eye, Blackie could see people outside the booth waiting for the phone. They began beating on the glass. "Things got outta hand."

"Not my father!" Didi wanted to get off the phone, to get away. "He loved Skip...."

Blackie heard it now in Didi's voice. The whole ordeal had worn her down, drained away everything. "OK, OK, Didi, we'll talk about it. I'll hold you, and it'll be all right."

Didi listened, tried to imagine Blackie's touch, which had made the tragedy of Skip's death bearable. "I can't right now," she stammered. "I have to think."

Blackie could feel her going, slipping away. "Please, Didi. No more talk. I'll make it all up to you." They were beating harder on the glass. "Didi?" The phone went dead. "Didi?" Blackie screamed into the receiver. They were forcing the phone booth open. They couldn't do that. She turned to see Crazy Charlie's shiny, patched head pressed against the door, and Waxy's ugly mug staring in at her.

Twenty-Nine

Blackie pushed back against the glass. "Whadda you punks want?" Charlie had finally gone haywire, she figured, after one too many lumps on the noggin.

"Stevie wants ya," he grunted, then retreated a little so she could pop the door open. He grabbed for her arm.

"Lay off," she muttered. It was the middle of the afternoon. Everyone gave them a wide berth.

"C'mon," Charlie insisted. The boss is waitin'. Car's outside." Stevie's big Hershey-bar-brown limousine.

"I ain't goin' nowhere with you." Blackie twisted away.

"That's what you think." Charlie reached inside his jacket. Stevie had said he wanted the lezzie and was fed up with excuses. They had to come through this time or else.

Blackie caught a glimpse of lead pipe, a rod on Charlie's hip, and Waxy moving in behind her. She pivoted on the balls of her feet. "You think you can sandbag me, you creeps, you got another think comin'."

"Stevie just wants to talk, Blackie." Waxy spread his arms wide to show no concealed weapons. "It won't take long."

Charlie eased in closer so she could trace the crease in his skull. "Yeah, make sure you're OK, after what happened to the colored boy and all."

"You mean Tyrone?" Since when did Stevie care about Tyrone?

"The squealer," Waxy giggled, then whined when Charlie cuffed him on the ear.

Blackie despised them both. "Who said Tyrone was a squealer?"

A sick little smile drew back the corners of Charlie's mouth. Richard Widmark without the looks. "It's *you* Stevie wants to see now, Blackie." He caught her by the wrist and doubled it backward. The pain brought her to one knee right there in the pharmacy. People ran for the street. "Now we're gonna get in the car."

Squealer, squealer. The word sizzled inside Blackie's brain. They knew, and if they did, Stevie did. That's what this was about. Stevie knew she'd ratted him out, to a dame who'd just hung up on her. It looked like curtains for Blackie's career. She'd be doing her next star turn at the bottom of the river. She struggled to her feet. "Lemme go. You got the wrong girl."

"Right, wrong." Charlie dragged her out the door. "You're comin' with us."

What a sap she'd been to ignore Renee's reminder: "First lesson, don't cross the boss." What a sap to believe Park Avenue had a real heart.

"Hold on, mister," a voice sounded over Charlie's shoulder. A lone cop on the beat, most likely a rookie, all blue eyes and apple cheeks. "This your car? Looks like the kid don't wanna go along."

"Family business, officer," Charlie answered quickly, then tried to throw the young flatfoot off track. "His old lady's lookin' for him."

The cop swung his billy club, looking Blackie up and down. "That so, kid?"

The silence was thick and gummy like hot asphalt. They had Blackie backed up against a wall. No matter how much she didn't trust cops, she feared a spin with Stevie's button men more. She dropped her voice into its lowest register. "I got nuthin' to do with them dirty stinkin' faggots."

The officer's eyebrows went up. "So that's your game, is it?" He poked Charlie with his nightstick, who let go of Blackie's wrist.

"Hey, you got us all wrong," Waxy intervened. "This guy's a dame."

"Whaddaya talkin' about, you pervert?" The patrolman collared Waxy.

Blackie didn't wait around. Swivel-hipping across Eighth Street through traffic, she sprinted down the avenue. Charlie darted after her.

"Hey!" The officer released Waxy and gave chase.

Blackie took the steps into the Fourth Street subway station three at a time. She bounded over the turnstile—the way she used to do as a kid when the cops weren't around—and plunged down another flight of stairs. She raced along the uptown Eighth Avenue platform, praying for a train going anywhere. There were none. She paused to look back and saw Charlie's round sweaty face a few yards away, and the length of lead pipe he brandished in one fist. Stevie's threat echoed in her ears: *Nobody talks about this to nobody.*

"I'll teach ya," Charlie shouted. People took cover behind the steel uprights, women shielding their children.

The A train roared into the station, lights flickering, and opened its doors. Loudspeakers bleated out an unintelligible advisory, and Blackie dived into the next-to-last car. Girls in sundresses, men in seersucker suits, and matrons—wearing hats and marshalling small boys in knee pants—pretended not to notice her.

From the window, Blackie watched Charlie veer toward

the closing doors, then gird himself for a leap between the cars, onto the narrow shifting platform that coupled them together. He wasn't going to let her slip out of his grasp.

But the cop was younger and fast. He jerked Charlie back by his coattails. "What's your hurry, soldier?"

As the train gathered speed, Blackie peered out to see the lead pipe fend off a blow from the officer's billy club. Charlie wouldn't go quietly. She took off her Dodgers cap and sat down. The doors opened and closed on 14th Street.

As long as she stayed on the train, banging and screeching through the darkness, she put distance between herself and Stevie's hoods. At 34th Street and Penn Station, she could hop a train out of town. But she had only a couple of dollars on her and no place to go. She could transfer to the Seventh Avenue train at 42nd Street and run to her parents in Brooklyn. But what would she tell them? Her father would never forgive her. By 59th Street, a plan was jelling in her fevered brain. Next stop, 125th Street. Now or never, time to make her break. She squeezed between closing doors to phone a number she'd sworn never to call.

"Lucille Martin's," said a voice on the other end, not Sundown's. Blackie asked for Renee. "Tell her it's Blackie Cole."

Renee was on the line in a jiffy. "Oh, sweetheart, thank God you called."

Blackie heard ice tinkling in a highball glass. Maybe Renee was having a little cocktail. Another promise out the window? "I hadda call." Even if she was stewed to the Mickey, Renee was Blackie's only chance. "I'm in a little jam."

"Baby, you don't know the half of it." Renee put down her glass. She wanted a drink, but she wanted Blackie more. "You oughta know Stevie was up to the house again this afternoon, shootin' his mouth off to Lucille. 'That Judas, Tyrone,' he sez, 'squealed on me and paid the price.'"

"Stevie said that?" Blackie gulped. "He's nuts."

Sunlight filtered through layers of curtain over the 12-foot French windows. "I tried to warn you, honey, all those wise guys are nutcases." Renee lit a cigarette. "Are you OK?"

"For now." Blackie paused, an easy target, to peruse the subway station. "Charlie and Waxy are on my tail. They got orders to rub me out."

Renee almost swooned. "Then it's true what Stevie sez. 'Next it's Blackie's turn,' " she rasped, " 'the double-crossing little rat.' "

Blackie's blood ran cold. "Renee, I'm at Columbus Circle, with just the clothes I have on and a few bucks."

"Stay right there and I'll pick you up in 15 minutes, by the newstand. "Whether Renee admitted it to herself or not, this was the break she'd been waiting for.

"By the park?" Blackie asked.

"On the corner."

"Come quick, OK? I'm scared."

Renee dissolved in adoration at Blackie's helplessness. "Sweetheart, you can depend on me."

Didi returned to the drawing room, her eyes swollen with weeping. On the sofa, her father had gone back to brooding over his newspapers. "You know," he said, "I believe O'Malley will sweep into office."

She looked down at him scornfully. "You've given up, haven't you?"

"I don't understand, dear." John Jay folded the *Times*.

"On Skip, on finding out the truth."

"Oh, Diana, how can you go on torturing yourself?" He got to his feet and took a step toward her. "For what it's worth, they seem to have gotten their man."

She turned and walked over to the windows. He followed her, the ring shimmering in the palm of his hand. "We have this as proof."

His words swirled around her like gathering storm clouds. Still with her back to him, she asked, "Does the name Victor Callahan mean anything to you, Father?"

Something shattered inside his head, like a window breaking. A shower of shards fell around him. Basil, the butler, would have them swept away. "Callahan?"

"Victor Callahan."

"I don't know, Diana." He kept his guard up. "Why do you ask?"

He did know, she realized with a start. She saw it in his face, that snobbish poker face. What was he capable of?

"That chap called Blackburn, or Blackstone, mentioned him to me."

"And he knows this Callahan?" Blackburn, or Blackstone, must be another unfortunate young man, like Victor, with nothing to show for himself. He didn't like to think of Diana associating with that class of people.

"They've met, I believe," Didi hedged.

"But I'm afraid I don't know either one." The smoke screen was dense. John Jay plopped down on the sofa. "Is this important, Diana?"

"I think so, Father." She scented confusion. "Did you hire Victor Callahan?"

He shrank from her penetrating glare. He had underestimated his daughter, and thought to amend his argument. "That's it, darling. There was a young man at the paper, on the loading docks, I believe."

"He works at the newspaper?" Didi sat down beside her father.

"We gave him a job as a favor to Judge Valerio." That should shut her up. "A veteran, he said."

"A protégé of Judge Valerio?" Her father's side of the story provided tantalizing details.

"Certainly not so much as that," John Jay laughed. "Just a young man down on his luck."

Didi lit a cigarette. "So you gave him a hand up?"

"We have helped many former servicemen find their places—"

"He was some shell-shocked riffraff," she interrupted, "and you hired him to spy on Skip!"

"You don't know what you're saying, Diana," he bluffed. "You know nothing about it." He paused. "Owen had a problem, you know."

"And this was how you chose to help him."

"It was a subtle plan." John Jay pretended to be impervious. "I had to avoid any hint of scandal, for Owen's sake as well as the rest of the family."

Scandal, blackmail. It all had a familiar ring. She'd sold out cheaply. Skip had fought back.

"At any rate, Victor's disappeared, so there's nothing to be gained from this."

"Disappeared, did he? Didn't you wonder why?"

"Of course." It was time to terminate this discussion. He dropped his head into his hands. "Diana, you have no right to question me like this."

"Who am I supposed to ask?"

"Please, Diana." He begged, and she saw that he was old. Dry white flakes like stale oatmeal nested in the corners of his mouth. As a child she'd idolized him, longed for his touch as a balm for her scrapes and bruises, her loneliness.

"I'll be going now, Father."

He seemed not to hear. "Yes, it's over. Owen won't be coming home." He got up and started for the elliptical staircase. "I'm going upstairs."

Thirty

A sedate town car, silvery in the sunlight, sped down Blackie's block. Didi didn't wait for the chauffeur to open the door. Still swathed in pale blue Chantilly lace down to her calves, she sprang from the car. She would wipe the slate clean, apologize for doubting Blackie, for being a coward. Blackie wouldn't be in a rush to get to the club. They could talk things over, like the redhead at the Waldorf. Blackie would explain, or maybe she'd never heard of her. This town was full of lunatics.

"Don't wait for me," Didi commanded the chauffeur. The afternoon sun reflected off the river and up Christopher Street, splashing over Blackie's building. Inside, the smell of garlic simmering permeated the downstairs hallway and rose up the steep winding stairs. Mildewed wallpaper framed Blackie's door. Didi paused a second to catch her breath, then tapped with a small fist. "Blackie?"

There was no answer, but the door swung inward on its hinges. Didi nudged it. "Blackie?" She took a step inside and caught one foot on the brass floor lamp, fallen across her path like a sapling in the forest.

Shadows filled the room. Didi righted the lamp and turned it on. "Blackie?" she called louder. A pipe rattled in the bathroom.

Didi hesitated. The lamp wasn't the only thing out of kilter. She turned toward the bed where several deep slashes crisscrossed, spewing feathers and cotton wads. Bedraggled fragments of black broadcloth, hacked into strips, trailed back to the closet. Blackie's tux. Inside, more of her clothes hung in tatters on their hangers. Didi drew back. This was no burglary.

On the floor by the armchair, Didi's foot slipped on something hard and slick like ice. She looked down and gasped. A silver frame with rounded edges lay in a nest of broken glass. She recognized the full serious face, dark hair pulled back, but scratched and mangled. Blackie's sister. Her children and the old couple stared out, helpless and forlorn. Didi hadn't seen this photograph of Blackie's family since her first visit to Christopher Street. She bent over and picked up the frame.

Didi had begged Blackie not to go back to the Candy Box, but Blackie wouldn't listen. Now she was in real danger, threatened by shabby, desperate people like those Didi had seen in depressing movies where the hero failed.

Perhaps shady characters had overpowered Blackie, abducted her. In the bathroom there was no sign of a struggle. At first glance, nothing seemed amiss in the tiny Pullman kitchen, except for the old enamel table. Scrawled in black across its surface, Didi read RAT, then saw the open bottle of shoe polish in a near corner, spilling dark viscous liquid onto the floor. She felt sick to her stomach.

One more time Didi looked around the room where Blackie's touch had comforted her, where pleasure and love had been hers for a few moments. She'd let Blackie risk everything, but she'd never intended it to end this way. She would have to learn, like Skip, not to care what people had to say.

Discretion, her father had said. She was sobbing.

Didi had to find Blackie before it was too late. She hurried out the door and down the steps. She would go to the police, hire private detectives. She would find Blackie Cole, or her name wasn't Diana Fletcher-Payne.

Renee's sling-back pumps clicked down the broad polished aisle of Grand Central to the Concourse. She wore a beige linen suit, a circular enamel pin with pavé diamonds sparkling on her lapel. Her face shimmered like the silvery image on a movie screen as she and Blackie passed under the clock.

For their trip out West, Renee had dressed Blackie as a butch Cary Grant, in blue blazer and cream-colored flannels. Her shirt sported blood-red rubies at the French cuffs. Before settling on that outfit, they'd tried Blackie out in what she called her girlie clothes—penny loafers, straight black skirt, and a plain white blouse, with short sleeves and open neck.

"That's all you got to wear?" Renee asked cheerlessly. "You look like a nun." She laughed a brittle laugh. "But those gams! You oughta show 'em off more often."

Red-faced and shy, Blackie decided to travel in drag. With a lush pout, Renee told her, "You can wear any damn thing you wanna, honey. There's no place I wouldn't go with you."

"It's late," Blackie said. "I'd better try my folks again." A few minutes before, she'd called Mr. Holman's candy store— his telephone was the closest one—and asked him to send word to her mom to come over. She dialed Brooklyn from a pay phone.

The candy store was on Pitkin Avenue, at the neighborhood's heart. Mr. Holman sold egg creams, Cel-Ray tonic, and long salt pretzels, while a hundred other open shop doors beckoned the jostling crowd on the sidewalks with the promise of a bargain.

"Mr. Holman?" Blackie said. "It's Blanche Cohen. Is my mom there?"

Magda came on the line. "What is it, my darling? Are you all right?"

"I'm great, Mom. I just wanted to tell you I got a chance to go out to California, leavin' right away."

"So far away?" Magda asked. "Will you be gone long?" She kept an eye on her youngest grandchild, hot wet nose pressed against the slanted glass candy cases.

"If things pan out, I could stay a while. They say it's beautiful there, Mom. Palm trees and sunshine."

"Hold on, darling." Magda turned back to Sam Cohen, who was worrying her for news.

"You in some kind of trouble, Blanche?" he shouted into the receiver. "When are ya comin' to see us?"

Blackie's eyes filled with tears. "You shouldn't worry, Daddy. Everything's fine." If she told him her story, about the Mafia and a gay boy dead in a toilet, what could he do?

"You were always a good girl, Blanche," Sam mumbled.

She wanted to run home, but it was too late. "How's Doris and the kids?"

Magda took back the phone. She'd decided not to question her daughter's good fortune. "Fine, everybody's fine." She tapped her heel merrily on Mr. Holman's scrubbed wooden floor. "You'll be goin' to Hollywood, my darling? Am I right? Just like in the movies?"

"Yeah, Mom, Hollywood."

"Maybe you'll be singin' too? Such a beautiful voice."

"I hope so, Mom."

Renee nudged her from behind. "Time to go," she whispered.

"Gotta go, Mom. I'll send you a postcard as soon as I get

there." She hung up, as a terrible weariness engulfed her all at once.

Renee had enough energy for both of them. She took Blackie's arm to buoy her up. For a kid who'd never been farther than Atlantic City, Renee thought she was doing all right. She had it all, and Blackie too. On their way to the train, the arcade shops flashed by.

At a newstand Blackie slowed down, her eyes lingering over the headlines. One hit her like a roundhouse right to the jaw. She stumbled and picked up the evening paper. "Killer's Rampage Over," she read, then a single-column story:

> A Greenwich Village shootout ended a citywide manhunt for the killer of a teenage girl murdered last month in Yorkville. Police say they have conclusive evidence connecting Tyrone Miller of Harlem to that homicide, and to other unsolved crimes. In a dramatic chase to avoid capture, Miller fired on officers, who returned fire, fatally wounding him. Miller was pronounced dead at the scene....

"Hey, buddy, you wanna buy the paper or what?" A flunky strode out from behind his stand on barrel legs.

"No, no..." She thought Titanic would read the same shameful story. With bennies and booze he might be able to put it all behind him. She thought she never would.

Renee took control. "Sure, sure, mister, we'll take a paper." She folded it into a big straw purse with woven rafia flowers. "There you are."

Around a marble corner, Renee and Blackie stepped onto gray and red carpet that led to the gleaming stainless steel coaches of the 20th Century Limited, pride of the New York Central. Overnight to Chicago with air conditioning and breakfast tomorrow morning on the Super Chief for Los Angeles.

"I don't know if I'll be doing much singin' for a while," Blackie said.

"Aw, c'mon," Renee encouraged. "We'll call up Danny and Doc in California. Didn't they say you'd always have a place in the Peacock Revue? Now that's the big time!"

As they hurried down the platform behind their porter, photographers swarmed one of the cars.

"Wow, will ya get a load of that!" said Renee.

Through popping flashbulbs, they both recognized the celebrity posed on the steps for the cameras.

"Boy, oh, boy!" Renee exclaimed. "We're on the train with a movie star!"

Blackie looked over at Renee. She didn't want to spoil her fun. "You got it wrong, baby," Blackie said, with a hint of the million-dollar smile that had charmed audiences at the Candy Box. "That movie star's on the train with us!"

"All aboard!" The cry pulsated down the platform.

Renee snuggled against Blackie's sleeve. "This is just the beginnin', sweetheart."

Blackie turned her head once, half hoping to see Didi rushing toward her, half expecting Charlie and Waxy instead. She'd played out her trumps at the Candy Box and with Didi, and lost. It was time to move on. Even in the movies, poor girl didn't meet rich girl, fall in love, and live happily ever after.

As Renee lifted her narrow skirt to step up into their Pullman car, Blackie caught a glimpse of long silky legs. Maybe Hollywood wouldn't be so bad after all.

About the Author

Lisa Davis has lived for a long time in Greenwich Village and loves to write about it. Her fiction and nonfiction have appeared in *The Persistent Desire: A Femme-Butch Reader, Sister & Brother: Lesbians & Gay Men Write About Their Lives Together, Queer View Mirror 2, New York Sex,* and *Early Embraces II*. With a Ph.D. in comparative literature, she has taught in the state and city University systems of New York and frequently publishes translations from Spanish, most recently in *The Vintage Book of International Lesbian Fiction*. Other high points in her life include meeting Fidel Castro and almost drowning in the Colorado River. You can E-mail her at underthemink@aol.com.